DAZED
and
DIVORCED

Rom-Com on the Edge Prequel

Carol Maloney Scott

http://carolmaloneyscott.com

Dazed and Divorced

Copyright Carol Maloney Scott 2016

Formatting by Rik - Wild Seas Formatting
(http://www.WildSeasFormatting.com)

http://carolmaloneyscott.com

To My Readers,
Thank you for sharing the fun!

CHAPTER ONE

Claire

"Honey, why are you making a sandwich on the floor?"

Shannon looks at me with her big brown eyes and says, "Why are you *sitting* on the floor? Is that happy juice in your cup?"

I ignore the child's question and say, "Sweetie, you're getting mayonnaise all over the place."

"Mommy, Claire is sitting on the floor and Sammy is licking my sandwich!"

The little Pekingese is now getting in on the action while Mommy is preoccupied and the other lady (me) isn't taking charge.

I know this looks bad, but I am *not* drunk and sitting on the floor in front of the refrigerator, at my best friend's house, in front of her little girl.

Jane and I *are* sipping on Pina Coladas, but she makes them *so* weak. My ex-husband, Ron, was very anti-drinking, and therefore I have spent the better part of my life sober. Finally, I can live a little now that he's history.

I just decided to sit down for *one* second, and pet one of the many furry creatures who live in this house. For some reason, little Shannon likes to make her own sandwiches on the floor, especially when neither of her parents are paying any attention to what she's doing.

Jane comes barreling into the kitchen, carrying a package of hot dog buns and sweating. "Shannon, what are you doing? We're going to eat dinner in a little while. And Claire, are you seriously sitting on the floor in front of my refrigerator? Again? You did that on Memorial Day."

"I just sat down to pet the dog. Calm down. I'm not corrupting your child with my happy juice, and I can't help it if you have a barbecue every weekend in a vain attempt to match me up with an eligible man."

I wanted to add, 'and you're lucky I came back after last week.' I have endured *two* fix-ups with Mike's friends in as many weeks!

Jane shakes her head and starts cleaning up the mess Shannon has made. She's an adorable little girl, and most five-year-old kids wouldn't have taken the initiative to make their own sandwich. I give the little chick an 'A' for effort.

It's the first Sunday in June, and my best friends and next door neighbors, Jane and Mike, have invited me over for a barbecue. Again. They feel sorry for the divorced girl, but Mike has to be running out of unattached friends.

I'm not saying that I don't appreciate their attempts to introduce me to available men, especially since I've been doing such a poor job of finding any on my own, but I'm a little worried that 'newly divorced' is a huge red flag. I've been separated for a little over a year now, and in my experience, many people in my situation take a while to stabilize.

Last weekend, Pete (newly divorced) was nice enough, but spent the whole day talking about his ex-wife. And crying. Not all-out bawling, but I spotted some eye moisture.

Now of course I didn't make it any better by

drinking a bit too much, but could I help it? And then Jane and Mike got all sanctimonious and cut me off when I yelled out that my underwear was getting uncomfortable. I was just trying to situate myself on one of their side chairs in the living room. I can't help it if they buy stiff furniture.

Overall, I am a very stable person. I know so far it doesn't sound that way, but I have a good job in human resources at Bella Donna Press, I own my own home (well, I am trying to buy Ron out of his share as part of the divorce settlement), and I still manage to maintain a decent credit score, despite a slightly manic shoe addiction.

But being divorced is no walk in the park, and now that I'm in my mid-thirties, I'm worried that it isn't going to be easy to find a man to share the rest of my life with. Hence, the fact that I am sitting on Jane's kitchen floor waiting to meet the next bachelor—two fucking weeks in a row.

But this time I was *really* just petting the dog. My hangover last weekend was evil, and I'm not eager to repeat it.

I know I'm probably making getting back out there harder than it needs to be, but I'm especially concerned about my prospects with the opposite sex because I'm not able to give a man one of the things…

Mike appears in the kitchen, exasperated as always, and says, "Jane, can you keep control of things in here? I took all of the dogs out, answered about a million e-mails and voicemails, and now I need to go pick Tom up."

"Why are you picking him up?" Jane questions her frazzled husband, while offering me her hand. I allow her to help me stand up, and attempt to wipe any dog or sandwich debris off my white shorts.

"He feels weird coming here by himself, and I'm just trying to help a buddy out. Besides, I need more gas for the barbecue, so I'm going to pick that up on the way."

Mike turns to me and says, "Hey, Claire Bear, you understand, right? Tom just needs a little push, and I promise he's much more fun than Pete. He *was* a wet blanket, if I do say so myself. Now try to lay off the happy juice for just a little while longer. Or at least until the two of you can get drunk together."

He laughs and Jane shoots him a dirty look.

"What? They can party today—Tom's not driving and Claire only has to stumble next door. She was fine last weekend. We overreacted, Janie. You'll see—this is gonna be a great day. Tom's a fun guy, just like me."

Mike grabs his keys off the kitchen counter and kisses Jane on the head. "See you chicks in a few." He runs out the door in his usual whirlwind.

Jane sighs and says, "Shannon, why don't you get Joey and come play outside? Claire and I'll sit on the front porch and watch you."

"Yay!!!" Shannon goes flying up the stairs with her curls bouncing.

"Oh, to be so young and innocent," I say as I refill my happy juice.

Jane is the best at making these, and unlike wine, I can drink these all day and stay sober, and avoid having a headache the next day. Well, usually I can. Last week things just got out of hand. And besides, she is clearly making them very weak today. I know what she's up to.

"Come on, let's go sit on the rocking chairs. I think I need some happy juice, too." Jane pours herself a drink and grabs a bag of barbecue chips, dumping them in a bowl.

It's officially summer now, so we don't have to eat anything healthy. Not that I do most days, but my mother and doctors are after me about my bad habits.

We get situated on the porch, and watch the kids grab their scooters and bikes from the open garage. There are already several other groups of kids playing in the cul-de-sac.

We wave to a couple of other moms, doing the same thing we're doing. They're all dressed in 'mom' attire, most likely from Target. I'm the only one in white shorts and a sequined purple halter top with matching sparkly sandals. Perhaps I am trying too hard, but as my mother says, if I let myself go in the fashion department, what's next?

Good old Mom.

At first I hope no one comes over to crash our conversation, but they won't. I don't have anything in common with these suburban mothers. Plus, they all know my history and I am like a bad luck charm for their 'married with children' bliss.

When things first started to go wrong for me, they came over with casseroles and fruit baskets. But after things spiraled further down into more seriously fucked up territory, they started bowing out of 'Operation Cheer Up Claire' one by one.

But not Jane. She's the only one who sees past the lifestyle differences, and befriended me when she and Mike moved in next door. Now she's my best friend and confidante.

Jane places the bowl of chips on a wooden end table and begins rocking. 'So, I think Tom sounds like a good possible match for you. He and his wife had a Christmas party last year. He was nice, but she was a bitch. He's probably glad to be rid of her, and they split up right after the holidays, so he's technically not 'newly' divorced."

She knows this is a hot button for me now. "What did she do?" I ask.

Why does everyone always say that exes are terrible people? I can't possibly always be lucky enough to meet the good half of every former couple, but everyone says their divorces were the other party's fault. Although, Pete from last weekend would have taken his ex back, that's for sure. But that's unusual. Most claim that they were married to Satan. Or Mrs. Satan.

And hmm…come to think of it, I guess I do that with Ron. I do make him the villain.

"She was just…hold on…Shannon, watch for cars! I swear, the way people drive in this cul-de-sac. And it's always the people with no kids."

Jane finishes her rant and catches my eye. "Oh, I'm sorry, Claire. You know I don't mean you."

I do know that she doesn't mean me, yet I can't help but feel a stab of sadness. It happens any time someone mentions children, pregnancy, babies, or anything having to do with what I can't have.

"So, anyway…the ex-wife. She berated him all night. She rolled her eyes when he and Mike were joking around, and she looked me up and down like my outfit wasn't good enough for her big, fancy party. And the worst part was how she was shamelessly flirting with all of the men."

She lowers her voice, as if Mike and Tom can hear her in the car on the way here. "In the end, I think she was screwing more than one of Tom's friends. To be honest, I was even a little suspicious of Mike for a while."

"No, that's insane. Mike would never cheat on you."

Although he is always on the phone, late for social events, and just generally ADD about everything. Hmm...no, I refuse to believe it.

"I know you're right, but it was such a big scandal, and it was hard to believe any man in our circle resisted her clutches." She peers out into the street again and screams, "Joey, put that down. What is that? It looks dirty..."

My mind wanders while Jane monitors her offspring. I'm not really worried about Tom and whether or not he's a good match. Truthfully, I just don't see any man being 'the one.' I'm already jaded and I've barely begun the search.

Ron and I had been together since high school. He waited for me to graduate from college and come back home to our small town in the New York City suburbs, and then we got married. After a few years, we moved down here to Richmond, Virginia together. We bought a house and started thinking about a family. Then the trouble began.

"Claire, what are you thinking about?" Jane studies my expression with her concerned mom look. "Oh, and Tom has no kids, but Mike said he's past the point where he cares. He's in his early forties, and since his wife didn't want any he gave up on that dream a long time ago. You'll be on the same page."

I sigh and shift in my porch rocker. She really needs to get cushions for these things. The slats are already digging into my skinny butt. I smile and then frown as I think of Ron complementing my butt.

Ron…if only he could have been a little more understanding. I know the miscarriages were hard on him, too. But were they really? After the second one it felt like he was giving up on the idea of having a family. Kind of like Tom, I guess. And me, too, now that I am truly and completely unable to try.

I smile weakly at Jane to reward her for her efforts. She means well and just wants to see me happy. Like my nutty mother, who keeps trying to set me up with retirees from her church. Well, not quite, but the thought of me dating any man who could remotely want kids someday scares the crap out of her.

I guess I can't completely relate to that overprotective mother gene, as much as I wish I had gotten the chance.

I munch on a chip and say, "I'm sure he'll be great. So how far away does he live? Mike's been gone a while."

Jane gets up and grabs my empty glass off the table. "You know how unfocused he is. I'm sure he stopped to get coffee and he's yacking with the convenience store clerk. He'll remember Tom when he texts and asks him where he is."

She laughs as she goes inside to retrieve even more happy juice for both of us.

Mike *does* disappear a lot, and Jane never seems troubled, but maybe I am just looking at it from my very limited experience with men. Ron is the only man I've ever been with. I was sixteen when we met, and thirty-four when we separated last year. I shouldn't make judgments about other relationships.

Besides, Ron wasn't friendly enough, or motivated

enough, to leave the house for extended periods of time and talk to anyone. Mike is just a very outgoing person with a lot going on.

Mike and Ron have remained friends after our split, but without the 'cruise director' wives to make plans for the four of us, I don't think they have remained as close as me and Jane.

However, I do know that Ron talks to Mike about me, and if Tom or any other guy turns out to be 'the one,' or even worthy of a real date, Ron will hear about it from 'Loose Lips Mike.'

However, Mike's lips close up conveniently whenever I casually inquire about Ron's status. He *has* to be dating, but I do get texts and phone calls from him about things that clearly don't matter. As if he's looking for excuses to contact me.

I don't care if his new neighbor reminds him of the lady we rented an apartment from when we first got married. Or that he turned all his underwear pink when he washed them with his red towels.

Is he trying to keep his foot in the door?

It doesn't matter, because whether or not Tom, or any other guy, works out for me, Ron's feet, and the rest of him, are staying outside my door. All of my doors. Even the one that is beginning to desperately need a visitor.

CHAPTER TWO

Claire

"**M**ommy, Claire needs a Band-Aid for her boo-boo!" Shannon wails and runs in circles.

If it wasn't for the overall festive atmosphere (minus the wailing), I would say Jane is annoyed.

"Shannon, you and Joey can go up to Laura's to play with the kids. I'll watch you walk over there."

Jane shoos the kids out the door and glances back at me, pursing her lips. I know that look.

"Okay, have fun and be good. Tell Miss Laura to call Mommy when you're ready to come home, and I'll send Daddy to get you." She shuts the door and mutters under her breath, "If Daddy ever gets his ass home."

I continue to study my finger, which seems to be bleeding a little, as Jane comes at me with all sorts of first aid gear.

"How did you cut your finger? Let me see. Oh, it's not that bad. Shannon made it sound like it was gushing blood like Niagara Falls." Jane grabs my wound and...

"I cut it...ow, that hurts." I absolutely hate when anyone puts alcohol on cuts. I didn't cut it on a rusty nail in a landfill—it's fine!

"I was trying to be helpful and cut up the limes for the guys' Coronas, and the knife slipped."

"Are you kidding me? You could have cut your finger off. Are you drunk?" She tightens the Band-Aid and gives me that 'mom' look again.

"No, I am not. If you must know, I got distracted by the bird. I think he said my name."

Parrots are such weirdos. They're always staring at you like they want to kiss you or peck your eyes out. "Come to Polly, Claire!" Yuck.

Jane purses her lips and says, "You're a nut. And where the hell are these men?"

Since I have no idea, I slump down in one of the not-so-comfy side chairs in the living room, and attempt to dig my phone out of my tiny pocket.

Hmm…Ron has texted me three more times. He wants to know where I am. I was told not to tell him because he wasn't invited.

Jane shakes her head and grabs her own phone. "Mike has been gone for over an hour. This is getting…Claire, *what* are you doing? Sit up in that chair. You look like a drunk contortionist. We are not having a repeat of last weekend."

"I am not drunk. And you should buy different chairs. Ones that are made for actual humans."

I glance down at my body, and yes, it is twisted a little funny, but I need my legs to be elevated. I feel a headache coming on. Oh shit, I dropped my phone. Now where is it? I think it's under the chair.

I sit up and lean forward, hanging my head off the edge with my butt sticking up…ooh…that makes me dizzy.

Perhaps I *should* slow down on the drinks. They could be deceptively stronger than I think due to the fruity, tropical deliciousness. But Ron isn't here to control me, so I will do what I want. The kids are gone and I only live next door. Like my friend Rebecca at work always says, 'live a little, Claire.'

"Claire, do you really want your ass pointed towards the front door when the guys get here?" Jane shakes her head.

I'm getting tired of her lectures.

Before I can answer, I hear an unfamiliar male voice.

"Well, if I had an ass like that, I'd want it to be the first thing—"

Just as I right myself, phone in hand, Jane blurts out, "Where the hell have you been?"

I check my clothes to make sure everything is covered and where it's supposed to be, then turn to find the guy who was commenting on my ass. I don't know if I should hug him or...ohh...what's going on with his hair?

"Take it easy, honey. I had a few other stops to make first." Mike tries to kiss Jane, but she turns her face so all he gets is part of an earlobe.

Jane sighs and says, "Hi, Tom. Nice to see you. I guess you must have recently moved to Canada."

Mike mimics Jane behind her back.

Tom comes to his buddy's defense and says, "Oh Janie, don't be silly. You know Mike lives by his own timetable." Now he fixes his gaze on me and says, "So you must be Claire."

Jane can't resist sparring and says, "Yes, she's the one with the ass that should be...hey, what did you do to your hair, Tom?"

I'm relieved that Jane has noticed, and it isn't just an effect of the happy juice. I was worried that I was hallucinating.

"Do you like it? I wanted to hide the grey, like you ladies do...well not either of *you* because you're *far* too

12

young. But that bitch Helena dyes hers. Do you know she is like forty percent grey? Of course she says that's *my* fault. Anyway, I was going to get one of those men's hair kits at the grocery store, but then I said…no way, go to the pros. So I went to Helena's salon, and they did me up. What do you think?"

He poses, snapping his head from side to side in a bird-like fashion.

And I thought the parrot was creepy.

I wait for Jane to comment. I have never seen this man so I thought maybe he normally has blond frosted highlights in jet black hair. And what's with the wavy part on the top? Oh my God, I think Helena's hairdresser gave him his ex-wife's hairstyle.

Jane wrinkles her brow and says, "Hmm, let me see the back. Oh, the back is shaved. It's a…different look."

I didn't see the back. Oh my God, he just needs black lipstick and a leather mini skirt to complete his look.

Mike seems to be the only one who doesn't think it's odd that his middle-aged male friend resembles a punk rock groupie. At least she didn't give him a Mohawk, although that would be more masculine.

"Hey, Tom is trying to be hip. He's out there looking for chicks now. He can't go around with a boring haircut like mine. Now, where are the kids?"

Mike glances around as if he wants to change the subject. Gee, I wonder why?

Our friends discuss their little people while Tom brings the case of beer he was carrying into the kitchen, and then comes out to properly greet me.

Now I see his outfit more clearly. It's like his head lost a couple of decades, and all of its common sense, but from the neck down he looks the grandpa of the guy on

13

top.

I shake my head in disbelief. The Hawaiian shirt is silly, but the sandals with socks are the kicker. Doesn't he know anyone who can help him with his fashion choices? Or buy him a mirror?

"Claire, I am so sorry the discussion about my new look distracted our hostess from properly introducing us."

He glares over at Jane, who is still questioning Mike, and now has moved on to nagging him to get the grill going before Claire drinks all...

Is she kidding? At the rate this day is progressing, I may request a Pina Colada IV.

Jane

"...and then she just walked out, didn't even leave a note."

Tom is dangerously close to accidentally stabbing Claire with his steak knife, trying to tell his pathetic tale of woe. I thought he would be better than Pete. How the hell long does it take people to get over a divorce?

We should have gone with barbecued chicken. At least that way our inebriated friends could only hurt themselves with their own fingers.

Mike has been watching the exchange between Claire and Tom with an increasingly uncomfortable expression. He looks like he does when he hasn't pooped in three days.

I am trying to signal him into the kitchen with my eyes, but so far he's still glued to the verbal game of 'woe is me' ping pong.

Claire scrunches up her face and almost misses her mouth with the tiny piece of steak she has managed to spear with her fork. "That's sooo sad. But at least her lady parts didn't dry up and fall out, like mine."

Mike turns a mild shade of purple and tosses his napkin on the table. "Jane honey, would you mind helping me in the kitchen?"

I grit my teeth and reply, "I thought you'd never ask, sweetie."

As I rise from my chair, I can't help but say to Claire, "Honey, your lady parts didn't *fall* out. You just…"

As I wring my hands, Mike grabs one of them and drags me to the kitchen, and a much needed conference.

As we reach the relative privacy of the kitchen, Mike rubs his face and paces the floor. "Okay, clearly alcohol was a bad idea for the sad sack duo out there. Promise me we'll be together forever, Janie? My liver won't survive."

"Oh, shut it. This is serious. Hold on…" I perk my ears, like one of my many canine babies and hear Tom say, "Who the hell wants kids anyway? They just suck the life out of you like their ungrateful bitch mothers…"

"Ouch, he may not make it out alive if we don't get back out there soon. So what's the plan, Janie?"

Mike looks to me to fix this, as always.

I'm sure Claire is regaling Tom with her stories of miscarriage and hysterectomy, and it sounds like he's missing the sympathy gene.

Or he lost it at the bottom of the sixth or seventh Corona he's downed. His own cheap beer hasn't been touched. Where does Mike find these guys? Claire would probably do better on fuckedupsingles.com.

I suck in all the air I can manage, and exhale before addressing my exasperated husband. "Okay, obviously we need to cut them both off. This is feeling like Groundhog Day for a good reason. Two weeks in a row of this crap is more than my nerves can take."

"Agreed, but we'll have to salvage tonight by giving her virgin drinks again. She will have no clue at this point. And Tom can just pass out and sleep it off."

"Oh goody. That will be awesome when the kids get home, but I suppose we can say Tom got tired. Shannon falls asleep on the stairs on the way to bed. They'll buy it." I roll my eyes, knowing Mike thinks I'm really proposing that plan.

Mike continues to pace the kitchen floor, as if he can walk his way to a better solution. "You barely put any alcohol in those drinks anyway. She has the booze tolerance of a mouse. And Tom is just—"

I wince as Tom screeches, "well at least your husband wasn't screwing half the county!"

I squeeze my temples to ward off a headache. "Claire is not used to drinking. You know that. Ron is one of those tattle talers, isn't he?"

I watch Mike grab the sink and double over. Either he's having a heart attack or...

"What is so funny?" I demand.

He throws his head back and grabs my arm, shrieking like a little girl. "It's *teetotaler*! You made it sound like he tells on...hahahahahaha..."

"Whatever!"

I listen for more yelling, and the silence is more concerning than the heated debate over whose life sucks more.

Mike wipes his eyes and pouts. "I'm sorry, honey, but that was hysterical. Whew."

He makes a big show of collecting himself, like my humorous stupidity is just too much for him to handle.

Jerk.

He rests his palms on the kitchen counter and grows more serious. "No, Ron wasn't completely anti-drinking, but he likes to stay in shape. And you can see what he was dealing with. She's such a lightweight, and apparently one too many times holding her hair while she threw up in the bushes led him down the sober path."

"Okay, point taken. Now I am going to whip up a virgin batch and you can bring Tom home. He's a big boy and can sober up on his own couch. We really need to get the kids from Laura's and I would prefer both drunken idiots gone by...oh my God, was that the doorbell now?"

Ron

I can't believe I'm doing this, but Claire's texts have become increasingly bizarre and incoherent in the past few hours. Plus, I find it highly suspicious that she's even responding to me. Normally I get silence, or she uses my contact as an excuse to further criticize me, and tell me what a shit husband I was.

I know she was probably sworn to secrecy on where she was today, and I understand.

It's uncomfortable for the friends, especially couple friends, when there's a breakup. I don't expect to be invited when they have a get-together. I spent the afternoon on my friend Jeff's boat. Claire never really connected with his wife Roberta, so I kept *those* couple friends. Mike and I still talk once in a while, but the guy's a little too hyper for me.

I'm about to ring the doorbell again, but now I hear footsteps, barking and lots of yelling. The door swings open and a hysterical Claire is shrieking, "Well then you're just another insensitive, asshole man! No wonder your wife was blowing—"

She stops when she sees me standing in the doorway and folds her arms in defiance. She hates to be caught crying.

"Hey Ron, as you can see this isn't a good time." Jane smiles and rolls her eyes towards the scene behind her.

Mike is trying to get some guy up out of his seat, and Claire is doing all she can to avoid making eye contact with me, even though just twenty minutes ago I got a text saying something about saving her from the skink man.

Oh, *now* I see...autocorrect error. Definitely a different animal, not a small lizard.

"Yeah, this looks like *loads* of fun. I'm so disappointed I didn't get invited." I point at the wobbly douchebag and say, "Who's this asshole? Is he making my wife cry?"

"Hey, I don't like your attitude. The name is Tom and..."

And he hits the floor. Good thing Mike is there to awkwardly grab him by the arm, which now may be removed from its socket. How much did these two drink at an afternoon cookout?

Mike eyes me apologetically and says, "Hey, man sorry you had to witness this. Things got a little out of hand here."

He tries to pull Tom up to standing, but it's hopeless. Instead he drags him to the couch and throws him down on the pillows and dog toys. Several squeakers are engaged, which brings a couple of dogs to Tom's side. Maybe their slobber will sober him up.

"So what the hell is going on?" I shift my gaze back and forth between Jane and Mike, with my arms folded.

"Basically Claire's a lightweight and Tom...well, he's going through a tough time. He's gonna sleep it off, Jane's gonna walk Claire home, and I'm gonna flush my head down the toilet."

I groan and shake my head. "I can walk Claire home. You guys have your hands full with Pepe Le Pew here."

After a two second silence everyone busts out laughing. Even Claire's tear stained eyes smile, as she gives in to the irony of the joke I couldn't contain. I mean—what the fuck is up with this dude's hair?

"He's a drunk skunk!" Jane holds her legs closed like she's about to pee, and now Claire is pulled into the hysterics, screeching like a hyena.

Jane catches her breath and says, "Holy crap, that was funny. Good thing Tom's out cold. Listen, I'm going to get Claire home. There's no need for you to do that, Ron. Why don't you guys relax and have some dessert? The kids can stay at Laura's a little longer. There's peach cobbler on the kitchen counter."

Jane points to the baked goods, but I have something else in mind.

"Thanks, Jane, but I can take my wife home. She asked me to come get her."

Our friends both turn to look at Claire, and she averts her eyes, but manages to stand and collect herself. "Yes, I texted him earlier. But I'm feeling a little better now. I don't need anyone to walk me across the lawn. I'm fine."

Jane folds her arms across her chest and huffs. "Ron, I hate to add to the drama, but Claire is not your wife anymore, and you should stop calling her that. It makes it even harder for her to move on, and as you can see the pickings are slim enough—"

"She *is* still my wife. You haven't told them, Claire?"

Claire rubs at her makeup smeared eyes and quietly says, "He hasn't signed the divorce papers yet. So *technically* he's right."

Now they all glare at me, and I say, "What? I can see you two are doing a bang up job setting her up. That cartoon character on your couch is sooo much better than me, right?"

Everyone becomes silent and stares at their feet, and Claire finally says, "I'll go with Ron, guys. We have some stuff to talk about anyway. No need for you to worry."

She grabs her purse off the floor, and hugs Jane. "Thanks for everything. I know you guys mean well."

I shake Mike's hand and he says, "Good to see ya, buddy. We need to go to Hooter's for wings some time. I'll call ya."

Mike is a pro at pretending everything is fine when it is one-hundred-percent the opposite.

Claire brushes past me to the front porch, and as I quietly close the door I hear Jane say, "You're right. We better stay married."

They better, because they can't even find a date for someone else. However, they could make their lives a little easier by serving iced tea at barbecues.

At least their house wouldn't transform into a dive bar at closing time every weekend.

CHAPTER THREE

Claire

"**R**eally, I'm fine. I don't need anyone walking me home."

We're standing on the front porch, and Ron gives me that look I've seen many times before—the dismissive one that makes me feel like a child.

A very pissed-off child.

"I just want to make sure you make it into the house okay, and that you do something to prevent the massive hangover you're headed for. Remember in a past life how I used to take care of you when you got a little…out of control?"

He raises his eyebrows like a big, controlling, self-righteous jerk.

"That was *high school*, Ron. Mostly. A few times in college. *Maybe* once or twice in our first…hey, give me those keys—"

He grabs my key ring and unlocks the door. "While I do want to help you out, I also want to go to work tomorrow, and watching you fumble with those keys for the past five minutes wasn't inspiring any confidence."

I walk through the front door with as much dignity as I can muster. I do feel a little spinny, and I *am* regretting the last several Pina Coladas. I never would have had so many if Mike hadn't brought that, that…oh my God, his hair…

"What is so funny?" Ron is gaping at me while trying to suppress a smile. He always said my laughter was contagious, from the first time he heard it in study hall in eleventh grade.

"I was just thinking about Pepe Le Pew. Hahahahaha…"

I can't stop laughing at the absurdity of the whole situation. I am done with Mike's friends—and I need to forget *this one* ever happened.

And to think, I was actually letting someone *that messed up* make me cry over—"

Now the laughter has switched to tears, as it so often does lately. You would think I had my hysterectomy last week, instead of last year, considering how hormonal and emotional I feel at times.

Ron's smile also switches to a frown. I know how much he hates crying. Maybe this change of mood will prompt him to leave so I can curl up in my bathtub, and talk myself out of the funk I've sunken back into.

"Hey, don't cry. Let's sit you down over here and get some aspirin."

He lightly touches my shoulder and slowly marches me to the couch.

I reluctantly plop into the soft cushions, while he heads to the kitchen to look for the non-existent painkillers that don't do a thing. I don't like drugs, not even over-the-counter ones. Most of them are as useless as tic-tacs in curing any of my ailments.

Except Excedrin. That shit is amazing, but Ron thinks they're too strong.

I hear him muttering to himself in the kitchen. "How could you not have any aspirin? Okay, I found these Advil. I obviously bought these, but they're not expired yet. Take four, no never mind…three. You're so tiny. And drink this whole glass of water."

I take the pills and the water from his hands, briefly consider distracting him so I can throw them in the potted plant that's dying on the end table, but relent and swallow them.

"Do you ever water these plants?"

I slam my glass down on the coffee table, a little harder than necessary, and say, "I'm fine now. You've done your duty. I don't need any *more* help today."

I can't help but roll my eyes in the direction of my well-meaning, but delusional neighbors.

Instead of doing what I asked, he sits down next to me, causing me to recoil deeper into the corner cushion.

He rubs his forehead and sighs. "I really am just trying to help. I haven't been over here in a while, and I can see lots of things you've let go in the house, and I don't understand why you insist upon buying me out. And I also know that when you drink—"

"I don't know why you insist upon coming to my rescue when you know I need no contact with you in order to—"

"In order to what? Get over me? That means you're not over me. And you drunk-texted *me* and told me you were stuck in the house with a…hold on."

He pulls out his phone, and I cringe as he begins scrolling through what must be humiliating proof of my bad choices today.

"Here we go. You said, and I quote, *'pease come save me from dunk skink man with gandpa pats.'* Then you sent me about a million sad faces and then the baby emojis."

"Stop. I get it. I'm a mess." Even the skunk humor isn't funny anymore. "Maybe if you would just sign the divorce papers, I could move on."

"Hey, obviously I'm not stopping you from dating, if that's what you want to call that. And it's not stopping me, that's for sure. Two can play your game."

I wish I was more clear-headed so I could keep him from skirting the issue. "It's not a game, and if you're dating, then *you've* moved on. So just sign!"

He stands up and takes my empty glass back into the kitchen. He returns a minute later with a refilled glass of water, and an apple, cut up into pieces, and some cheese and crackers.

The fact that he isn't willing to argue with me is unnerving. I feel like I'm yelling at myself. He knows I hate that.

"I'm shocked that you have this much fresh food in the house. I guess your mother must have been here recently."

"No, I don't need my mother to grocery shop for me. And you're trying to change the subject with food."

I take a bite of the apple because even though he's annoying me, I'm starving.

He's also not wrong. About my mother. I do need her to bring me healthy food. I keep gravitating to the Coke and donuts. It's a good thing I have the metabolism of a hummingbird.

He sits down again, this time on a chair, and says, "I still love you, Claire. Other women mean nothing to me."

He shakes his head and the wrinkles in his forehead deepen. "You think I was so insensitive about your pregnancy losses and the hysterectomy, but as you can see, other guys are worse."

I stare at the food until it goes blurry and reply, "So

I guess I should just give up and join the convent. If we never actually get divorced, I think they might take me. And since you won't sign the freaking papers, that might be my best option."

His jaw tightens and he says, "No, what I'm saying is that they were *my* losses, too, and maybe, just *maybe*, you could stop being selfish long enough to see that. I don't deal with loss the way you do, but that doesn't mean I didn't care. And I was willing to consider adoption, but you're hung up on your fears. People don't just take their babies back."

I open my mouth to respond, but I am so tired of having this argument. Of trying to explain how it isn't the same for me, and that I needed more from him. And that it doesn't matter if my fears are real because they are real to me.

Instead I softly say, "Please just sign the papers. I'll worry about the house. And other men. All of it. It's my life."

"Fine. You can continue to date skunks, and any other member of the roadkill kingdom."

He jumps and runs to the door, slamming it before I notice he left his keys on the coffee table.

Shit. So much for his dramatic exit.

I make the effort to get up and walk to the front door. He opens it as I reach for the knob, and I run straight into his chest.

"You forgot your…"

Crap, now *he's* teary eyed. Dear Lord.

"Ron, I'm sorry."

I have no idea why I just said that. That kind of sums up our whole relationship—me saying what I think will make Ron happy, and keep the peace. It further solidifies my belief that I need him to sign the papers so I can loosen his grip on my heart.

But I'm not telling him any of that. And since he can't read minds, his face softens at my sudden conciliatory attitude and he says, "You know where to find me, Claire Marie."

Ron

I take the keys from her little hand and grip them tightly in my fist. That woman is so infuriating!

I knew she would unravel—she has no idea how to be on her own, and none of her friends are strong enough to whip her into shape. Although if her mother had any idea…

I walk to the end of the driveway to get into my car as the sun is setting. I have to be up at five in the morning to sort UPS packages for my route, and now I'll need to hit the workout room in my apartment complex to get out some of my frustration before I'll be able to sleep.

I could also call the chick on the third floor, but if I'm serious about getting Claire back, I need to lay off other women.

At first when she pushed me out of the house, I was stunned and hurt, but quickly realized that I had a *lot* of lost time to make up for. Claire and I started dating in high school, and I never cheated on her. We were both pretty inexperienced—she more than me—but we were only sixteen.

So at first I enjoyed the chance to expand my horizons, so to speak. But now, it's getting boring and I miss my beautiful, crazy, insecure wife. She drives me nuts with her emotions, but I'm the only one who really knows her.

And whether or not she wants to admit it, she needs

me.

I keep asking Mike if she's had any serious prospects yet, but it seems like she's been unsuccessful in finding any guys worthy of even *dating*, let alone any more.

On one hand, I would love to get her back before she sleeps with anyone else, but then she will torment me about my other women. At least we'd be even if she got some action.

But knowing Claire, she's not going to have casual sex, and if she meets a serious possibility, I will never get her back. So there's no ideal situation.

I don't want her to suffer with asshole men, but it seems like she's been a magnet for them so far. She doesn't get that the crying over her infertility isn't attractive to guys, and she's driving her friends insane.

I shake my head and put my phone back in the cup holder. I was going to text her something nice, but I have to draw the line with chasing. I have some pride.

A knock on the window scares the shit out of me.

"Hello, Ron. What brings you here?"

Our neighbor across the street is in the army, and he always looks like he's ready to salute. He's home so infrequently, and he's so weird and unfriendly, I never remember his name. Mike calls him 'The Commando.' Makes zero sense, but that's Mike.

Maybe my first order of business after getting back with Claire is selling this house, and starting over in a different neighborhood. This is the most boring side of town. If we're not having any kids, there's no reason to live in a suburban cookie-cutter cul-de-sac for the school system.

My neighbor is still standing next to my car, and I can't be rude and drive away without acknowledging him, but 'Army Guy' (that's what *I* call him—Claire knows his name) and his wife are the nosiest people on this street.

She's one of those judgy types who's constantly inviting you to her church and praying for your soul. And he thinks he's the neighborhood watch, as if anything bad *ever* happens in this cul-de-sac full of families with little kids.

He stands up ramrod straight, despite the fact that I am sitting in the car and can't see his face. I would get out and talk to him, but what kind of a whack-job can't bend over?

Whack-job. That's Claire's word. I am constantly reminded of her. I have spent my whole life with her. How can I get over someone I've loved since I was old enough to know what that means?

I look up and remember someone is standing next to my car, even though his crotch is at my eye level. I slowly lean my head out of the window, which makes this even more awkward. Luckily he moves back a couple of steps so there isn't any crotch contact with my face. Talk about starting a new neighborhood rumor.

"Hey...there...I was just...um...visiting Claire. She was over at Mike and Jane's and—"

"Was she inebriated again? My wife has been praying for her, and for Michael and Jane. We have invited her to church. Perhaps you could convince her to join us. Susan is a member of a solid women's group. Their fellowship would be a good influence."

He clears his throat and apparently didn't pause long enough to think through his next statement, and adds, "Of course the best thing would be for you to assert yourself and move back into your home."

28

I sigh and pull my head back inside my car, like a turtle retreating into its shell. It's not that I don't feel comfortable standing up to 'Army Guy.' He's in good shape, but I'm younger, taller and bigger. However, I find it's best to ignore jerkoffs.

Does he think I should drag her by the hair back into our cave? When I first moved out, I explained to him that Claire has rights, and I'm not going to force myself on her if she wants me gone. He just stared at me like I was speaking Martian.

And anyway, I prefer a subtler approach to getting what I want.

I wave my hand out the window and start the car. "Later, man (again, don't know his name and 'Dickhead' will just start a fight and he owns guns). Thanks for your concern. I'll let Claire know about the church group."

I smirk as I leave him standing there in the street.

Yeah, Claire will be at the ladies' church meeting. Ha! She may be a mess emotionally, but she would have no problem telling 'Mr. and Mrs. Stick Up Their Asses' where to go.

CHAPTER FOUR

Claire

"No, Jane, I'm not mad. I promise. You didn't pour the happy juice down my throat."

Jane called on my drive into work this morning, full of apologies about yesterday's unfortunate weekend barbecue.

"No, I didn't, but I did let my husband try to set you up with yet another pathetic prospect. I had no idea Tom was in such bad shape. After he woke up on our couch, Shannon asked him if he was wearing the wig from his Halloween costume."

I laugh again at poor Tom's hair. I am now able to call him 'poor Tom' because I am over my pity party, and I have decided that he's not someone I should allow to make me cry.

However, I am running the mind eraser over last night, so I wish Jane would drop it. I don't want her to feel bad, so I say, "That's hilarious, but really you couldn't have known, and Mike was just trying to help. And besides, I realize that I'm not the only one with problems."

"Well, I'm glad you can see the humorous side of things. So, did Ron stay awhile after he walked you home?"

I roll my eyes at my friend's poor attempt at subtlety. She called to get some scoop, as much as to apologize for causing me to want to scoop *out* my eyeballs yesterday.

I hesitate to respond as my attention is now on the insanely busy intersection that leads to my office. Bella Donna Press is located in the congested, trendy side of town, about forty-five minutes from our less sought after neighborhood.

"He did...but he didn't stay long." I sigh as I pull into the overflowing parking lot. If I could just learn to get up early like most normal thirty-something adults, I could get to work before nine. Well, I aim for nine-ish.

"You really need him to sign those divorce papers. Did he say what's holding him up?"

My breath catches as I recall Ron standing very close, telling me he was still in love with me. "No, just being jerky Ron. I think he wants to make me pay. You know how men are. They either do what Ron's doing, or they make unfortunate choices and turn into a skunk."

"You're bad! Anyway, I know you're probably at work by now, but I have the best idea to solve your problem. Or at least make you feel better."

"I am walking into the office and swiping my badge right now, but I can't wait to hear your latest *best idea.*"

Jane is full of ideas. She's a stay-at-home mother to a five-year-old and a seven-year-old, and while Shannon is still home all day with her (I think she should have gone to pre-school but nobody listens to me), she's a pretty independent little girl. Jane has lots of idle time on her hands and she loves to cook up schemes, but always for me.

I want to tell her to focus on shaking up her own life. Mine is already vibrating like a washing machine on the extra dirty cycle.

"You mock me, but who else is looking out for you. What was your mother's advice? Pretend to be Jewish so you can join J-Date because Jewish men are good to their wives?" I can hear the sarcasm in her voice, but my mother was dead serious.

"She wasn't serious." I can't let her think my mother is that much of a whack-job.

I wave to Amanda at the front desk, and she smiles like the little innocent cherub she is. She won't be quite as perky when her bad decisions come back to kick her...oh my God, what happened to my earlier positive attitude?

Jane changes the subject back to her plotting. "So anyway, *my* idea is the best! You'll love it. What time will you be home? Come straight to my house and I'll explain."

Ron

"Tennis after work, buddy?" My overly enthusiastic co-worker, Mario, joins me in the morning on the loading dock, already planning my night.

"I figure I'd rather go out and hit some balls instead of stayin' home and gettin' mine busted. Stella's got it out for me ever since I questioned her bikini last weekend. I mean, I'm opening the pool for the season. Who wants to see that?"

He cracks himself up, but Stella actually looks good for an older woman. They have a weird relationship. After raising their kids, it seems like they live pretty separate lives.

They moved down to Richmond from Long Island a few years ago, and with the huge difference in real estate prices, they were able to sell their 'dilapidated shack' and buy a mini-mansion with a pool here. He's close to retirement age, in great shape, and one of the few guys at work I can talk to.

"Sure, we can hit the balls around a bit. And I think Stella looked pretty hot."

I smirk as Mario shakes his head and scrunches up his face. "That's the problem—everyone encourages her."

Claire looks great in a bikini. I sigh, and remember how I left the ball in her court last night, and I need to keep busy so I don't accidentally drive over there again. She needs to think about what she's doing. Long and hard.

My face must betray my turmoil, because Mario slaps me on the back and says, "What's eatin' ya, kid? You still lettin' Blondie get to ya?"

I hesitate, but what the hell? It's not like there are many people I can talk to. All of my buddies are pretty much in my life to hang out and share interests, not to boo-hoo and analyze shit, like the women on that stupid show Claire used to love. All they do is sit around talking about what assholes men are, yet they're screwing a different one every episode. And what kind of a man wants to be called 'Mr. Big?' I'm guessing he was really 'Mr. Tiny.'

Shit, if I don't take action soon, Claire is going to end up like those women. I know it was only a show, but my sweet, innocent Claire might decide to change. What she's doing is clearly not working. Before long she'll be having sex in the city, the suburbs, the office...

Mario is heaving packages into his truck with the help of one of the temp guys, who he waves away so I can be encouraged to spill my guts in relative privacy.

"Yeah, I hate to admit it, but I'm having a hard time

letting her go. But in my defense, she sends so many mixed signals!"

Mario smirks and smacks me on the back. "Kid, that's a woman for ya. They never say what they really want, and when they do it's so wrapped up in trickery you don't know which way is up. But listen, if you want her back...and you do, right?" He widens his eyes and nods his head.

I gulp down my pride and check to see if we're still alone. I feel like such a douche.

"She says she wants me to sign the divorce papers, but yet she texts me to come to her rescue when she's drunk or needs help with something. And she usually responds when I text her, even though she says she wants no contact. And you should see the guys she's trying to date—it's ridiculous. If she really wanted a man, she could attract one. So I don't know what the hell she's doing."

Mario nods his head like the wise counselor he believes himself to be and says, "So what you need to do is nothing."

I blink my eyes several times and blow out a puff of air. "Are you kidding me? That's your big 'man of the world' advice?"

"Yep. If you keep chasing after her, she's going to keep playing games. Now when I say nothing, I don't mean *nothing*."

This is incredible. I should have just asked one of the women in the office for advice. This sounds a lot like trickery to me, and at least they're more likely to speak *Claire's* language.

I wish I would have read that stupid relationship book about the planets Claire tried to push on me years ago—women are like Jupiter? And men are…I can't remember. It was probably Ur*anus* if it was written by a woman. I hope it was because what guy…

Before I get my head back in the conversation, Mario continues. "Stop telling her how you *feel*, or that you want her back. Just act cool. Be her friend. Nonthreatening like. Let her think you have given in to what she wants, but you're such a great guy that you have no hard feelings."

He glides his hand in the air to indicate the smoothness of his plan.

"No offense, but you're a nut." I slam the truck door closed and jangle my key ring. "Be a friend? She doesn't want me around at all."

Mario raises one bushy eyebrow again, and twists his lips to the side. "If she didn't want you around she would erase your number, change her locks, and ignore your every attempt at contact. If that didn't work, she'd slap you with a restraining order. What has she done to get you to sign the divorce papers except whine about it?" He folds his arms across his chest and gives me that smug look he has when he's sure he's on to something.

Except this time, I think he's on to something.

I lean on the back door of the truck and stare at my feet. "I think you're right. So just be friendly? You know, come to think of it, I saw a lot of things she could use help with in the house."

"There you go." He smacks me again and says, "And tell her you *are* going to sign the papers. If she's liking you again, she won't even notice that you're not doing it. It's not like she's got any serious prospects lined up, right? I bet she'll eat up the attention if you're not making her feel pressured in any way. Mark my words."

"Yeah, she's really fucking up on the serious prospects front. I thought I was meeting some whack-jobs."

There's Claire's word again.

"Oh, and that reminds me. One more thing—no matter what, do not tell her about all the other women you've been...*seeing*."

"Hey, I had every right to make up for lost time. I was faithful to her for so many years, and then she just pushed me out—"

"Whoa, save that anger for the court tonight. But you hit the nail on the head. You have done nothing wrong, and that's why she doesn't need to know the real deal. And if you're lucky you'll get to her before she starts doing the same thing. Just be the guy who's around, but give her some space. You're buddies with the best friend's husband, right?"

Maybe a drink and some wings at Hooter's with Mike after work today? I could swing by to pick him up after tennis. I'll have time to get home and shower. I get off early enough to play tennis first. I'll time it around the time Claire gets home from work. She'll think I'm coming over to bug her and declare my love again, but nothing will be further from the truth.

Claire

I slide the key in my office door, as I try to hold onto my purse and laptop. I don't know why I bring the computer home every night, as if I have *so* much work to do. I barely have enough going on to stay busy during the workday. I fear Bella Donna is a sinking ship.

I push the door open, and drop my belongings on my desk. I sigh as I catch a glimpse of the old-fashioned nameplate on my door, which causes my stomach to turn slightly.

Claire McDonald Ratzenberger.

That's a mouthful, right? But no, I didn't hyphenate as a young bride. I happily took Ron's name and assumed I would be a Ratzenberger for life, and raise little Ratzenbergers.

Since that dream has blown up, and I find myself trying to force my husband to sign divorce papers, I am struggling with the name thing. I could just drop his name, but since we're not divorced yet, I figured I would pull my Irish maiden name back out and dust it off. Once the divorce is final, I'll drop Ron's name and prepare to live my life as a truly single woman.

I keep telling people, including myself, that I'm divorced. Separated feels the same as divorced, or at least I think that's true. Will be true.

Or perhaps I am just walking around in a daze, and when reality hits me like a sock full of bricks, things are really going to go south.

My mother thinks I should just stay a Ratzenberger, because after all I'll be remarried in no time, and I'll take the new Prince Charming's name.

She clearly isn't paying attention to my dating experiences thus far. To be fair, I haven't shared much with her, but at the rate I'm going I will surely retire from Bella Donna Press before I add any new names to my door.

I place my purse under my desk and open my laptop. Now what's my password? How do I forget this after every weekend?

"Hey, how was your weekend? I'm hoping better than the last one."

My co-worker, Rebecca, is obviously referring to

'Weepy Pete,' the name she assigned to last weekend's blind date fix-up.

"Well, I hate to say it, but it wasn't much better...I did the crying this time."

I go on to fill her in on the basics of Tom, his hair, and my unfortunate alcohol consumption. I leave out the part about Ron. She's always telling me I need to cut the cord with him and move on.

Spoken like the true, professional single girl she is.

"Oh my God, how could Mike not know one normal, single man?" She stops laughing at my misery long enough to pose that obvious question.

Rebecca doesn't understand why I am having such difficulty with men. She's in her mid-forties and never married. She's quite attractive with her auburn hair, slate blue eyes and enviable figure. Come to think of it, I look like a little boy next to her. Ugh...

"Claire, you're beautiful, and there is no reason you can't meet a bunch of nice, normal prospects. I'm telling you, you need to join Meetup."

Rebecca has been hounding me to join her singles' meetup group ever since Ron and I split up, but the thought of meeting a bunch of strangers in such a forced environment creeps me out. It sounds almost as bad as online dating, which I have also avoided like spiders and salads.

"Thanks for the never ending offer, but I am going to pass for now. I think we have bigger problems. Honestly, I'm worried about our jobs."

Rebecca and I comprise the human resources team, and a few years ago they split our duties. I am in charge of recruiting and training, and she is responsible for employee relations and benefits. I'm not sure which one of us got the worst end of the stick.

Dealing with people in this industry isn't easy, but at least we aren't on the editorial staff. The authors are complete, neurotic whack-jobs. What is it they say about writers and house painters? Yep, all hitting the bottle.

And as if obsessing over the status of my career isn't enough, I am still trying to sign into my computer. Maybe this is an omen. Three failed attempts. Did I recently change my password? A few more tries and I'll get locked out, and have to call IT.

"Well, if the editorial staff wasn't stuck in the dark ages maybe we could publish something other than cookbooks. Due to a little thing called the *Internet*, not too many people are spending money on recipes. And now I heard we've signed someone to write *gluten-free* cookbooks. Apparently no one can eat bread anymore without shitting themselves. It's a big thing."

I am grateful to have a friend at work who can be so blunt, especially at this conservative company. Yes, HR is a challenging profession for my slightly crude and unfiltered pal.

However, Rebecca and I both grew up in the north, where cursing at work was the norm, especially in New York. Never once did I hear anyone complain about someone using the 'f-bomb.' What does that even mean? Hearing the word 'fuck' is similar to being blown into pieces?

Rebecca grew up in Rhode Island, and apparently women there also have what many of our co-workers here refer to as 'potty mouths.'

I roll my eyes at her while banging away at my keyboard, and say, "Following trends is a good thing. I'm sure we're on to something with that."

That's not my password, either! Oh my God, one more try and I'm locked out of my freaking computer. Dammit!

"And then we have those sweet, *clean* romances. As far as I'm concerned, clean is for children and eating utensils. Hey, are you listening to me?"

I look up and say, "What? Yes, I just can't login and now…shit, I'm locked out."

I mess up my hair in frustration and then instantly regret the eggbeater look. Rebecca stares at me as if I've lost my last fruit loop.

Which I have.

"You'll have to call IT. It's not that big of a deal." Rebecca crosses her arms across her ample chest.

"Yes, obviously." I run my fingers through my hair in anticipation of a visit from a member of the male species. All of the IT employees are men. I'm not interested in any of them, but I also don't want to look like I just rolled out of bed or had sex in my office.

I pop open my compact mirror, close it in defeat and continue. "I know those books are silly to you, and I don't read them either, but I'm sure there's a market for them. There are plenty more women like my ultra-conservative neighbor across the street. And anyway, Bella Donna Press has a wholesome image to uphold."

We would be my mother's book supplier if she wasn't so into military history, which is obviously not sweet or clean. It's funny how she picks and chooses what's offensive.

However, I'm not going to bring up the subject of mothers, because Rebecca's mom is much older than mine, but a wild woman. It's too early in the morning to hear about an eighty-year-old lady who reads erotica.

Rebecca wrinkles her nose as if sweet and clean is stinking up the place. "Between you and me, if Tim would stop chewing gum and remodeling the office, he would have time to make better business decisions. Every time I see him, he's talking to a contractor or a decorator. We have no money to buy new furniture and artwork."

She gestures to the meager décor in my office, and even though the threadbare carpet and ugly, brown tweed chairs are in need of replacement, I see her point. I do have one picture of an otter on my wall that's kind of weird, but cute. Or maybe that's a beaver.

Oh well, back to the problem at hand. I shuffle around in my purse, find my phone, and begin typing a message to IT. Who says I can't multi-task?

I look back up at Rebecca and say, "I know, he's out of his mind. The gum thing is bizarre. Have you seen his office? There are piles of gum everywhere. It looks like we're preparing for a 'free pack of Bubble Yum with a purchase' book promo."

Rebecca shakes her red mane and says, "And he isn't fooling anyone with that 'if I chew gum, I won't eat' crap. Have you seen his stomach?"

Rebecca often refers to middle-aged men's mid-sections with various maternity references. It's a big pet peeve of hers. I wish she would find another analogy, because any reference to pregnancy still pings my heart in a bad way.

But I understand her annoyance as a single woman who's in shape, and wants an equal partner. She says all the older single men she meets want Victoria's Secret models, but look like walking advertisements for beer and pork rinds.

Perhaps she *is* bitter about her dating life, even though I just assume her big boobs and snarky wit attract the best men. The whole time I've known her, she's been branded a cougar. Her last serious relationship was with a guy my age, but that ended several years ago.

I could never be a cougar. I worry enough about my ability to make a guy my own age happy, since my lady parts *have* dried up and fallen out. I don't care what Jane says. I may be overly dramatic about it, but she's the one walking around with fully functioning baby-making equipment.

I snap back to reality, knowing I need to commiserate with my colleague before she goes back to her office to deal with her latest playground monitoring, I mean *employee relations*, case. Some of the things people report to HR are unreal…

"Yes, I know. He looks pregnant, at least six months, right?" I tell her what she wants to hear, but maybe the poor guy just has a slow metabolism, or he's stress eating.

I do the opposite, but plenty of sad people chow down when they're in a bad place. After all, he's the captain of a sinking ship, and I've met his wife. Not exactly a charmer.

Rebecca laughs and I glance past her to see…oh great. Seriously? This is who IT sent to help me? He must have gotten a notification that the ditzy blond in HR can't remember if her password is the one about puppies or unicorns, and he couldn't resist personally coming down to mock me.

"Hey ladies, now you both know that not every man can have my abs. Come on, punch them and see."

Justin stands up straight and tall, and pretends to start untucking his shirt, which even *he* wouldn't do in the office. I glance over at Rebecca and her eyes have widened. I have a feeling that if I wasn't here, she would encourage him to continue, even though she's old enough to be his young mother. Since I value our friendship, I never mention that fact.

And why the hell does he have to be so nosy? But, yikes! We *should* close the door if we're going to say shit about…

"You really should discuss these matters with the door closed. I don't know if our CEO wants his mid-section challenges so freely discussed." Justin smirks and his green eyes shine with mirth. He loves himself so much I bet he has a picture of himself on his office wall, instead of the muskrat. I mean, otter.

Justin is only twenty-four years old, and already manages the whole IT department. I hired him last year, straight out of Princeton. He's not one of those spoiled rich kids, but he's apparently brilliant in his field. He's also too good-looking to work at Bella Donna Press in Richmond. He should be in Hollywood. Or in politics. He is self-absorbed enough to be successful in either place.

"Yes, you're right, so please close the door for us." I don't need him to help me with my password reset. I'm sure he has more important things to do. I can call Marcus and he'll be over in a minute, and he will behave professionally, and not like an entitled little punk who…oh my God, did he just close the door and sit down next to Rebecca?

I clear my throat and say, "I meant for you to close the door so Rebecca and I can have some privacy." I raise an eyebrow as if my authority is going to convince him…wait, I don't have any authority.

Now Rebecca is standing at the door with her hand on the knob. "I have to run anyway. Someone is upset about other employees using their coffee creamer. I don't want a riot on my hands." She smiles and gives Justin a final once over before slipping out the door, and closing it behind her.

I do not need privacy to talk to *Justin*. Actually, I don't need to talk to him at all. Is it hot in here?

"So I guess you don't want to punch my abs?" He laughs and puts up his hands in surrender as he regards my glare. I'm guessing he's also amused by my surely tomato-red cheeks.

Leaning forward again, he says, "Hey, you're not logged in. Did you just get in? Wild weekend? I've heard about you divorced women."

So I guess he isn't here about my computer.

If inappropriate workplace flirting were a sport, he would be a gold medalist. But it's so hard to get mad at him when his blond hair is framing that chiseled face, and those big, strong hands are playing with my stapler.

I haven't stapled anything in years, but I may start now.

CHAPTER FIVE

Jane

"Jeez, Janie what time does Claire get home? These kids are starving. Look at Joey—his eyeballs are popping out from lack of nourishment. Don't worry kid, Daddy's gonna feed ya."

My nutty husband messes up our seven-year-old's hair, and smiles his usual goofy grin. Most women would be annoyed by demands for dinner, but he's just joking around. I don't mind—he makes me laugh and he's also a self-entertaining unit, so low maintenance.

I roll my eyes and hand Joey a bag of fruit snacks, which he drops on the floor, and I have to grab, before one of the dogs gets to them.

So much for my starving offspring. Speaking of that, Shannon has been awfully quiet…

As I search for my little one, I say, "You know Claire works way on the other side of town. She'll be here soon. Why don't you take the kids to get something to eat? By the time we get back from the country with our little surprise, it will be too late."

"Yes, dear. Kids, what do you want? Oh, there's the bell. I'll get it."

Mike opens the door to the usual symphony of barking and says, "Oh, hey buddy. Thought you were Claire."

My stomach sinks, and I quickly whip my head out

of the kitchen to see who's here. I hope it's not one of Mike's disastrous blind date friends, because Claire doesn't need that today. I should have told her to text me when she got home and I'd go over there to pick her up, but I wanted her to see everything laid out on the dining room table before we leave.

I relax when I hear Ron's voice, but only a smidge because Claire isn't going to want to see him, either. His car didn't vacate the cul-de-sac yesterday until quite a while after they left our house, and I can only imagine that wasn't an easy visit.

I pop out of the kitchen and say, "So what brings you by, Ron?" I know that's not the friendliest greeting, but I'm hoping we can get to the point so he won't stay long.

"Hi to you too, Jane. I just wanted to see if Mike felt like hanging out. I was just playing tennis earlier, and thought we could grab a beer."

Mike rubs his chin and says, "See the thing is, Jane is getting ready to go out and I've got the kids."

Taking the opportunity to get everyone out of the house, I chime in with, "You do all need to eat. Just grab the kids and…okay, you can't have a beer, but you could have one here. Later."

I thought Ron doesn't drink, but I'm not about to get into that debate, or remind him of Sunday's events, with Claire due here any minute.

Ron says, "Yeah, that would work. I'm starving, too. Where do the kids like to eat?"

He's being awfully cooperative. Hmm…

Before Shannon and Joey come running downstairs asking to go to Chuck E. Cheese, another voice interrupts our conversation.

"Hey, why is the door open? My mother would die

if she lived here. We were always told to keep the door closed or every—"

"Bug in the neighborhood will get in."

Ron finishes Claire's sentence. She looks at him with a puzzled look, as if she's hoping he isn't part of her surprise. Which he is not!

"Hi, are you here to see…?" She looks at Mike for an explanation.

Ron jumps in and says, "Are you *that* surprised to see me? Didn't you see my truck out front? Claire, you are always so observant."

He says this with a smile, but if I know Claire she's not going to find his teasing to be funny or endearing. I need to push them all out the door so I can show Claire the big surprise.

"Hey, Mommy, what's all this doggy stuff?" Shannon is holding the soft pink blanket with the paws on it, and the puppy teething ring.

Yes, Claire is about to become a puppy mother.

Claire looks at each of us for the answer, and Ron shrugs his shoulders to indicate he's not in on this plot.

"Jane is taking you to pick up your new puppy! Isn't that amazing?" Mike is looking for someone to high-five but the only taker is Shannon. Joey is bored and laying with his Matchbox car on the wood floor, apparently wasting away to nothing while his dinner destination hangs in the balance.

Claire blinks several times and says, "Seriously? A puppy? What kind of puppy?"

"Now I know it's sudden, but I thought it would be fun and a great way to…you know, take your mind off things." I smile at my friend encouragingly; however, Ron being here creates awkwardness I wasn't counting on. The execution of this surprise is not going according to plan.

My patience is wearing thin, and if I had super powers Ron would be reduced to a pile of dust by now. I glare at him in the hope that he will take the hint and get out of here.

I don't want to tell Claire that it's a good redirection of her maternal instinct with her soon-to-be ex gaping at her. I am trying to avoid *sad* tears today.

Mike jumps in and tries to diffuse the tension by saying, "Look at all this loot. This is going to be one lucky pup, that's for sure. Kids, go get your shoes. Me and Uncle Ronnie are taking you out."

He turns to Ron as the kids run off and adds, "Friendly's tonight, but next time I promise it'll be Hooter's." He winks at Ron, who is still watching Claire a bit too intently.

"I don't understand. When did you plan all of this?" Claire has finally approached the table and is examining the bountiful puppy layette.

"Let's sit down and talk about it after everybody leaves." I pull out a chair and ease Claire into it.

"Can you at least tell me what kind of dog?"

This is the best part because I know how much she loves wiener dogs. She's always showing me pictures of them on Facebook.

"She's a short haired, black and tan mini-dachshund."

Claire smiles faintly, looks at Ron and then bursts into tears. Before I can stop her, she's off to the bathroom, slamming the door shut.

Mike's mouth hangs open and he says, "What was that all about?"

"I don't know. She loves those little hot dogs. Ron, do *you* know?" I look at him for some possible clue, but since he's normally clueless, I doubt I'll have any luck.

It could just be the parallel to human babies, but it seemed like there was some other connection there, since the breed appeared to push her over the edge. I know Claire's never had a dog, so it doesn't make...

Ron says, "I have no idea." He pauses a moment, presumably searching his vast Claire database for an answer, and says, "No, I really don't know, except she might be upset about all this...stuff." He gestures to the table. "If I did this, she would be screaming at my insensitivity. You realize a dog isn't going to make her forget she can't have a baby, right? I know you meant well, but when I suggested getting a dog, I was the world's biggest asshole."

I slump into the chair Claire was previously occupying and feel a headache coming on.

Claire loves all my animals. Could I really have misread this one that badly? Or is there something else going on?

Claire

As I grip the vanity in the powder room, I study my slightly manic, weepy eyes. A puppy? Really? And a *wiener dog* puppy?

I know Jane is desperate to help me, and divert my attention towards something positive. And in her world, animals are the cure-all.

I get it, but it's more complicated than that for me. Plus, the memory trigger is just too much, especially with Ron standing there.

I don't know if the memory itself hurts the most, or the fact that his face didn't betray a glimmer of recollection.

I'm sure Mike and Jane are questioning him now, and he's standing there with his thumb up his ass, chalking it up to hormones and bad dating prospects.

Asshole.

I grab one of Jane's pretty hand towels from the basket to wipe my eyes because they seem to be out of toilet paper. Normally I wouldn't want to stain her good linens, but she should have some normal towels if she's going to make her guests cry.

That's not fair, either. I cry much more than anyone over the age of two.

I sit on the toilet lid and take deep cleansing breaths, like the woman on the yoga DVD, the one time I bothered to give it a go.

It was about ten years ago. Not the yoga DVD—the memory that sent me scurrying to the bathroom.

We had just bought the house, and we'd only been married about a year. Ron was hired permanently at UPS, and I had a good job with a staffing firm, earning commission on top of my salary. We were having fun decorating the new house and getting ready to start a family.

Or so I thought.

It turned out that Ron felt we were too young, and that we should become more established before trying to get pregnant. I saw his *logic,* but my baby cravings were off the charts and not at all logical.

I had what was probably an abnormally strong maternal instinct, and I worked as hard as I could to wear Ron down on the subject, so much so that we were lax at times with birth control.

After we were settled, and had most of the rooms

furnished with the essentials, Ron offered me a compromise—wait a few years for a baby, but we could get a puppy right away.

Ron had never been a huge animal lover, but I suppose he was anxious to get me off his back about a human offspring, but also make me happy.

Really I think it was the former, but regardless of his motive, I relented and we started to research dog breeds, and identify places where we could procure a little furry creature.

Since we weren't experienced in pet acquisition, we ended up at a pet store. In New York, such establishments had mostly become a thing of the past, but there was one in the next town over from our house in Virginia, and they had a fresh litter of miniature dachshund puppies.

We had already talked about how a larger breed dog, like a Lab or a Golden Retriever, would be a good dog for children, and how little dogs can be snippy and harder to manage with babies because they fear the quick movements, and sometimes intentional rough treatment, of tiny humans.

But when a wiener dog puppy is staring at you with those eyes, and jumping and wagging its little tail, well you just melt into a pile of goo. At least I did.

Even Ron put his macho exterior aside momentarily, and I could see he was enchanted by the miniscule creature.

We asked the shop owner if we could pet the little guy, and he took him out for us to hold and play with. They even had a small enclosed area near the registers where potential puppy parents could interact with the babies.

This thing was small! He was actually smaller than Ron's foot. Ron *is* a big guy, but he doesn't have an enormous basketball player foot. The puppy was teeny-weeny!

He was pouncing and biting Ron's shoelaces. He jumped on my leg and didn't make it to my knee. We kept looking at each other for confirmation of the other's feelings, and it was obvious we were both falling in love.

When Ron picked the little wiener up and I leaned in to pet him, he licked my face. Then he hid his nose in Ron's jacket, probably thinking we couldn't possibly leave him there after all of his flirtatious puppy manipulation.

But as we approached the sales counter, we both got hit with a dose of 'holy shit we can't just take this thing home right now!'

So we thanked the owner, and very reluctantly relinquished our new admirer. We said we'd think about it and do a little more research. I think the guy was hoping that we were young and naïve enough that we wouldn't realize these puppies were small for their age, probably from a puppy mill, and that you should only buy a purebred puppy from a reputable breeder.

Luckily, we were a little smarter, and once we walked out of the shop and started talking to friends and relatives, those were the kind of warnings we received. And don't even get me started with all of the guilt trips over not adopting a shelter dog! That added a whole new level of debate to our decision making, and even more complexity.

While we were hashing all of this out over the next few days, I noticed that my period was late. A hastily purchased pregnancy test confirmed that we were indeed expecting.

Ron was cautiously happy, but I could see a part of him was kicking himself for being lax, and for failing to close the deal on the puppy, and sign me up for the canine mother starter kit.

As soon as I knew I was going to be a mother of an actual human, all thoughts of a dog receded to the back of my mind.

At times I thought about the little guy at the pet shop, though. I felt terrible leaving him there. He loved us, after all. And it wasn't his fault if he wasn't bred from the best stock. He was so little, but surely with the proper veterinary care and love, he'd be fine.

One afternoon, about two months later, I left work early due to a bad bout of morning sickness, and decided to stop in and see if the puppy was still there. Logically I knew he wouldn't be, and other people would have picked up all of the pups in that litter by that time. But something pulled me back to the shop for one more look.

As I got out of the car, blood was dripping down my leg.

Needless to say, at that point I had more pressing things on my mind.

Jane

"Alright, she just sent me a text from the bathroom. She's fine, but she really needs me to make..."

I stop talking, but both men are still staring at me. Screw it. Ron wasn't invited to this party anyway.

"She asked if I would make sure Ron was gone when she comes out." I look at him pleadingly and say, "Please just go. For some reason, she's more upset than usual. And I need to find out if it's because of the puppy idea or if it's something else. But whatever it is, you being here isn't helping, and she's not going to come out and tell me what's going on."

Ron sighs and glances dejectedly towards the powder room. "Fine. I'll go. Can you let me know if she's okay later?"

Mike steers Ron towards the front door and grabs his keys. "She'll keep us in the loop. Now let's grab those two hooligans of mine and go get some grub. I'm starving. Kids, let's go! Friendly's!"

They come running, and in a moment they have kissed me goodbye and they're on the driveway, trying to open the locked car doors by hanging on them.

I wish I could go to Friendly's. I have a feeling Claire is going to be unfriendly when I attempt to wrangle her into the car.

Ron

"Shannon, you're not getting any ice cream if you don't eat your macaroni."

Mike is pleading with his daughter while his son is engaging me in a game of paper soccer with the rolled up straw wrappers.

It's a wild guys' night out.

Normally I would be a little better with the kids, but this night is not going according to plan. At all. I only came to see Mike as a way to run into Claire, and then when I was lucky enough for that to line up perfectly, the wheels fell off the bus.

I would think Jane would know better than to surprise Claire with a puppy. When I suggested that, I was the biggest asshole in the world. I guess Jane is now the second biggest asshole, but being Claire's friend, and a woman, she'll be protected from the full onslaught of Claire's hormonal wrath.

Speaking of which, she needs to see the doctor. I can't believe she is still hormonal, and if she is, he needs to give her something. Drugs. I don't know what, but they do something for this problem, or most men would be murdered in their sleep in middle-age by their menopausal women.

So because of all of this puppy drama, I didn't get to casually talk to Claire about helping her around the house, or start my "Operation Friend" campaign. And now I am stuck at Friendly's, eating a disgusting, greasy burger and watching Mike poorly referee his kids.

I don't know why they even *order* food for Shannon. It's a mere formality just to get the free ice cream sundae. They should just make their selection for her from the kids' menu, tell the waiter to throw it in the garbage once it's ready, and bring out the sundae. There would be less crying and approximately the same amount of real food consumption.

"So Claire was pretty upset. Jane thought the puppy was a good idea, but maybe it was too soon?" Mike signals for the waiter to take Shannon's nearly full plate away.

I say, "I would have advised against it, but she may come around once she sees the puppies."

Oh shit. I just remembered something.

Mike catches me staring off into space and says, "What's wrong? Are they behind us?"

He looks over his shoulder, as if Claire and Jane were going to come here and join us for dinner, after Jane dragged Claire out of her toilet hideout. She wanted to get as far away from me as possible.

And now I think I know why. Besides the already established reasons.

"No, I just remembered why Claire was probably so upset. A long time ago we looked at a dachshund puppy. Before the pregnancies."

Mike screws up his face and says, "Oh, that's probably it!"

He smashes the table more forcefully than necessary in agreement with my revelation, and the old ladies behind us jump. He turns to them and says, "I'm, sorry, my buddy just had a breakthrough. You know, like a mental...never mind."

The confused diners go back to their food, probably muttering about Mike's poor manners...and parenting.

I tell Mike the basic story of the little puppy that we almost adopted, before Claire got pregnant the first time.

"Wow. So after she got pregnant you just never revisited the dog idea." Mike smacks my arm across the table while Shannon and Joey dribble ice cream all over the place. "I think you cracked the case, my friend."

In a moment of weakness, I say, "Speaking of friends, I really want Claire to be my friend." I throw my napkin over my half-eaten food and say, "If she won't take me back, I still want her in my life. I was gonna offer to help her with some stuff around the house—"

"Oh, God knows she needs that. I've tried to help, but you know me? I've got two right thumbs and two left feet. Or something like that."

Memories of Mike's attempted household maintenance come back to haunt me.

One favorite was the time he secured the outdoor furniture (and grill) to the deck with dog leashes during a hurricane. Needless to say, the tables and chairs were flying into the side of my house after a few strong gusts of wind.

Luckily, we live far enough inland that the winds didn't also blow the *grill*, because that would have wound up *in* my dining room.

His defense was that he's from Rochester, and he only knows what to do about snow.

"Yeah, I remember that you're not too handy around the house, but luckily you make money with your brain, right?"

Mike goes on to tell me stories about his job as the head of Physical Therapy at a mental hospital. I always try not to make jokes about that, but it's challenging.

I'm not really listening anyway, as my mind wanders back to Claire.

I didn't get to tell her anything I intended tonight, but I think I know what to do to make her feel better.

Jane

Thank God I finally coaxed Claire out of the bathroom with assurances that the 'asshole' was gone. I'm not sure what Ron did this time, because he barely said a word. I thought she would be more upset with *me*.

Once we sat down and looked at the puppy on the breeder's website, Claire warmed to the idea. A little. She said she was at least willing to go look, and that she has always loved wiener dogs.

I knew it!

So now we are driving to the country, about twenty minutes outside of our town, to see the puppy.

Hopefully Claire will fall in love. I've already put down a deposit, and the breeder is expecting this dog to be taken off her hands tonight. She's got a couple of pregnant mamas and needs to turn her attention to new litters.

Claire and I also talked about the whole breeder vs.

shelter thing, so she wouldn't think I was being irresponsible. She agreed that she has zero dog training experience and the blank slate of a puppy will probably be best.

Then I made the mistake of asking if she's sure she wants a little dog, since men often prefer bigger dogs, and finding a man seems to be challenging enough (I didn't say the last part of that statement out loud).

She promptly replied that she doesn't give a shit what men want, and that since she is childless, alone and barren, she should get exactly what *she* wants.

I decided this was a good time to stop talking and get in the car, before her mood darkened any further.

Now we're almost at our destination, and Claire has been silent the whole way.

"Hey, are you doing okay?" I check in with her when I catch her staring out the window, as we pull onto the breeder's road.

She repaired her makeup as best she could, but she still has a little bit of a 'late night meth addict' look around the eyes. But only slightly.

Linda, the breeder, isn't going to notice. She just wants to find someone who will take good care of her puppy. She came highly recommended by my vet, and I have confidence that all will go smoothly.

At least on Linda's end.

Claire turns to me and sighs. "Yeah. I'm excited to see the puppy."

Her tone of voice and words don't match, but I am still crossing my fingers that it will be love at first lick. This dog is adorable! She's only nine weeks old, and her short black and tan fur is sleek and beautiful.

Claire's phone dings, and I hope it's not anything

that will set her off before we pull into the driveway. I almost want to swat the phone out of her hand and tell her a spider was crawling on her.

Oh wait, now she's smiling.

"Good news?"

She keeps grinning and tucks her phone back into her bag.

"Just a text from Ron. So let's go see the baby."

She gets out of the car, and I take a quick moment to lay my head on the steering wheel for strength, and text Mike.

"Claire got a text from Ron and is now all giddy. WTF?"

I add several emojis to soften the implied swearing. I always worry the kids are going to get a hold of our phones and adopt our language, but I could always tell them 'WTF' means 'what the fruitcake.'

Claire

'I remembered. I'm sorry it wasn't right away. Get the puppy, Claire. You can start over. You'll be the best puppy mom.'

I should still be mad, but Ron remembers. And he said he was sorry. That's a rare occurrence.

I'm *not* softening towards him, but somehow the fact that he empathizes with what I'm feeling, that *someone* gets it, makes me willing to give this puppy thing a chance.

It's not a baby replacement. It wasn't going to be ten years ago, and it's not now. It's just another good life experience I've been denying myself.

And Jane was so excited. She really cares, too. I owe it to her to be more enthusiastic.

"Jane, what are you doing in the car? Come on."

I wave my hand and she grabs her purse. I think I

startled her with my abrupt about-face, but I don't feel like sharing my text with her. She'll make a judgment about Ron, and me, and the divorce papers he's not signing, etc. It goes on and on...

Right now, I don't want to delve into any of the crap.

Just the puppy poops I'll soon be picking up in my yard.

CHAPTER SIX

Claire

"What? What happened?"

I flail around in bed and fall on the floor. Ow, I'm not in bed. Why am I on the couch? Oh yeah…Princess Pee-Pee Pants.

I survey the damage to my family room that has occurred in ONE night as a new puppy mother.

For some reason, I had this idea that puppies were much easier than human babies. After all, I know plenty of people who have dogs, and their homes are perfectly orderly and normal. Right?

What I didn't think about was the mobility of a puppy, the lack of diapers, and the existence of sharp teeth. All a human baby can do to wreak havoc is cry, and then you pick them up and they usually stop.

But not the little cyclone of energy that is a nine-week-old wiener dog, on the loose in new surroundings.

Within ten minutes after Jane left, Dixie (that's what I named her, and I thought it was so cute until I realized I should have named her Dark Destroyer) turned to me with a manic, playful glare as if to say, "Haha, the real dog mommy is gone, and now I will take my place as Queen!"

Really she just laughed at me, or so I presume, and proceeded to pee everywhere, eat my couch cushion, and gnaw on the windowsill.

I also badly stubbed my toe on a dining room chair while chasing her with my flip-flop in her mouth.

Apparently her preferred diet includes sparkly sequins.

And speaking of diet, she finishes her food before it hits the bowl. She was literally vibrating in anticipation of her meal.

I wondered if the breeder hadn't been feeding her, but she devoured more food right before bed. I know she's supposed to be on a feeding schedule, but I was desperate to get her to eat something other than my personal belongings.

I sigh and sit up on my disheveled couch, eyeing the small mound under the blanket. Apparently dachshunds are a burrowing breed and they like to sleep completely under blankets. It has something to do with being bred to crawl into holes and hunt badgers and other smaller vermin.

As I swing my feet onto the floor, I see a victim of such innate training. The tiny, soft squirrel toy Jane bought now has a missing eye, one arm hanging on by a thread, and his heart—I mean squeaker—has been silenced, removed and discarded by my miniature murderer.

When Jane called last night to see how we were faring, I was too embarrassed to tell her that Dixie had already made me her bitch.

If I can't even take care of a dog, maybe that's why my ability to have human children was taken away.

It's already seven-thirty and I still have to get ready for work, and drive forty-five minutes to the office. Awesome.

Jane and I did discuss what I would do with Dixie

during the day, and we decided that I would forgo the crate for now, and just contain her in one room. I picked my office because it's a small room on the first floor, and it has a couch and a view of the cul-de-sac.

Hopefully she'll sleep most of the day and not chew on everything in sight. Jane did also promise to come over midday to check on her, and let her out to potty, as if Dixie has ANY idea what that means.

In all of the drama of last night, I didn't really listen when the breeder was sharing directions on puppy care. She did give me a whole bunch of reading material, which I stuffed into my purse to review at work today. I'm sure I'm doing everything wrong, and little Dixie will become a perfect angel once her ignorant Mommy becomes enlightened.

As if reading my mind, a little head pokes out from under my soft blue afghan and yawns. Her little mouth opens wide enough to fit the fist of a small child, displaying her perfect razor sharp teeth.

She's SO damn cute.

This is why people can get through this hell. The cuteness is off the charts. Fortunately, she did sleep most of the night because I let her sleep with me on the couch, but that's not a permanent solution.

I pick up the little pumpkin and put her in her harness.

Well, actually I wrestle her to the ground as if she were an octopus or an alligator, breaking a sweat before I can secure her leash. I did listen to one piece of advice last night—dachshunds are very unreliable and don't respond to voice commands, so must be leashed at all times.

Wow, that's shocking!

I carry the little whack-job to the back door, in a vain attempt to get something out of her body before it all ends up on my floor. I lower her to the grass and for a moment, watching her sniff and romp, I forget my frustrations. Her sense of wonder at the world around her is astonishing, and her pure joy is contagious.

I just need to read the puppy training pamphlets. Jane caught me off guard with this whole thing, but I'm glad she did. It's a welcome distraction from worrying about finding a man—and Ron's crap.

After about five minutes of watching Dixie run around the yard, I am growing impatient, thinking about how late for work I will be.

"Come on, little one. Time to make your pee-pee."

Instead of squatting and taking care of business, she rolls over and shows me her belly.

Once again, the cute factor is mind numbing.

So I pet her belly and pick her up, taking her inside before she's had a chance to pee.

We come back inside, and as soon as I put her down and remove the leash, she's off and running.

How am I going to prevent her from destroying my carpet? I could try to contain her in the kitchen but the entryway is too big for the gate Jane lent me. There must be some solution.

I know! I think there were puppy pads in with the loot Jane gave me last night. She said she prefers them to crate training. Since I don't have a crate, they're my only hope right now.

I didn't try them last night because I told myself it seems preposterous that a dog would know that's where they are supposed to pee. However, it is equally ridiculous that they would know that outside was the correct place. She has spent most of her life in a box with newspaper.

Hmm…that's it!

The only problem is, who gets a newspaper anymore? I peek out my front window, keeping one eye on my mischievous charge. She's hopping up and down in the kitchen, waiting for her food. She's staring at the counter and crying, as if the food will jump down into her mouth.

"I'm sorry, sweetie. I can see you need to eat right away. Here you go!"

I pour the tiny bit of allowed kibble in her bowl, and it's almost gone before the morsels clink against the ceramic bottom. The bowl is adorable—it has little paw prints on it…anyway, back to my mission.

Ah, ha! My neighbors on the other side have a newspaper sitting at the end of their driveway. Joan and Rich are a working, married couple, and they are out of the house before the first light of day. Come to think of it, they also get home after dark.

Anyway, I don't think they give a shit about their newspaper. Sometimes there is more than one sitting there, and Joan has even complained that Rich lets them pile up for so long that she drives over the mound on her way to their garage. I don't know why they don't take two minutes to cancel their subscription.

I glance back at Dixie, who seems to be taking a rare moment of rest after inhaling her breakfast, and sneak outside.

Thankfully it's not yet time for the little kids to walk to the bus stop. I am usually stuck trying to maneuver around that menagerie when I'm driving out of the neighborhood.

I shouldn't be spotted now. I look both ways and sprint next door, swiping the newspaper quickly. I must look like a mental patient wearing the clothes I slept in, stealing from my neighbor's driveway. Luckily there is no one in sight, but anyone could be watching me out of their windows, wondering what insane thing I'm up to now.

I get back inside, sweating from my effort, and proceed to quickly and efficiently lay down a layer of pee-pee pad and newspaper over a large part of my office floor. That should definitely inspire Dixie to do her business in the correct place.

I carefully position her toys near the same area, and now I get a flash of genius. The gate can be stretched sideways from the couch to the bookcase, creating a completely gated section of pad/newspaper combo. Now I can contain her without any access to unprotected carpet. I add her water bowl and soft, pink blankie to my newly constructed puppy fort and admire my work.

Dixie has been laying on the couch this whole time, watching me intently. Her eyes widen as I pick her up and place her in her new daytime habitat. It's a plenty big space—way larger than a crate, so she should be happy. She can also see out the window as an added bonus.

I congratulate myself for my ingenuity, and head upstairs to shower and get ready for work.

In the shower I am hit with a new wave of panic. What if she gets upset and starts chewing on the couch or the windowsill again? But she does have a ton of chew toys in there, and she's probably tired. The sun also streams into a portion of that space, and dogs love to sleep in the sun. I'm over managing—she just has to learn and I must be patient.

I get dressed and put on makeup in a hurry, almost falling down the stairs because I didn't take the time to fasten the ankle straps on my shoes.

I rush into the office and find Dixie quietly laying in the sun, looking like a lazy movie star, soaking up the rays.

Shit, *now* it's time for the onslaught of elementary school kids, and their mothers, to meander up to the bus stop. I back my car out of the driveway with much trepidation, hoping the moms are watching their youngest, and most distracted, kids.

I stop at the bottom of the driveway when I remember I have bills in my purse I need to mail. I don't want my electric getting cut off, and if I take them to work again I will never remember to bring them to the mail room.

I step out of the car into a pandemonium of activity. Almost everyone on my street has young children. I wave to Jane, making the universal sign for 'I'll call you later' with the pretend phone up to my ear. Shannon waves too, but Jane takes her hand and starts yelling at Joey for running on the neighbor's grass.

I turn to get back into my car and scream.

Okay, I don't scream. It's more of a squeak, but my neighbor, Susan, scared me by positioning herself six inches from my mailbox. How did I not hear her sneak up on me?

I'm not sure why she's out here. I thought her kids were home-schooled. Maybe she saw my sneaky heist earlier, and she wants to lecture me on the evils of breaking the commandments.

"Good morning, Claire. Don't you look pretty!"

"Thanks, I'm off to work. Have a great day!"

I smile extra enormously and put one foot in my car when she says, "Actually, I wanted to tell you about something if you have a minute."

I would look at my watch if anyone wore watches any more, but I give up. She'll just hunt me down later and I'm already behind schedule.

"Sure, what's up?"

She goes on to tell me that her husband saw Ron the other day, and she was worried that I might be considering taking him back.

"No, actually I'm not. We're in the middle of divorce proceedings and—"

Before I can tell her to mind her own business, she says, "Oh, good. Any man who isn't able to open himself up fully to the healing grace of our Lord isn't worth your time. A man does not turn from his wife in her time of need. Yes, having a family is the purpose of the marital union. However, in times of such tragedy a man must accept his childless fate and comfort his wife."

She had me liking her for a second there, but as usual she went too far. She still doesn't really get the fact that Ron didn't leave me.

"I appreciate your support, but I have to—"

"Just one second. I promise I'll be quick. My church has a women's group that meets on Thursdays—"

"Oh no, I don't think that would be for me. I'm fine, really."

"I do think you would enjoy the group. We're not all married, and there are even a few divorced gals now. No matter how much a woman may want to honor her vows, she can't stop a no-good man from running out on her, now can she?"

I find myself nodding, and then get a flash of women sitting around knitting, sipping sweet tea and talking about the Bible. I won't fit in with that circle, nor would I want to.

"I don't think—"

"Before you say no, just listen. *This* Thursday we're running a speed dating event!"

I look at her as if she just said they were hiring a male stripper or organizing an orgy. Speed dating? At *her* church? I think one time she referred to dating as 'courting.' I suspect most of the women in her group churn their own butter and put chastity belts on their unmarried daughters.

"Speed dating? I've never done that. I think it would be awkward and…"

I'm running out of excuses that won't be insulting, but for some reason I'm thinking maybe it would be okay. I've never dated a man who goes to church. Maybe I'm missing something, and things can't get much worse. At least these men probably won't show up drunk and crying, with a skunk-do.

I sigh and say, "Okay, you've got me. What time?"

She claps her hands and immediately texts me the details. I hear my phone ding in my purse with impending doom. What did I just agree to do?

"You're going to love it! These events are so much fun. The married ladies had the idea in the first place, and we're running the event for all the singles in the church. But don't worry, everyone was also tasked with inviting people from outside the church, too, so you won't feel out of place."

I think I just agreed to attend a recruiting event for new church members disguised as a matchmaking party. However, I feel better now that I have this new information. Maybe some promising non-church members will come, too. I can't be the only sucker.

"Sounds great, thanks for the invite."

I make my apologies about needing to run off to work, and plan on zooming past the bus stop. Hopefully, the bus has already come and gone, and it will just be the gossiping mothers I have to watch out for.

Dammit, the bus is here, so I have to sit and wait for all the kids to load up before I can escape. Now it looks like somebody forgot their lunch, and we have a shoelace problem...ugh...

My eyes get a little moist as I watch my neighbor, Laura, tie her little girl's pink sneakers. I am really disliking this neighborhood more and more. The reminders of my loss are everywhere, but would I heal faster somewhere else?

I need to be honest with myself—there is no way to escape the existence of motherhood, unless I check out of normal society and go live with Buddhist monks or something.

And they take a vow of celibacy, so what good are they?

I take the opportunity to check my phone, and find out what time I am going to make a fool of myself on Thursday. I'm already mentally running through my closet, piecing together a respectable, but somewhat alluring outfit.

Before I open Susan's text, there's a call coming in from Ron.

Now he's *calling*. Really? What is so urgent?

I clear my throat and sit up straight, accepting the call just as the bus finally pulls away. At least this way none of the mothers can stop me and try to engage me in chatter—I have a phone to my ear.

"Hey, what's up?" Ron sounds too upbeat for this early, but then I remember that he goes to work so early, this is almost his lunch time.

"I'm just driving into work. I'm running late—our pal Susan grabbed me."

"Oh really? Did she tell you about her women's group?"

How would Ron know about the women's group? Susan said she was worried I was tempted to take him back. Does he know about the speed dating? Did she tell him to stay away from me and that she was trying to find me a man? She said Jake talked to him. Hmm…I wouldn't think Jake would get involved in domestic relations.

All of these people need to get a life and stay out of my business.

"She did mention something about…a meeting. So anyway, did you need something?"

I am not telling him anything. Somehow he'll use it against me. If he really wants me back, I don't want to give him anything else to become jealous over. With my luck, he'll register for the event and be one of my dates!

He hesitates a bit and says, "Well, yeah actually I wanted to talk to you yesterday when I saw you next door, but with the whole puppy thing…how's that going, by the way? I bet she's a doll."

Now I get sucked into puppy talk, and it's hard to make it sound like I have everything under control, but Ron is the last person to whom I would admit defeat or incompetence. He'll just file it in the 'Claire would have been a bad mother anyway' file.

He listens to my story and says, "She sounds adorable. I can't wait to meet her, but what I mainly wanted was to offer to help you with some stuff in the house."

Probably reacting to silence, he quickly adds, "As a *friend*. I promise I have no ulterior motive. I noticed some things that needed repair while I was over, and I want to help you out. I know you think you want to stay in that house, but eventually you may want to sell, and you can't let it fall into worse disrepair."

I hate to be suspicious, but my long history with Ron has taught me that he never does anything without a personal agenda. "Why do you want to help me? What's in it for you? I told you the other night—"

"I know all of that, but...I just feel bad about the way things have ended between us. And as I said, I really still care about you, Claire, but I shouldn't have said what I said about my feelings. I was just sucked in because you were so upset. I can't change the past, but you can let me do something for you."

So now he's saying he *isn't* still in love with me?

"Okay, Jeez. Let me think about it. Okay?"

He seems appeased for now, and I get him off the phone with promises to connect later, as I try to think of what excuse I can come up with for avoiding his call tonight.

Can't he just leave me alone? And I don't want him to be in love with me, so why do I feel worse hearing that he made a mistake in professing his feelings?

No matter how he feels about me, Ron *is* right (I hate when he's right!) about one thing. The house is rapidly deteriorating.

I don't understand how the absence of a man for less

than a year can cause the place to fall apart. Am I that inept?

Easy question—yes, I am. I don't have the money, skill or motivation to do anything more than basic cleaning.

When Dixie was chewing on the windowsill, I noticed how bad the paint job looks. I had always wanted to paint all of the rooms in the house pretty colors, but Ron insisted that white walls were best. Then everything matches, so he said.

The motivation behind that decorating preference is that we never need to buy anything new, because even all of the old crap from our first apartment matches white walls.

Ron is cheap.

He also doesn't like any of my color choices because he has no taste whatsoever in decorating. Or fashion. He wears brown shoes with black pants! And he doesn't own one garment that is anything other than black, brown, grey, or beige.

But I'm glad he called. Those white walls have been making me feel like I live in an asylum. No wonder I'm so agitated all the time. I need some nice soothing blues, a bold burgundy, or a striking hunter green.

That's it. That's my first household job on the list.

Unfortunately, Ron is not the man for that job.

One thing I promised myself when we separated was that I was not going to continue to fight with him, and we have wasted far too many years locked in battle over daily lifestyle decisions.

He will give me grief over the painting, even though he no longer lives in the house, and I'm done with that drama. I don't want to hear his opinions and lectures.

He was controlling and never really cared about what was important to me, even before I lost what mattered most...and things *really* fell apart.

It's nice of him to offer to help, but it's too little, too late.

Jane has a painter she's used in her house, and she said he does a great job, *and* he's reasonably priced. If I just stop buying shoes and eating out for a couple of months, I could afford to start on this project.

Of course I *could* paint myself, but then it would look like it was done by a drunk skunk in the dark.

Ha-ha...I know a guy I could call...

Kidding!

I dial Jane while at a stoplight.

"Hey, you know that painter you use? Can I get his info?"

CHAPTER SEVEN

Claire

"Hey, do you want to come to lunch with me and look at paint swatches?"

I stand in Rebecca's doorway with the grin of a woman about to go on a decorating binge. I haven't done it in years, and now I can actually get what I want.

Rebecca looks up wearing the little half glasses (when did she start needing those?) and says, "As much as that sounds like a wild time, I have a lunch date with Tony."

She goes back to staring at her computer, only this time she's scrunching her nose. I guess she must need even stronger reading glasses.

"Tony? As in, your ex, Tony? Oh my God, are you—"

"No, we're not back together." She takes off her glasses and blinks fast. "I wish I could see. I should be going to the eye doctor. Anyway, Tony and I meet for lunch at least once a month, just to catch up."

I narrow my eyes and ponder that one. I've been known to be a bit innocent about the meaning of Rebecca's code words. "Does 'catch up' mean—"

"No, I'm not sleeping with him, we're just friends. It *is* possible to be friends with an ex, especially one you dated for a short time. It wasn't anything serious—it never is with Tony."

Hmm...I've only met Tony once, therefore I can't speak to his intentions with women, but Rebecca is one to talk. She's one of the most independent, non-committal women I know. It's not that it's a bad thing, but it's not right to bash a guy for doing the same thing you do.

"So you're painting? Please tell me you're not going to do it yourself?"

"No, with the puppy—"

"You got a puppy?"

"Well, yes, and then Ron wanted to paint—"

"You're talking to Ron? Did he get you a puppy?"

Exasperated, I wring my hands and take a deep breath. "No, Jane got me the puppy. She's very cute—well, never mind." Rebecca has zero maternal instinct and is a cat person. "And Ron just offered to help me with some stuff around the house, but I'm going to say no. I called Jane's painter, and he's coming over tomorrow night to give me an estimate."

"Well, that was smart. The last thing you need is Ron in your life again. How about the painter, is he cute?"

"I don't think so—Jane didn't mention that. And why can't I be friends with Ron? You just said it's okay to be friends with exes."

Before Rebecca gets a chance to reply, I feel a presence right behind me, and I don't have to turn around to know who it is.

It's nice to know he doesn't only stalk my office, although when he didn't see us in there, he may have just come straight here. I don't know why he persists...

He says, "Are you two talking about boys again? I feel like I'm on the playground in middle school."

I mentally calculate that Justin was in middle school

when Ron and I got married, so I really don't see how his input is valuable.

Rebecca purses her lips and says, "Justin don't you have a server to fix or code to write, or whatever you people do over there?" She shakes her head and speaks directly to me again. "Men don't do anything for you without an agenda. He's either looking for a more favorable divorce settlement or he wants you back."

Justin steps to the side of me so he can see my reaction. He folds his arms and intently waits for my answer. Well, actually he's doing that in an obnoxious, flippant way.

I am not going to choose this time to tell Rebecca what happened with Ron the other night. His declarations of love are none of Justin's business, and it will just give him more teasing material.

I say, "No, I think he just wants to call a truce and be nice. In my experience, men are too lazy to…Justin, what are you doing?"

He has walked into Rebecca's office, and is writing something on a post-it note with one of her pens.

Rebecca glares at him and says, "Really, can't you go jot down your genius ideas in your own office? We're trying to have a conversation, and I'm going to be late for lunch."

"Sorry, I was just taking notes. This information about what men do and don't do is riveting. I must compare it to my own behavior later and see how I stack up."

He smiles as Rebecca points her finger at the door.

"Okay, I'm leaving." He makes it past me and then peeks his head back in. "Are you sure neither one of you want to punch my abs? I feel even more worried about how I measure up, now that I know Claire's hunky ex is back in the picture. And you're having lunches with Tony..."

"Okay, I'm off to see Benjamin Moore." I leave Rebecca's door open as I beat a hasty retreat.

Justin is still standing there, and says, "Who's Benjamin Moore? Another admirer?"

I really question his genius IQ. A smart guy would have gotten the hint to leave us alone already. Maybe at another point in my life I would have been flattered by the attention, but someone like Justin is not interested in me. Or Rebecca. I think he's just bored. Don't geniuses get bored easily?

I sigh and shake my head. "You know damn well it's a paint store. Now go back to your office and behave."

"Yes, Ma'am. You know, I could help you, but you know how guys are? Then you'd have to...never mind."

He disappears down the hallway and I swallow the comments I would like to yell as he walks away.

He's right in a way. Our generalizations about men are silly, but we've had a lot more experience than he has...well, at least Rebecca has.

But I have more concentrated experience with one man for a long haul, and that's got to count for something. Unfortunately, I have to call that man and decline his offer. I guess that's when I'll be able to see his motives.

Ron tends to get angry when things don't go his way.

Ron

Things are really going my way. I finished my route early today, and I'm looking forward to relaxing by the pool in my apartment complex.

I'm sure Claire has spent most of the day thinking about my offer, and what a nice guy I've become. I just need to make sure I hold back and let her come to me now. Being pushy and controlling are a couple of her complaints about me. She doesn't understand that I know her so well that I know what's best for her. The events of the past year make it painfully obvious that she doesn't make good choices on her own.

I throw my keys on my kitchen counter and scroll through the messages on my phone. Nothing from Claire yet, but it's early. She won't be off work for a couple of hours.

I should go check my mail before I change into my swim trunks. Whew, I should also take a shower, even though I'll need another one after using the community pool. At least we don't have too many little kids in this apartment complex, but there is always the pee factor to consider in a public pool.

I purposely rented in one of the fancier communities after I moved out of our house, even though I hate to waste money. If I have to live in an apartment, it needs to be a nice one.

It's a newer complex behind the Walmart shopping center. I know right away that makes the fancy factor plummet in a lot of people's minds, but it's convenient to be near some shopping, and it's still close to work.

I grab my mailbox key off the counter and my phone starts ringing. Claire. Yes! I pick up the call and head out to the group mailboxes right across the hall from my unit. I frequently forget to pick up my mail, and then find out my driver's license has expired or I missed out on pizza coupons.

"Hey, Babe what's up?"

Okay, I need to dial it back a notch. 'Babe' is not a 'friendly' name. I wouldn't ever call Mike or Mario 'Babe.'

My assessment is confirmed as it takes a moment for Claire to speak.

"Um, hi. I just wanted to let you know that I was thinking about your offer, and I have decided to hire a painter. Not that I don't appreciate it…"

I put the key in my mailbox a little more forcefully than necessary as Claire continues to babble nervously about how if she needs something small fixed, she might call me, but I helped her realize that the painting was the most urgent thing that needs to be addressed.

Yeah, I bet. It's just because she knows how much I didn't want the inside of our house to resemble the rainbow flag or a daycare center.

As I get ready to respond, I am startled by a hand on my…what the fuck?

I cover the phone as if it's the one that was attached to the wall around the time I was born, and whisper, "Knock it off, I'm on the phone."

Claire says, "Ron? Are you there? Who are you talking to?"

"No one, it's just Mario." That was smooth. Mario is clearly someone. "He came by to drop off my tennis racket. I left it at the…" I grab Stacy's hand and guide it away from my…

"Oh, well, I'll let you go then. But you understand about the house, right? I do appreciate you wanting to help, but I think it would be best for our…friendship…to leave it to a—"

"Yep, I totally get it." I dance out of Stacy's grasp and now she's wagging a package in front of me and licking her lips. Did she just pull that out of her mailbox?

Claire pauses again and says goodbye.

Shit, I really wanted to try to talk her out of it, but…

"Stacy, what are you doing? Get inside before the kids get off the school bus, and someone calls the cops."

She follows me into my apartment and pushes me up against the closed door, covering me with her mouth and hands.

I know that doesn't *sound* bad, but I haven't gotten a chance to address the 'Stacy' situation, now that I've decided that I want Claire back.

Just as roughly as she started molesting me, now she grabs my ear and her touch turns painful. This woman is about as opposite from Claire as I could have veered, which makes sense for a casual, rebound buddy.

I refuse to use the common term for what we're doing because I said I would never stoop that low.

She reaches under my shirt and pulls an underarm hair.

"Ow, you're crazy. Stop it." I hold her arms and try to calm her down.

She says, 'So, who were you talking to? And why am I suddenly Mario returning a tennis racket?"

I release my grip and use this as an opportunity to get away from her, making it to the relative safety of the middle of my living room.

I'm a big guy, but Stacy is almost six-feet tall. She has chestnut brown hair (I think that's what you'd call it), which curls into an unruly, sexy mess. Her eyes are green and her body is to die for. She's like one of those warrior princess women on violent cable TV shows. In deep contrast to this persona, she's a librarian.

Yep, I went with the fantasy woman.

"Stacy, you need to calm down. I was talking to Claire, if you must know, and I didn't feel like explaining anything to her."

"Claire? You lied about me to Claire? Since when are you all chummy with her? Is she just trying to get you to sign the divorce papers?"

Sometimes I kick myself for telling Stacy too much.

And then other times, like now, I lie.

"Yep, she's still busting my balls about it, and I'm not going to give her any ammunition to get more out of me than she's already asking for."

She's actually not asking for anything, and I have nothing to give her. I just know that as a divorced woman in her early forties, Stacy is about as bitter as they come about these things, and she's constantly telling me what her ex did to her, and how I'm too soft with Claire, blah, blah, blah...the things I do to get some action.

But this is some amazing action.

Still, I wonder if I haven't bought myself a bunch of trouble. Stacy and I aren't *dating*, and she isn't one of those women who pretends she has more commitment from a guy than she does. I thought she was fine with what we're doing.

But as it is plain to see, she has some possessive feelings towards me, even if it's just a pride thing.

No matter what, there is no way we could be in a relationship. She's way too volatile and untrustworthy. She's cheated on the last several guys she's dated, including her husband, but according to her, *he* was the asshole.

One day, I expect to hear that she was fired for coming on to one of her library patrons—like a college kid looking for help with his term paper.

She's almost ten years older than me, and I'm the oldest guy she's been with in *years*. Not that I'm knocking the cougar thing—she's just not…like Claire. In any way. And I'm beginning to realize that I appreciate some stability.

Stacy now dissolves into a forced pout, and comes running at me again, this time hopefully for more desirable molesting with less pain.

Shit, what am I going to do about this?

"Well, hopefully you'll get this resolved soon. Even though I enjoy my independence, I could see us going places when you're a free man."

She starts kissing me again, which is a good thing because she can't see the expression on my face.

How could I possibly have gotten this woman so interested in me that she thinks we have a future? I'm not even that nice to her. I never even call.

Hmm…I *have* been going about it all wrong with Claire. I *should* let her come to me. Isn't that what Mario said?

But then again, Claire and Stacy only share female anatomy, and not too much else. No plan will have the same effect on both of them.

This one is psycho, I do know that for sure, as I feel blood forming on my lip.

"Jeez, Stacy. That hurts." I touch my lip to inspect the damage. It's like kissing a very attractive Rottweiler.

I'm losing my mind. Now she's pouting again and opening her package. The one she was waving at me in the hallway.

"I got something for us."

She pats the couch to motion for me to sit down, and

begins to open up her sexy treasure chest. Lingerie, massage oils, a few things I don't want to admit that I've never seen, and don't know how to use. But the last item is the worst.

She holds up a box with a big heart on it.

"This is a 'love' heating pad, you know...to mimic a hot stone massage."

Oh, that's not so bad. I thought it was some kind of romantic gesture...

She turns the box around and reads from the back, 'express your tender love for your partner with intense heat applied directly to..."

I stopped listening at 'tender love.'

I am fucked in all the wrong ways.

CHAPTER EIGHT

Claire

Berry Cobbler. New London Burgundy. Monticello Rose.

I can't stop staring at my pretty paint swatches. I was so excited in Benjamin Moore yesterday, and I spent all last night pouring over the choices, holding them up to my walls and furnishings.

I don't know why I didn't do this sooner. It's like I've been in limbo. Definitely in a daze.

And the worst part is that I've been sending this message to Ron, too. I haven't made any concrete steps to move my life forward since the separation. That's why he won't sign, and maybe he thinks he's still in love with me. Or I'm in love with him. I am behaving more like a grieving widow stuck in the past, than a confident woman who has made a life affirming decision.

So I'm starting with paint. And a puppy. I just need to keep the puppy out of the paint, which is why I called Joe, the real painter.

I was thrilled that he was already free to come over tonight. I'm going to get estimates for all of the rooms, but I think I'll start with the dining room. It's not very big, so it shouldn't be a huge expense, and I've always wanted a red dining room.

Ron said he didn't want to be reminded of blood while he was eating his dinner. Meanwhile, we ate in the dining room about three times a year.

This is why I'm so proud of myself for saying no to Ron. I need to cut the cord. Ron and I will never be friends like Rebecca and any of her exes. She's right, it's just not the same.

While I am patting myself on the back for handling Ron and the house, my skills as a puppy mother are still questionable. That's a bigger learning curve.

My brilliant idea with the newspaper the other day only resulted in shredded newspaper and puppy pads. The pee was conveniently deposited on the actual carpet. I think she was proud that she figured out how to get to her real toilet, despite the challenges Mommy set up.

Good game, Mommy. Let's play some more.

I broke down and called Jane. After she was done laughing, she brought me a puppy pen. It's a wooden structure with slats and basically acts as a circular cage.

I put it in my kitchen and it seemed to do the trick today. Sure, she peed and pooped in it, but I can deal with that for now. I need to figure out this potty training thing, but in the meantime I'm saving my carpets. If I hadn't been so stubborn, Jane would have helped me from the start.

This is a lesson for me — know when to ask for help!

I watch Dixie playing on the floor in her pen, and smile at her. She immediately whimpers and jumps on the gate. Wow, that actually moved a smidge. She's a strong little thing, but there's no way she could ever knock it over. And her legs are about two inches long, so she has no future as an Olympic high jumper.

I decide to let her out for now. There's no reason to keep her locked up. The painter will be here soon, and she'll want to greet him.

The doorbell rings and I scoop her up so she can't run out the front door.

"Come on, Dixie. Let's go meet the nice man."

She wags her tail as I open the door.

"Well, hello there. I'm Joe."

I firmly grasp Dixie with my left arm, and shake his rough hand. Ron's hands are pretty rough, too, but this guy has done some serious physical labor in his life.

"Hello, thanks for coming at such short notice."

I move out of the way and gesture for him to come in.

He walks in and touches Dixie's paw. "Hello there to you, too. What's this cutie's name?"

I put her down and she immediately jumps on Joe's leg, not even reaching his kneecap. I'm surprised she didn't recoil when he grabbed her paw — dogs don't usually like that type of touching.

"This is Dixie. She's only been with me for a couple of days."

He bends down to pet her and she rolls over to show her belly. From this vantage point, I can see Joe has paint on his slightly balding head. It looks like the room he was painting today was a sunny shade of yellow.

"She's a doll." He stops petting her and slowly stands up. I notice he does so with a bit of effort, but he's not a young man and I'm sure all that hard work takes its toll. I can barely lift *my* lazy butt up when I bend down.

"So what have we got here? You're lookin' to paint the whole place?"

He gets out a stained, crumpled up notebook, pulls a pencil from behind his ear and smiles at me.

He has a nice smile, even though his teeth are a bit stained from smoking. Jane assured me that he never smokes in the house, and he is very trustworthy.

He better be because if he's here while I'm at work, Dixie will be here, too. But he certainly seems like an animal lover. After all, he'd have to be if he worked at Jane's house.

I lead him around the house, and show him all of the rooms I would like painted, including the foyer and upstairs hallway, which has a cathedral ceiling. He assures me that he has very tall ladders and lots of experience with heights.

He also tells me about other houses in the area he's worked on, which makes me feel even more confident. He's been doing this for years, and while he may be a little rough around the edges in his appearance, that's to be expected. He's not going to paint in a suit.

I'm just not used to having strange men working in the house. Ron did everything or it didn't get done. He would never have paid someone.

As we talk, Joe tells me about dogs he's had, and how he wished he had time for one now, but they're a lot of work. I even share some of my mishaps so far with Dixie, and he reassures me that I'll get the hang of it.

"We are *owned* by the puppies, but eventually they learn who's the boss."

He laughs and Dixie looks at him as if to say, 'Sir, you've never had a wiener dog.'

I'm enjoying our chat about the house, the neighborhood and dogs so much, that I didn't notice how late it's getting. I'm meeting my friend Audra for dinner downtown, and I need to get going. I tell Joe I need to wrap this up.

"Sure thing, little lady. I have all the notes I need, and I can get back to you by tomorrow with the estimates. "

I thank him and walk him to the door.

"Bye little girl. Don't give your mama so much trouble." He pets Dixie's tiny head and whistles on his way back to his work van.

What a nice guy.

I switch gears and grab my furry baby, setting her down gently in her wooden prison with food, water, a blanket, toys…she should be all set.

"Okay, Dixie. Mommy's going out now. I'll be back soon."

I run a quick comb through my hair and swipe on some lip gloss before running out the door.

The drive downtown is actually only about twenty minutes, and I quickly text Audra that I'm running a few minutes late. We're meeting at a Spanish restaurant, which is not my favorite. Actually, I've never been there. I hate Mexican food, but she swears this is nothing like it. I guess I do believe her, but I am so squeamish about foreign cuisines, especially if they are spicy. I ate Thai food one time and almost spontaneously combusted.

Okay, really I just spent a lot of time in the bathroom, and my tongue was scorched for a week.

I pull into the parking deck and seek out a good spot. If I don't pick one close to the exit I end up walking around looking for my car with a sign on my back that says, 'please abduct me, I'm a moron.'

Luckily it's not too crowded so I can get a spot on the ground floor, within shouting distance of the attendant. I walk out onto the street and notice I have a message from Joe already.

Wow, he's quick. I would have thought he would e-mail the prices to me, but he may not be high-tech enough for that. Or maybe he just wants to tell me the price for the dining room, since I said that was my top priority. I do want to get on his schedule since he's pretty busy, but I'm at the restaurant now so it can wait.

Audra is sitting at the bar sipping something amber colored in a small glass. I don't know too many women who can drink straight scotch or bourbon, or any of the hard liquors. I can do a shot if I'm cajoled into it, but it burns a hole all the way to my stomach.

She's British, but I don't think that has anything to do with high alcohol tolerance. She's also a vegetarian and a physics professor at the university downtown.

She's an unlikely friend for me, being that I drink wine or girly drinks, I love a good steak, and I almost failed physics in high school.

The only time I remember waking up in class was when the teacher dropped a bowling ball on the classroom floor. This was supposed to illustrate some scientific principle, but it just gave me heart palpitations and a stronger dislike of the class that my father and guidance counselor forced me to take.

But I digress.

"Hellooo, it's so good to see you. How have you been?" Audra speaks in soothing tones and her accent is comforting. We haven't gotten together in a while, and the last time I saw her I was quite an emotional wreck.

Yes, worse than I've already shared, but let's not talk about it.

I join her at the bar, and lay my purse down on a stool. "I'm fine. Is our table ready?" I give her a hug and feel her lean, muscular frame. I'm a thin girl, but I'm squishy. Audra has a tall, athletic body, sort of like a bigger ballerina.

She also has the most gorgeous naturally grey hair. She's in her early forties, but apparently premature grey runs in her family, and she chooses to embrace the natural look. Overall, with her sparse makeup and conservative pant suits, she's also the opposite of me in the fashion department.

"It *is* ready, but I was waiting for you. You look great. Shall we sit down?"

The hostess gathers our menus as Audra settles her bar tab, and we all proceed to the front of the restaurant. I should have known she'd asked for a spot by the window. She loves to people watch. She's rather introverted, but she likes to observe. I suppose that's why she's a scientist.

We settle in and begin chatting about our jobs and what we've been doing so far this summer. We're able to order quickly and our food comes out a short while later.

Surprisingly, the waiter steered me in the right direction, and the paella I ordered isn't hot at all, and is actually quite delicious. Who knew?

Audra takes a small bite of her vegetarian bean salad and says, "I absolutely must get to the sea this year. Do you fancy a little trip?"

She always refers to the beach as 'the sea.' It makes it sound so much more exotic and adventurous.

We talk about planning a long weekend away, and I add, "I wish we could get Rachel to come with us."

Rachel is our mutual friend. Audra and I met through her when Rachel and I worked together, and they lived in the same apartment building. That was before Rachel married George and began having babies.

They have a little boy named William, and a baby girl named Anna. Close to my age, she's now a stay-at-home mother.

"Oh, I meant to tell you—I stopped by to see her yesterday and she said she would love a hen's night. What do you think?"

Audra sees Rachel often, even though they have completely different lifestyles and schedules. I can't imagine Rachel has time to go out and party.

"Really? She'll leave the baby?"

"Well, she's almost six months old now, and Rachel has been out a few times without her. She's pumping her milk. Anyway, she said she'd love it if the three of us could go out on Friday. She wants to go 'clubbing.' I said I wouldn't know much about that, but that you might have some ideas since you're out far more than I am."

Audra is single, never married and has no children. Kind of like Rebecca, but Audra rarely dates. Her last real boyfriend was years ago, before we met. She prefers to stay home with her cat and read. I think being in class all day drains her energy, and she would rather spend some time alone than go to a noisy club.

But I can't see Rachel wanting to go to a club either, or George approving of that, but that's another story.

"Actually, I don't go 'clubbing,' but there is a nice place not far from here with a more upscale feel upstairs with a more mature crowd, and a real 'club' downstairs."

"Oh, that sounds brilliant."

I pause and think of how to describe the place I'm talking about. Of all people, Justin actually reminded me about it. He says he goes there with his friends—downstairs, of course.

Why would he want to hang out upstairs with people like me and my friends? He gets enough of that during the work week. I'm sure if we went to the upstairs bar we'd never run into him. Plus, young people always go out later, and I'm sure Audra and Rachel will be ready to go home by ten.

I put down my fork and say, "I think it would be a good bet that Rachel won't want to go downstairs. When she sees all the half-dressed, barely legal kids lined up to get in there, I'm sure she'll be happy to take her leaky breasts upstairs with the rest of us old people."

Audra laughs and spits out a couple of beans, which makes her laugh harder. I am just hoping no beans shoot out of her nose.

Now that image has me dying laughing. It's a good thing it's not crowded in here or we'd be making a scene, but it feels good to laugh.

We compose ourselves and decide to propose a night out at The Tobacco Warehouse on Friday. It also might be a 'brilliant' place to meet some decent men.

This week is looking up—I have my speed dating thing on Thursday, and now these plans on Friday. And once I leave here I am going to call Joe back, and soon I'll have my beautiful berry colored dining room. Maybe it will inspire me to host dinner parties.

Okay, that was taking it a little too far. There's no magic dust in the paint.

Over dessert we talk about Dixie. Audra adores animals, so she 'oohs and ahhs' at the pictures on my phone, and she's so happy for me.

We wrap up with an after dinner cordial—well actually, Audra does. I've had some wine and I can't walk home from here. Audra lives a few blocks away, and as much as I will offer to drive her, she'll say that an evening 'constitutional' clears her head.

We hug goodbye outside the restaurant with promises to arrange Friday's festivities. I let Audra take the action to get back to Rachel. It's not that I don't want to talk to her, but frankly I've been feeling terribly guilty that I haven't been to see the baby yet. I've never wanted to be one of those women who shies away from babies because she can't get pregnant, or for that matter, brides because she can't find a husband.

Unfortunately, I am now that woman. Perhaps this outing on Friday will break the ice. I'll apologize and get my ass over there to see the little cherub.

I can't avoid babies forever, and Rachel is also a loyal friend. Besides, Audra said I shouldn't even worry about it. Apparently Rachel has been so scatter-brained since the birth that she probably thinks I *have* been to visit.

I safely get to my car and lock myself in, while looking for the ticket to pay the parking fee on the way out. Oh, yeah—Joe. I better call now before it gets too much later.

Before I dial, I decide to listen to his message. Since I grew up in the era of the answering machine, I feel obligated to listen if someone has taken the time to record a voice mail.

And besides, maybe it will give me all the information I need, and it doesn't even warrant a call back.

"You have one voice message. First message."

There's the usual pause and then...

"Hey there beautiful..."

Uh oh, did he dial the wrong number? I shouldn't listen to a message that was meant for someone...

"I can't stop thinking about your eyes…"

Why am I not deleting this? I feel like the peeping tom of voice mails.

"…they're so soft and brown, like melted chocolate…"

I gasp and look in the mirror. My eyes are a little chocolaty!

"…and that little dog was such a sweetie, just like her mama…"

Motherfucker! Now it sounds like he fell asleep. Is he drunk? I hear a faint hiccup and then…

"…I would sure like to take you out some time…and I've got some good ideas for colors for your bedroom…"

I am going to kill Jane!

"…I reckon you should save the red for a more private space, if you know what I mean?"

I think my paella is going to make a resurgence after this, and I know I should hit delete *now*, before he follows that up with a visual I can't soon forget.

"…they say red is the color of passion…so if you want…oh son of a bitch…where'd that table come from…sorry Baby, I just hit my head because I'm drink…drunk on your smile…"

Mercifully he either dropped the phone, he's unconscious, or he accidentally deleted my number and can't call back.

Oh my God, it doesn't matter because he knows where I live! I suddenly feel like I need to shower under scalding water for an hour. How could he have good references from my neighbors?

Now I realize that I never checked into that, and I remember Mike joking about how painters always drink. I got that stupid stereotype from him, but I didn't think that would translate into this sort of behavior, and he paints a straight line and shows up on time. Jane would never knowingly recommend a creeper and a pervert!

Unless of course this one has enough morals to lay off married women. I punch the steering wheel and have a quick foot stomping tantrum before backing my car out of the parking space and heading home.

I am praying that Joe isn't sitting outside my window with a radio, singing love songs, like in that eighties movie.

If so, the cops will have to get involved and that could be ugly. Of course, some of *them* could be cute.

I know—if he calls again I will tell him Ron and I are getting back together, and he's going to take care of the painting.

But I still feel badly for lying.

It's funny how I hesitate to go on the offensive. So many women are raised to be nice girls. *He's* the pervert and I'm trying to figure out how to avoid hurting his feelings. My mother didn't teach me that, though. It must have been societal messages.

I hate to think what Mom would suggest doing to him.

I reach for my phone to call Jane to fill her in, but decide to wait until I've calmed down. She should know so she doesn't give his name out to anyone else, but I'm not in the mood to deal with it.

I still want my red dining room, and I know how to get it. Of course I could find another painter, but if Ron wants to help me so badly, maybe I should let him. I can set boundaries. Once again, I am hurting myself because I am afraid to be assertive with a man.

I think if he spends a little time at the house, and around me, he will see why we aren't together, and he'll finally sign the damn papers.

Feeling much more in control, I plan to call him when I get in, once I take care of Dixie's mess and take her outside for another fruitless round of 'please go pee-pee outside for Mommy.'

I drive into my cul-de-sac slowly, but it's not like there are many hiding places for cars, and I don't see Joe's van, or any other suspicious vehicles. Just all the people who live here, tucked in on a boring Wednesday evening in suburbia.

For once, I am grateful for the peace and quiet. Maybe I should just stay here—after all Audra is always complaining about her partying neighbors in the city, and…

Jesus, Mary and Joseph…was there a woodpecker in here?

I hold onto the kitchen counter for strength, and survey the scene. Dixie is still in her enclosure in the kitchen, and she's wagging her tail and jumping and spinning like she always does. She has most certainly peed and pooped in the far corner of her assigned space, which was to be expected.

What I hadn't counted on was that she would turn into 'Mighty Wiener' and push the wooden enclosure, from the inside, all the way to the center kitchen island.

You would think that wouldn't be such a big deal— she didn't make it to the carpet in the family room, and so the island just formed a needed road block. An obstacle.

Unfortunately, the wood is also a good fang/nail sharpener, and my overgrown, furry termite has chewed an actual, fucking HOLE in the island. I can see my dishes in the cabinet, which opens on the other side!

I've seen pictures of dogs chewing their way out of doors and dog houses, but I thought they were bigger dogs. Or it was just a joke for the cameras. Or the wood was like paper and they lived in some sort of falling down shacks.

But no. It seems the average, unattended wiener dog puppy can actually chew and dig its way to China.

At least to *my* china.

CHAPTER NINE

Claire

Maybe if I sit very quietly for the next ten minutes no one will come in my office, and I can sneak out without anyone seeing me. I have been avoiding people all day.

Luckily Justin had some big meeting with the other executives so he's been out of sight. And Rebecca took one look at me this morning and brought me Excedrin and a Coke. Only a true friend would bring me double caffeine products *and* accept my silence regarding the problem.

Normally I love to commiserate on my problems, but last night was just a double whammy.

After I breathed into a bag (not really, but it was close), I cleaned up Dixie's mess as best I could. I called Jane and told her about Dixie and Joe. She laughed at the former, and apologized profusely for the latter.

She gave me the name of her pet sitter, who also does one-on-one pet training consultation. She also reminded me that she can come over and check on Dixie when I'm out, although that won't solve the larger problem. Dixie needs constant supervision until I get a handle on her lack of potty training and destructive behavior.

I think Jane also secretly feels guilty for pushing me to get the dog in the first place, but she's mainly afraid I'm going to give her away.

I would *never* do that. Even though she is playing my last nerve, I love her already. She's badly behaved, but she's adorable and cuddly and I can see she already needs me.

How could I ever get rid of her?

Melody, the pet sitter, sounds like a sweet lady. I'm wondering how much it's going to cost now that I'll have my own personal wiener whisperer, but with the money I am saving on painting, I should still come out ahead.

I called Ron at lunchtime and he returned the call right away. It sounded like he was in the UPS truck with the wind whipping through the semi-open vehicle.

I didn't tell him about Joe because I don't really want Joe to die, or Ron to end up in jail. That will only magnify my troubles.

I told him the prices were kind of high, and if he was still interested in helping, maybe we could work something out with the settlement and the amount I will owe to buy him out of the house. If I finance the work in that way, it will be cheap long-term, and Ron will be properly compensated for his time. I still have the problem of the hole in the island, but that's not critical, and I would rather hide it from Ron, if I can.

By the afternoon I'm starting to feel a bit more in control of my life, and I'm able to get some work done.

Work is frustrating lately. We've been trying to hire an editorial assistant for ages, and we just can't attract a talented young person to this staid, boring company. Amanda is timid so she settled, but I don't think she's very career focused. Hence, why she's ended up as our front desk receptionist.

And our CEO, Tim needs an administrative assistant. Again!

But who am I to talk about career focus, as I pack up my laptop and prepare to sneak out early, even though I came in late, *and* took a long lunch.

I am justifying this behavior by telling myself that if they want me to work a full day, they need to give me more real work. I could handle much more responsibility. Come to think of it, this is yet another area where I don't want to rock the boat and I accept less.

My self-psychoanalysis ends as I peel out of the parking lot and hurry home to change for tonight's exciting event—church speed dating!

Tomorrow night's 'girls' night out' to The Tobacco Warehouse is all set. Audra said Rachel is beside herself with anticipation, and she's been sending Audra pictures of potential outfits all day.

That makes me a little sad because in the past I was the one who had that kind of relationship with Rachel. I am eager to patch things up.

The problem is that I feel like all I do lately is patch things up. I don't even have time to figure out why so many things are full of holes, when something else gets shot up.

At least tonight is a clean slate. I don't know any of these people, except for Susan, and no one will have any pre-conceived notions about me.

It's also a controlled environment, and we're not allowed to give anyone our contact information. After the speed 'dates' we all turn in a sheet with our picks, and then we get e-mails with a list of people who were interested in us. The church ladies will only provide contact information with each participant's permission.

As I pull into my driveway, I feel a sense of calm rush over me. Like I've turned a corner. Jane brought her spare crate over this morning (she doesn't believe in them but has them for when dogs get sick) because I think she was up all night worried about Dixie's fate, our friendship and my sanity.

Not necessarily in that order.

I gave in because after all, what the hell do I know? I don't know if I 'believe' in crate training, but I do believe in living in a house that isn't completely destroyed.

It will put a Band-Aid on a problem, but I don't see how putting her in a different container constitutes 'training?' I know there's more to it than that, but I am not home to work on it.

So I thankfully agreed to lock Dixie up before I left for work, and Jane promised she would come over and check on her every hour.

How could that end up being a disaster? Maybe Jane taking her outside will get her used to it. Jane has tons of experience with dogs and for the most part, hers use the outdoor facilities.

She last texted at four and said everything was fine, and supposedly Dixie peed outside, and Jane reminded me that I shouldn't worry because dogs won't poop in their crates.

This is the part I don't understand, but the experts say that dogs see the crate as their house, and they won't poop in their houses. However, Dixie has no qualms about pooping in *my* house, where she also lives. And how will she know it's *her* house? Are we going to have a mortgage closing? A house-warming party?

I have been reading some of the literature from the breeder on training, and it does seem like there is something real in all of this madness. I am still holding out hope that I can do this myself, and won't need to call in the pro for a house call. It's only one tiny dog.

I walk in the front door and I can already hear the crate bars rattling. I feel like I've kept her in prison all day, but then I remember how many visits she's had, and she's just excited to see me after…oh, come on!

I stop a few feet from the crate, which is in the kitchen. I am far enough away to change my mind and run back out the door, but still close enough to smell the poop carnage. I can also see it. Smeared all over the crate, the blanket, the toys *and* the dog. She actually has a piece of poop partially covering her *eye*!

My dog's vision is blocked by her own shit!

I want to scream, punch something, and cry—all at the same time. Instead I swing open the crate, grab Dixie, and throw the smelly jail cell into the backyard, along with all her other disgusting belongings.

I hold Dixie as tightly as I can without hurting her, or getting shit smeared all over me, which amounts to holding the whole dog with three fingers as I carry her upstairs. I head to my bathroom, then change my mind and switch to the guest bathroom.

I fill up the tub with water—well just a few inches—and submerge Dixie while trying to find some kind of shampoo or soap that won't harm her skin. It would have made sense to assemble my supplies *before* I got her out of the crate, but I'm working on adrenaline here. I have single Christians to speed date in about twenty minutes!

Dixie is whining at top volume as I rinse the poop and attempt to lather her with some cheap shampoo left over from the last time Ron's mother came to visit. That shows you how often I come into this room. It's pretty mild shampoo, so it shouldn't hurt her.

I feel sorry for the poor baby, but the mess is making me late. I planned on changing my clothes anyway, but I didn't plan on wearing dog stink cologne, and now I'm worried that some poop essence may have shot up into my hair.

Somehow I manage to rinse most of the shampoo out of Dixie's fur, and grab a towel from the rack after letting all the water out of the tub.

Now I realize she still has more suds that need to be rinsed, so I have to hold her wiggly body still while spraying her with the handheld nozzle. She doesn't seem to be as upset about this method, but is shaking like it's below zero in here.

"Oh Dixie, I'm sorry but you pooped yourself so badly. I know the air conditioning is cold. We'll get you dry in a minute."

I pick her up and wrap her in the towel, wrestling with her in order to get her dry. Sitting on the floor, I finally give up and let her run off down the hall. I peek around the corner to find her shaking her body violently and rolling around on the carpet.

Hopefully there is no more poop on her body, or next I'll be calling the carpet cleaner.

Or I could skip all of these smaller steps and just bring in a wrecking ball. At this rate I won't owe Ron anything to buy him out of the house—the value will have sunk so low it will be a better settlement for both of us to just set it on fire.

I realize I'm being a tad dramatic, but now I have ten minutes and I'm feeling panicky. I hope lateness isn't one of the seven deadly sins.

Or is it? Let's see—there's greed, lust, sloth—yep,

this could be interpreted as sloth, and I'm not going to tell them I'm late because my dog had shit in her eye.

I let Dixie continue to use the hallway carpet as her personal towel, and run back to my room to change clothes, and fix my face and hair. I pull on a cream knit top that comes up to my neck, but is form fitting enough to be stylish. I pair it with a brick red, flared knit skirt with a pattern of black and cream geometric shapes. My lightweight black cardigan and black kitten heeled pumps complete the outfit.

The jewelry I'm wearing will have to do, and under no circumstances am I wearing stockings. If they are offended by my bare legs, they can kiss my ass. I pull my skirt down a little, but my knees are showing and if that's a sin they can refer back to the ass-kissing invitation.

I almost run out the door before doing anything with Dixie. The crate is lying in the yard, so that's out. I gave Jane the 'super strong' wooden enclosure back, and the pet gate just locks her in a room where she can destroy carpet, woodwork and furniture.

Making all of those assessments in a split second, I grab her wiggly, damp body and plop her on the couch with a clean blanket—the soft blue afghan, and a few toys that escaped Shitstorm 2012.

"Bye, Dixie. I surrender."

Mentally letting go of that problem for now, I run out the door, pulling on my sweater.

Susan's husband, Jake is across the street watching me almost fall down the porch steps trying to put my shoes on, and I realize that his wife has probably already been at the church for half an hour.

I bet Jake could help with Dixie. If I didn't think he

would scare her to death, I'd ask him to check on her. She could use the fear of God…or the army. 'Private Dixie' reporting for duty!

Ugh…she's never going to listen to me, I'm about as scary as an ant.

Oh my God, that reminds me. I hope I didn't leave her food out—that might attract ants.

CHAPTER TEN

Claire

By some miracle (no church pun intended) I am here with about thirty seconds to spare. The whole way in the car I have been sniffing my hair to see if it smells like poop.

I am so paranoid now, and everything smells like poop. I think the stink may have just lodged itself in my nasal cavity, and other people won't smell it. I wish I had some perfume to sniff in order to neutralize my over-taxed sense.

Right before I get out of the car I stick my hand lotion bottle up to my nose and snort it like nose spray...or cocaine.

Not that I've ever snorted any drugs, but the guy walking by my car with his mouth hanging open seems to think he's caught me in the act.

Great, he's probably my first 'date.' He looks a little old—maybe he's in a different group. Wait, did Susan say there were different age ranges?

I throw the lotion down, massaging some of it into the skin around my nose—can't ever have too much moisture—and head inside.

The church building itself isn't very church-ish looking, but it's a non-denominational Christian church. But not one of those 'high-five stoked for God let's meet in a movie theater' churches.

I pause to read the name on the building since I never can remember. When Susan starts telling me about it, I usually zone out.

It's not that I'm opposed to church, or religion in general. I was raised Catholic, and like many of my faith I have fallen away from the Church, and now that I am soon-to-be divorced, I don't see much of a place for me within the spiritual community of my youth.

So I'm kind of like a holy fish flopping around out of water.

Okay, so it's the Southside Bible Church of Our Savior. The flashing neon marquee outside tells me so (how did I miss that when I pulled in?), as well as information about Bible study, an upcoming play about the life of…I didn't catch that, it's moving too fast. Oh crap, they have a divorce support group. I need to dodge that one.

Feeling less confident than I did when I hastily accepted this invitation, I walk into the main lobby and see a table with a bunch of women seated, and people gathering around filling out forms and putting on nametags.

"Oh Claire, you made it!"

Susan grabs me as if we are old friends, as opposed to awkward neighbors who regularly ignore each other. However, I do think she means well, and it was nice of her and her fellow church ladies to organize this event.

Scanning the room while caught in her bear hug, I am pleased to see that none of her buddies look like Dana Carvey playing the 'Church Lady' on Saturday Night Live.

"Yep, I'm actually looking forward to it."

This is a tiny little bit of a lie, but how bad can it be?

Shit, is lying also one of the seven deadlies?

Ron

Claire called today, and asked me to paint for her. I knew she would see that was the best solution. She said the painter was expensive, and I'm sure she realized that she can't afford it. Or at the very least it will cut into her shoe or 'girls' night out' budgets.

She also babbled about paying me back by adding to the amount I get from her when she refinances the house, and buys me out.

That's a nice story, but I paid no attention because that's never happening. I don't even know if she will qualify for a mortgage that size on her own, and regardless I fully intend to be moving back in soon.

Unfortunately, I still have to live in my apartment for now, and there's the Stacy issue. I was so mad at myself last night for giving in to her, but she just makes it so damn easy.

I tried to open my mouth to tell her that she was coming on too strong, or even that I have decided I want Claire back, but none of those words would form as she started putting the tricks in her sex toy package to work.

I am especially susceptible to this sort of thing because Claire and I never did stuff like that. After we get back together, I intend to add a little spice to our lives.

The problem is if I tell Stacy about my intentions with Claire, she might tell her about us and ruin the whole thing. Plus, I have told Stacy A LOT of stuff about Claire and our marriage.

But in my defense I hate therapy, and I was licking my wounds, and she was licking...other stuff...so I relaxed and started talking, and once I saw I had a sympathetic ear, it was all out on the table.

Well, usually the bed, but sometimes the table or the couch. Once on the patio…

Anyway, it's not like I'm cheating. Claire and I are separated, and she is trying to get me to sign divorce papers. She's *actively* dating, or whatever you would call what she's doing, and if she hasn't slept with any other guys, it's not because she doesn't want to.

Even after ticking off that list of reasons why I'm in the clear, I'm not. If Claire finds out about this, my chances are shot. Stacy is the type of women that other women despise, and now I can see she's developing actual feelings for me. I got involved with her in the first place because she didn't seem to have any feelings, at least not in the romantic department. But now she's left her 'love massager' at my place. Thank God Claire has never been to my apartment, and never will.

I'm working late today to pick up a little overtime. They asked Mario and he laughed for about five minutes straight, and then kept cracking jokes about it all morning.

"Youz jokers want me to work until *five* o'clock? What do I look like—some kind of Superman Delivery Guy?"

He then ran around as if he was wearing a cape, leaping in the air. I'm not sure if he was insinuating that guys who work overtime are ass-kissers or have homosexual tendencies.

Knowing my politically correct buddy, he meant both. The managers can't wait for his retirement.

I just shook my head at his bullshit, reminding myself he doesn't know better, but it's up to human resources (Claire used to get hot when I told her about

Mario's behavior) to tell him to knock it off, not me. Once the manager told him that they actually *needed* him to work later than five, and he said he was going to 'piss himself' from laughing, and went outside to smoke.

I felt bad for Bob—he's a newly promoted supervisor and he sweats every day trying to get someone to cover the extra runs when people call in sick.

So this time I volunteered. It's not like I'm in any hurry to get home and see Stacy…

Oh, shit…I forgot about this house on this route. I filled in a few months ago for Craig, and the woman at this house was…well…let's just say she likes a man in a uniform. And let's also say it was around my lunch break time anyway…and let's add that it's a deserted sort of street, so not many people would see a UPS truck parked in one place for too long and call the office…

Yes, I had crazy 'delivery man fantasy sex' with a bored housewife—like in a bad porn movie.

I know, I know…my choices have been less than stellar. But that's what happens when your wife, *the only woman you've loved since the eleventh grade*, decides to throw you out of your home because she can't recover from losses that are not even your fault.

And I do want to point out that even though I referred to her as a 'housewife,' she's not married. At least I'm pretty sure she's not. She said she was home on disability, but she seemed pretty 'abled' to me. I'm not sure what kind of work she does that she was able to convince the government she couldn't do it. Because even if she was a contortionist in the circus she was ready to report for duty.

I stop the truck before I get to the end of her road. Since it's summer, it's not dark yet and I don't want to be spotted. I could just throw her package at the front door and run. She won't know it was me. I turn the small box over in my hands—it's not especially heavy and it's not marked with any 'fragile' warnings.

I cut the engine on the truck and begin to sneak down the road. Well, really I'm just walking at a normal pace, but I intend to sprint when I get closer to the house, especially if I see a car in the driveway.

I'm almost to the house now...what the...?

I do a double take when I see a FedEx truck parked on the side of her house. Unbelievable! I guess all the delivery guys must have their own slot. I wonder when the mailman fits into her schedule...

I momentarily wonder if Craig is on her regular agenda, but shake off that thought. He's pretty old, and I think he might be a Mormon, so I doubt it.

With renewed energy (since I was saved by a horny FedEx guy), I heave the package at the front door, skulking away like I'm stealing it instead of delivering it.

Right before I turn to make my getaway, I notice the return address on the box...and it's the same shop where Stacy ordered her goods.

There's nothing wrong with a little help in the bedroom, but I am noticing a disturbing pattern in my behavior, especially when I spend the rest of the ride back to the office thinking about how I'm going to be able to sneak into my own apartment.

Claire

"Let's get you set up with your name tag and your seating assignment." Susan grins and leads me by the wrist to the entry table.

"Mary, this is my neighbor, Claire. The one I was

telling you about."

Mary lowers her reading glasses and smiles, then frowns, then smiles again. The first smile was the more genuine one, and now I'm wondering what Susan told her about me to cause her to conjure up a fake welcome, once she realized who she was meeting.

"Welcome to Southside Bible, Claire. Have you ever done speed dating? I'm guessing you've tried it all." She clears her throat and I notice Susan's nostrils flare. "I…I mean, you've been single a while now, right?"

"Almost a year, yes. And I've never tried speed dating. Is that my nametag?"

Mary isn't much older than me — she's just dressed a little less stylishly. But in all fairness, she is sporting a rather large wedding ring set, so she's not here to hook a man.

Seriously, did I just use that phrase? 'Hook a man?' That sounds like something my mother would say.

That reminds me, I really need to call my mother. I told her about my new puppy and she was all excited. I just hate the way everyone is treating this dog thing like a baby substitute. I am going to cringe when she refers to Dixie as her 'grand dog.'

I slap my nametag on my shirt, and stake out my seating assignment, but before I can make it over there Susan points out a couple of women to me.

"Now, don't look now, but the other two divorced gals in our women's group are over there. One of them is painfully shy — bless her heart — and the other is, well…let's just say you're the belle of the ball tonight. I bet every man here wants your contact information after we're done."

I thank her for her vote of confidence, but I don't

have the heart to tell her that I have set my expectations very low for this event. I am not a prized cow hoping to get a lot of bids on my milk.

I smirk to myself when another woman sits down next to me. We start chatting and I find out that her name is Tammy, and she attends a different church, but her neighbor invited her to this event. She's probably in her late forties, and I am once again noticing that this seems to be an all-ages event. Luckily I don't see any men old enough to be my father.

Tammy looks at the ceiling and says, "My husband—God rest his soul—has been gone a few years now and everyone is telling me it's time. Even my children."

Why did the widow sit next to me? I don't do well with death. I never know what to say, so of course I go with the normal condolences, and she tells me how he was sick for a long time and now he's with the Lord. She seems okay because she moves on to questioning me pretty quickly.

"So what brings a pretty girl like you out here?"

"Oh, that's nice of you to say, but we can all use some help, right?"

We share a laugh and I continue. "I'm just having a hard time finding men I connect with, so I figured why not give this a try? I've been single almost a year now, and I am really in need of some…companionship."

I adjust my words at the end there because this woman may not appreciate hearing about how I am sex-starved. I could have added that if I was a loose woman I could just go out and bang some random guy, but that is not something a widow at a church speed dating event wants to hear.

I must be getting desperate if I'm sharing these thoughts with strangers.

Apparently I hit a nerve because Tammy's face lights up and she grabs my wrist (are hands off limits in church, but wrists are okay?), and exclaims, "Yes! Companionship. I so miss long walks with Don, and watching our favorite shows together at night."

She smiles at me and I nod my head, and then she starts laughing again. "Oh dear, I just realized I think you meant a different kind of 'companionship.' Am I right?"

Okay, so she gets it. I don't know why I assume that just because someone is a little older than I am, and a church-goer, they wouldn't have any interest in sex. That's a horrible, narrow-minded stereotype. I admonish myself and lower my voice to a more conspiratorial tone.

"Yeah, I'm having a hard time going this long, but I don't want to just have sex with anybody."

She turns purple, and now I really don't know what to do. I thought I was being subtle — where is the middle ground here? I needed more coaching before I was let loose on these people.

The organizers look like they are corralling the last of the singles into place, so hopefully I can end this conversation soon.

Tammy fans herself with her note pad and says, "Well, no of course you wouldn't want to do *that*. How long were you married? You must have had a very short dating period before your wedding if you're having a tough time…you know…for not even a year."

I am still nodding, but I don't understand what she means. Why is the length of the dating period…?

Oh, I get it…

"Do you mean that since I waited until marriage that I should be able to wait now?"

"Yes, but I do see that now that you've had intimate experience with your husband, that you would want it more than when you were an innocent young girl, but we also have more self-control now, don't we?"

I'm silently willing Susan to start the proceedings, but now I'm a little scared of what I'm up against. Do the men here think like Tammy? That seems impossible.

I am about to lie and agree with Tammy, but then I decide that's a bunch of crap. Why should I lie to her? I'm a grown woman in my mid-thirties, and it's 2012!

"Tammy, you see…I dated my husband for almost eight years before we got married. We met in high school."

"You waited eight years?" Her eyes widen and then she leans back in her chair and purses her lips. "Oh, no you didn't. Did you? Just a few?"

I shake my head and just as Susan asks for everyone's attention, I lean in and grab Tammy's wrist, saying, "Yes, a few…months."

Well, that ends that budding friendship.

It's funny because normally when I tell other women that I've only been with one man my whole life, they are shocked for the opposite reason — not *enough* experience.

I never thought I'd find myself in a place where *I'm* the slutty one.

I should have brought Rebecca — that would have been fun, and it would have ensured that I receive no further invitations to the Southside Bible women's group.

CHAPTER ELEVEN

Claire

"Hi Abel, I'm Claire."

I take the hand of bachelor number one. He doesn't shake it properly, and I wonder if he's one of those men who doesn't shake hands with women.

I refrain from making any jokes about his name, such as 'what are you 'abel' to do?' Since I do know enough about the Bible to know it's a biblical name, he probably wouldn't find it funny. Plus, I think it could also be taken suggestively.

Why is this environment making me so paranoid about everything I say?

"I'm sorry, what did you say?"

Abel just asked me a question, but he's a bit of a low talker.

He says a bit louder, "What is your favorite Bible verse, Claire? I find it's good to have one to fall back on as a personal token of faith."

Abel is about my age, he's attractive with closely cropped light brown hair, darker brown eyes and a pleasant smile. He's wearing the khaki pants/polo shirt business casual uniform, but he's probably just come from work.

But seriously—my favorite Bible verse? I don't suppose explaining to him that most Catholics don't read the Bible would help in this situation.

"Um...I don't really have one." I fidget in my seat like a misbehaving preschooler and ask, "So what do you like to do for fun?"

Abel makes a face as if I have just told him I like to fornicate with the devil.

"Fun? Claire, fun isn't the reason we are here. We're here to serve the Lord. Now, I'm not saying we can't enjoy things like mission trips and hymn singing. Maybe a few innocent games if we have little ones. Have you been on any mission trips?"

I take a deep breath and look around the room. There are at least twenty men here. I can't keep this up if they're all like this, but maybe this guy is just over the top, and some will be less...intense. After all, Susan did say that a lot of the people here tonight are not church members. I can be polite for a few minutes at a time.

I smirk as I hold back my response to his question. I don't think he would like it if I said, 'yeah, I'm on a mission to get...'

"Okay, times up, speed daters. Gentlemen, move to the left."

Susan has saved me from any further spiritual grilling. It's a good thing it's 'speed' dating. I glance down at my phone in my purse out of nervous habit, and when I look back up Abel has been replaced by a tall, slim, blond guy in a suit.

Abel didn't even say goodbye or give me any parting travel tips, and I never found out his favorite Bible verse.

But there's no time to mourn the end of that short relationship.

"Hi, I'm Claire." I extend my hand assertively this time. This guy smiles, but doesn't reach for my hand, so now it's hanging there awkwardly. This could, however, be a germ-phobic problem, and not a weird aversion to touching women he's not related to.

"I'm Cain. Nice to meet you."

Abel. Now Cain. I *know* the connection there. I just need a moment to think about it…yes they were brothers. One of them killed the other, but I don't know which way that goes. Asking him would be a bad idea.

The main thing I remember from Catholic religious instruction was learning what infractions were considered mortal sins. There were lots of them, and I am probably going to hell, even with my very limited experience with men.

Cain smiles and says, "These things are so awkward, aren't they? I just went to one at my church last week, and I didn't meet a single woman I clicked with. Can you believe it?"

He's a nice looking guy, but it's hard to imagine he didn't like *any* of the women he met. However, I don't have high hopes, either.

"That's a shame. So you're not a member of this church?"

His face pales and he says, "Oh no. You're not, are you?"

Now I'm confused again. Is he looking for a church-going woman, or is he hoping to hook up with one of the more secular types in the bunch? Maybe I'm misjudging him. He can't be held responsible for his name, and lots of people give their children biblical names. I think Abel just soured me on this experience early on, and set me off to a bad start.

This guy's church could be one of those more liberal churches where everyone is questioning their beliefs and they welcome anyone, like those 'high-five, woo-hoo' ones I was mentioning earlier.

I better answer before our short time is up, or I'll never know.

I laugh and say, "Oh no, not me. I was beginning to think everyone here was—"

"This church is *way* too loose in its morals for me. I found out when I got here that some of the people participating in this event tonight aren't members of *any* church. Can you believe that?"

"Okay, speed daters, time to switch again!"

Now it's Mary's cheerful voice that saves me.

I'm really glad I didn't get to hear about the rules in his church. I am actually surprised that men like Abel and Cain would still be single in their thirties. I thought most very religious people got married young. Makes me wonder what's wrong with these guys, other than the obvious incompatibility with me.

I eye the front door, but I can't jump up and run out. It will screw up their numbers, and I don't want to cause a scene. Besides, the guy who saw me inhaling the lotion is pretty far down in the rotation. I *should* probably escape before I have to meet him, so I'll give it a little more time.

The next guy has just sat down...well, he's trying to. The poor guy is a little large for these seats. I think they gave us the chairs they use for Sunday school classes.

"Hi there, I'm Warren."

His friendly smile almost makes up for his size. I hate to be like that, but I'm a small woman, and Warren is pretty heavy. He carries it well because he's tall, but I just don't see myself with someone this large. He does seem very nice, so I smile and say, "Hi Warren, I'm

Claire. Having fun so far?"

"Yes, I've met two very nice ladies. But did you see that spread of food over there?"

Warren is eyeing the after-event buffet like it's way more enticing than any woman. It's too bad because he has a nice face, and aside from how he looks, he's really harming his health. It's easy for me to say because I'm so naturally small, but I feel like Warren is a heart attack waiting to happen.

"I didn't actually notice. What do they have—like fruit and veggie trays?"

I know that trying to steer him to healthy choices isn't going to help much since he's had a lifetime of eating the wrong things, but it can't hurt.

Luckily no one is here to remind me of my donut fetish, except for the little bad fairy on my shoulder who reminds me of all of my shortcomings.

I don't really hear this fairy, it's just an expression.

"Oh, I guess they have fruit and all that, but I came for the shrimp. My co-worker, Mary, invited me and she assured me there would be shrimp. And cake. So you didn't notice any shrimp?"

I turn to look, but I can't see what's on the table. "I doubt they would leave shrimp just sitting out—"

"Hey, I know! If we pick each other tonight, you wanna hit Golden Corral after this?"

Before I can politely decline his offer to visit the poor quality trough eatery, we've switched again. I almost wish the women were the ones on the move because I feel like a sitting duck watching the whack-job parade.

Here's number four. I can't see his nametag…okay, there it is…I'm finally remembering that we are all wearing nametags.

His name is Jed. I think that's also short for a Bible name. Jedidiah? Jedi…something. Not like in Star Wars.

Oh hell, now I'm smirking because I can't get the Beverly Hillbillies song out of my head. Damn Nick at Night! *'First thing you know, old Jed's a millionaire…'*

I'm trying not to hum the tune as I say, "Hi, Jed, is it?" I squint to make sure I'm reading it right.

"Hello, yes. And your name is?"

He is staring at my face, which I guess is a good thing, right? My nametag is above my left boob, but they are currently quite covered up so he could look at it without being improper.

I point to my nametag. "It's right here. Claire."

He keeps his eyes fixed on my face. Oh no, maybe he's like that crazy mother in the movie, *Carrie*, who refers to her daughter's breasts as 'naughty pillows.' No wonder that character went completely insane. Pretty soon there is going to be a horror movie named, *Claire*.

Jed clears his throat and says, "So, Claire are you here in pursuit of marriage and a family, as prescribed by our Lord?"

I once again look at the daunting line of potential suitors still slated to come my way and sigh. "I'm not really sure how to answer that. I'm just trying to meet people since my divorce."

Jed winces, and is probably already praying for this sullied woman…

"But you surely want children?"

I lean back in my seat, finally relaxing my posture. This is unbelievable. The last thing I expected was to discuss my darkest problems at fucking speed dating! But since Jed's not even in the neighborhood of a possibility, I fold my arms and say, "I would have loved them, but I can't have them."

I expect him to apologize for bringing up a touchy subject, or to express his condolences. Or to tell me that God must have a different plan for me, and that I should come on his mission trip to a malaria-infested jungle to find my calling.

Instead, he places his hands on the table in front of him and grows very serious. "Claire, we must pray that the Lord will bring you children."

I smile nervously now. "No, prayer won't help me. I had a hysterectomy."

He jumps back as our shift change is loudly announced again by Mary.

As he stands up, he says, "I see. Well, since you have allowed the devil's work to be done to your body, I don't know that you can be—"

A tall, attractive man appears beside psycho Pastor Jed, who obviously has abortion and hysterectomy confused, and says, "Okay, buddy. Nice speech. Let's move it along. I need to meet this beautiful blonde."

Jed moves on in disgust and the somewhat hot, new guy sits down, and I immediately start laughing. It starts as a smirk but I can't hold it in.

"And what's so funny, Miss…Claire."

His ability to read my nametag on my chest without fear is a good sign, but it's *his* name that's got me in stitches.

"Hello, *Christian*."

He now seems to get the joke and says, "Yes, it is rather humorous that my name is Christian and I'm the least holy one in the bunch tonight. Are there some nutters here or what?"

"I'll say, but let's not waste time on them. Were you

invited here by one of the church ladies?"

"I was."

He nods his head in the direction of my seat neighbor. I wonder how they know each other, but I don't want to waste time on useless chatter with the one normal guy here.

"Me, too." I am suddenly at a loss for words as I take in my new speed date's dark hair and eyes. I can also peek at his firm chest from here, and his forearms and hands are strong and remind me of Ron's...ugh...why am I thinking about Ron at a time like this?

"Hey, Claire, I have an idea." He lowers his voice and continues, "Between you and me, I'm not seeing any good pickings in either direction you or I are headed tonight."

We both look in the direction of the singles we haven't met, and I have to agree that it looks dismal.

I turn back towards Christian and say, "What were you thinking?"

I am already feeling a little light-headed with excitement and I haven't even had a drink. That's a good sign—and Rebecca keeps telling me how I need to loosen up and take chances.

"I propose we get the hell out of here." He eyes the door to the parking lot and our freedom.

"Really? Just get up and run out the door?"

I thought he was going to say let's go outside of their rules and exchange information now, or plan to meet after we're done here. Something spontaneous and romantic.

But I guess running out of speed dating hand-in-hand with a handsome stranger is pretty romantic—it feels like a movie scene.

I steal one more quick glance down the row to my left at the men coming up next, and I catch the eye of the guy from the parking lot. I'm not looking forward to him telling me about a church sponsored lotion snorting rehab he can recommend, so I look Christian dead in the eye and say, "Okay, but you lead."

Before anyone even seems to look up from their own captivating partners, Christian has grabbed my hand and we are in the parking lot, laughing our asses off. I also notice he has a nice one.

"That was sensational. I can't believe you agreed." His smile is huge and I am overjoyed just seeing someone happy because of something I did. I haven't had much of that lately.

I wipe my eyes in case my happy tears have smudged my makeup, and say, "I am *trying* to work on my sense of adventure."

We are still standing in the parking lot, and I'm kind of surprised that none of the church ladies have followed us out here to admonish us for breaking the rules. However, it's more likely that a round of applause and prayers of thanksgiving have erupted due to the departure of the two heathens.

Really, I do consider myself to be a believer…I'm not sure exactly *what* I believe, but I've never been made to feel like a terrible person before at any church function. Those people are complete whack-jobs.

Christian runs his fingers through his thick hair and points to his car. "I'm over there. Do you want to follow me and get a drink first?"

I look in the general direction of his vehicle, and think a moment before saying, "First?"

I feel stupid now that I've blurted out the single

word question, because I'm sure he means dinner. It's a little late, but he probably also came here straight from work and didn't get a chance to eat. What else would he mean? I really need to stop expecting all men to behave like extreme stereotypical caricatures.

It suddenly dawns on me that his name is Christian, like the guy in the 50 Shades...okay, now I am really being ridiculous. He just wants a beer and some nachos, not a spanking.

I relax my shoulders again, and Christian says, "Before we go back to my place. Or your place would be fine, too. I usually don't invite myself to anyone else's house. You know, my mother taught me *some* manners."

It takes me a second to shake off the irony of mentioning his mother's etiquette lessons, while exhibiting the outright balls to assume that a woman he just met at a church speed dating event is agreeing to have sex with him because he suggested leaving said event.

I purse my lips and take a deep breath. "I'm not going home with you, and I am absolutely not letting you come to my home."

His raises an eyebrow and smiles even more. "So you wanna do it in the car? What a wild one you are! It looks a little secluded over there—"

He shuts up and rubs his bicep after I smash it with my overloaded purse, like a comedian dressed as an old lady in one of the variety shows my parents watched in the seventies.

"Ow, what was that for? Wait, do you like it rough?"

"No, you stupid asshole! I'm not having sex with you anywhere! Ever!"

I go to smack him with my purse again, and he

retreats, covering his face.

"Well, you should be more clear. What the fuck…" He glances at his cell phone and dials a number.

My mouth hangs open in amazement as I hear the beginnings of a booty call conversation.

I couldn't make this shit up if I tried.

I stomp to my car, get inside, and toss my bag on the passenger seat. I am so mad that I don't even stop to get something to eat, even though I know my choices at home consist of peanut butter and frozen pizza.

Those are two separate choices—I'm not going to eat them together.

As angry as I am, I can't blame Susan or anyone else. I'm just not used to being single, and I seem to be going about it all wrong.

When I was married, I had my share of troubles, but at least I didn't have to open myself up to the abuse and insanity of total strangers.

As I pull into my driveway, I almost tear up at my sentimentality for the past. Instead of strangers, the man I loved was the one who…but was he really *that* bad? Or *did* I let the baby troubles push him away?

Speaking of babies, if Dixie has done anything destructive I will lose my mind. I left her on the couch, and now I'm regretting that decision.

I open the front door and she comes running to me, slipping on the wood floor and smashing into the wall again. She's going to knock out what little brains she has.

"Hi, Dixie. Did you miss Mommy?"

I kneel down and let her jump on me while I try to pet her wiggly body.

"Okay, let's see what damage you did this time."

She follows me into the family room, and amazingly

I don't see much out of place. The pillows on the couch are a little messed up, and oh...another other little blanket is on the floor. It must have fallen down when she jumped off the couch. It's all wet.

"Oh, Dixie, you pee-peed on your blankie."

I can't get too mad at her because I know even young children sometimes wet the bed, and that it's often an anxiety thing.

"It's okay, sweetie."

As I'm talking she walks over to the blanket and pees on it again.

"Okay, I'm not saying you should keep...hey, I know."

I grab the wet blanket with two fingers on my left hand, while I scoop Dixie up with my right.

At the back door I add the leash and harness to my left hand, and manage to get the back door open. I lay the small piece of stinky fabric down in the yard, wriggle Dixie into her harness and plop her in the yard, too.

I don't know if she has any more pee left in her — it seems like she's an endless fountain of it — but it's worth a shot to complete the experiment. I rub the grass with the blanket, hopefully coating it well with the scent, and then put the blanket on the back deck steps.

And sure enough, my little sniffer notices a familiar odor in the yard, excitedly inhales the aroma and pees on the *actual grass*.

"Yay, Dixie! You peed in the grass!"

I quickly grab her to give her a reward. All the books say that reinforcement of desired behavior should be immediate because puppies have the attention span of a flea, especially this stubborn little head banger.

I put her down on the kitchen floor, continuing my

theatrical praise routine, and put a small amount of peanut butter on a spoon.

She is in licking heaven.

Her little pink tongue darts maniacally to ensure she savors every last drop of the treat.

As soon as I can see there isn't a trace left, I put the spoon in the sink and kiss her on the top of her head, lavishing her with one more round of praise as if she just invented flying cars, instead of just peeing outside.

She runs off in search of a toy. My little one loves to murder her toys when she gets excited, and she deserves to celebrate by shaking the head off a stuffed squirrel.

I survey the pickings in my freezer and pull out a small frozen pizza, as planned. I pre-heat the oven, and think about Christian, who is probably already having sex with another woman, not even bothered anymore by my rejection.

What a bunch of shit.

I pour myself a small glass of red wine, and go off in search of…well, so much for celebrating small victories.

Sitting in the middle of my family room carpet is a nice load of poop. Dixie is wagging her tail as if she is expecting more rewards for an even better gift.

I sigh and get out the paper towels and the rug cleaner.

Hmm…but can I really blame her? I am a lot older, with a much bigger brain, and while I may know where to go to the bathroom, there are many other lessons I'm not learning too swiftly.

CHAPTER TWELVE

Ron

"Oh, Ronnie, it's so great to have you here. It's so hard for me to help with the boat—I'm just not strong enough. And now that those ungrateful boys are teenagers, they don't even care about going boating with their Mama and Daddy."

All I'm doing is holding the damn rope and my friend's wife, Roberta, is acting like I'm lifting the boat over my head. She didn't act like this last weekend, and I don't know what's gotten into her.

She comes up for air and then continues to ramble, "Look at those arms—have you been working out even more? Well, of course you have now that you're back on the market."

I smile because what the hell else can I do while I'm waiting for Jeff to park the truck and trailer, and rescue me from his admiring woman.

"I do hit the gym, but really anyone could hold the boat, it's not like it's going anywhere."

I met Jeff playing softball years ago. Neither of us kept it up, but he's busy coaching his sons and running a car dealership, and I got sick of it.

Now she's laughing. I'm really not funny, and that wasn't even an attempt at humor. Where the hell is…oh here he comes now.

"Hey, thanks man. Roberta, get your ass in the

boat."

Jeff playfully smacks her ass, but her eyes are still trained on me, like I'm going to suddenly walk on water. I don't remember her being like this when she used to sit in the stands and cheer on the softball team with Claire.

She is also plenty strong enough to hold onto the boat. She's not a huge woman, but she's no tiny little thing. Like Claire.

A strong wind might blow Claire off the dock if she tried to hang onto the boat. And my water-adverse wife would not like that.

Yes, I am still referring to Claire as my wife because that's what she is, and I intend to help her to resume that role. She sent me a friendly text last night, making plans for Saturday. Yes, it's just plans to paint her dining room, but there was talk of dinner. She wants to cook, but I won't let her. Claire hates cooking, and frankly my stomach isn't a fan of Claire's cuisine. Besides, I want to show her I've changed and I appreciate her, so I am not going to put her to work.

Jeff starts up the boat and soon we're trolling away from the dock. Before he cranks up the speed, Roberta is fussing to make sure we've all applied our sunscreen, and we have drinks in our hands.

"Ron, which beer do you want? I brought several varieties, and oh…do you need me to put sunscreen on your back?" Roberta has taken off her cover-up and well…let's just say that very little is currently covered up.

I just took my shirt off because I'm on a fucking boat, and it's HOT out, but now Roberta has moved up to a new level of ogling. This is insane—I'm in decent shape but Jeff's not a fat slob, and dammit…I do need sunscreen on my back, and Jeff isn't going to want to do it. This time last year Claire would have taken care of it for me.

"Um…sure, I don't want to get torched out here."

Jeff is laughing, and I'm not sure if he thinks it's funny that I need sunscreen or that his wife is openly flirting with me?

"Roberta, you just treat everyone like a little kid. She's somethin', isn't she?"

Okay, he thinks this is *maternal*. Wait, maybe it *is* maternal. Definitely it is. She just feels sorry for the single guy and she wants to make sure someone…

Never mind. The way Roberta is rubbing the lotion into my back is not at all maternal. I need to stop her before she moves to my front…

"Okay, thanks. I'm good." I turn and grab one of the offered beers out of the cooler.

"Come here, honey…let me do you." Jeff grabs his wife around the waist and starts rubbing lotion into her exposed skin. I also don't remember Roberta wearing a bikini, and it's really a bit much for a woman her size who's had two kids.

She did not act like this last weekend, and I don't know where this is coming from.

I man the steering wheel and avert my eyes, giving them some privacy. Unfortunately, Roberta catches my eye and I'm not sure if the look of lust is aimed at her husband's touch…or the want of mine.

I just wanted a peaceful day on the boat. I am avoiding Stacy like the plague, but she's been texting me. I can only stay out for so long, but so far I've been strategic in avoiding her. Hopefully I'll be back at my own home soon, and Claire will be on the next boat outing to put an end to Roberta's craziness.

"Ronnie, do you want some chips? I also brought some fruit. Bananas?"

I sigh as she peels the yellow fruit and starts…oh my God…

"Roberta, would you leave the guy alone. He knows how to help himself. Why don't you go read your book in the sun until we get to our favorite spot?"

She pouts but takes her towel and her paperback to the front of the boat, where she spreads out…okay, I'm not looking anymore.

I briefly get a memory flash of Claire in a bikini and swig my beer. She was never a big fan of boating, but she loved the pool. I wonder if she's still going to the one in our neighborhood. Hey, technically I'm still a member. I think I even still have my pool pass buried somewhere in my wallet. I could go some time and hang out with Mike when he brings the kids.

I'm getting ahead of myself. That may be too obvious and pushy.

Jeff interrupts my scheming thoughts and says, "So, cheers man. Your second boat outing of the season. You should be able to get in a lot more time on the water now without the little scared wife." Jeff pops off the top of his beer and flicks it into the trash bag his lovely bride has so conveniently provided for us. Such a good *mother*.

"Yeah, well you know how Claire is with water. She can't swim."

Jeff laughs and resumes his post at the wheel, gunning the motor and zooming down the river. Roberta has finally sat down, but probably just so she doesn't go airborne.

Jeff ignores Claire's fear of water and says, "Hey, is

Claire still driving that crappy old car? I could get her in a new one, no problem. But of course if she's got a bigger house payment she might not be able to afford it. You didn't give her a raw deal, did you, man?"

Now we have to yell to hear each other over the noise of the engine and the wind, but I'm sitting close enough to Jeff that we can still have a conversation. I am choosing to pretend I didn't hear that last question, and I laugh and point to some kids flying off of a tube up ahead.

Jeff is easily distracted and doesn't even notice when I don't answer. Instead he moves on to the next grilling topic.

"You know you could have brought a date on the boat. It would have kept Roberta occupied and you know we'd like to meet whoever you're dating. Be supportive and all."

Jeff makes a sharp turn for no apparent reason, and Roberta yelps as she's tossed around at the front of the boat. Jeff yells out, "Sorry, honey. I just love how smooth this baby takes the curves."

I forgot what a show-off Jeff can be. Maybe that's why he doesn't care about his wife showing her body—it's just an extension of his collection of things he's proud of. I hate to admit it, but I'm a little jealous that I don't have much to be proud of. No kids. Boring job. I'm being kept out of my home. This plan to woo Claire back better work.

"There have been a number of women, but no one I want to encourage."

Jeff smiles and says, "Okay, I see what you're gettin' at. Keepin' it casual. That's what I would do if…well, you know."

He peers up at Roberta, who is enthusiastically waving at a bunch of nearby boaters. I know it's the *boater's code* to wave, but I'm noticing that when it's a boat full of men, she's waving with more than her hands. Maybe she's having a mid-life crisis.

"That Roberta is getting wild, between you and me." He lowers his voice and leans in closer. "You know the late thirties is a peak sexual time for women. I'm exhausted. But I'm sure you're having more fun with the variety, right man?"

There's that age-old belief that the grass is greener on the other side. He thinks he'd love to be in my shoes, but he'd be crying in his beer just like all the rest of the divorced men. Of course I would never admit to feeling that way, so I'm glad we're playing this game. I'd much rather be the object of jealousy than sympathy.

We tool around the water a bit more, and Jeff settles at their favorite spot. It's a shallow, sandy area, and is usually pretty crowded with other boaters.

I help Jeff with the anchor and stabilizing the boat, but my mood has soured with all this talk of my exciting bachelor life. I'm so tired of talking about other women when all I want is my life back.

I glance over at Roberta, who just dropped her book, clearly on purpose, and leaned over to get it. Seriously? I look away before the decency laws of the state of Virginia are violated. For God's sake, there are kids out here.

She grabs one of their many flotation devices, this one is a tube with a drink cooler in the shape of a flamenco, and gets in the water with her book.

I need to jump in and get wet. The temperature just keeps rising as my mood is taking a nose dive. I scan the area and take in the scene as I lower myself into the river. The water is still cool, even though it's hot out. It's early in the season and this huge bathtub takes a long time to heat up.

I set my sights on a bunch of women in bikinis. They are all blond and remind me of Claire. Maybe not current Claire—more like ten years ago. Seeing them with their guys makes me think back to simpler times when *we* could splash in the water, drink, joke around with our friends. As long as it wasn't deeper than three or four feet.

"Hey, stop ogling those skinny, young girls." Roberta startles me with her scolding, and she laughs.

"I was just looking at the log in the water over there."

"Oh, Ron. I know what you were doing. You miss Claire. I can see it written all over your face. My husband thinks you're out having the time of your life, but I know better. Hell, you're not even affected by *my* girls."

She lovingly points to her own breasts, which are barely contained in the fabric that's holding on for dear life. Actually, it looks like she borrowed Claire's bikini and squeezed into it.

Luckily Jeff is still on the boat, choosing a radio station, and he's missed his wife's comments.

I smile and exhale. "I don't know how Jeff deals with you, but you are one of a kind."

I raise my beer to her wine cooler and endure an awkward silence while she keeps smiling at me.

"Okay, yes, I miss Claire."

Just as those words leave my lips, I hear a light splash behind me.

"Are you serious? I thought you were well over

her." Jeff is munching on a sub and shaking his head. "You haven't signed those divorce papers yet, have you? You never mention it anymore, or the house. Wasn't she supposed to buy you out? You're stuck in limbo, aren't you?"

"Jeff, leave him—"

"No, he's right." I cut Roberta off and face my friend. "I am…was…in limbo. But now I have a plan."

I proceed to tell them the whole story. Why not? I'm sick of pretending and if they don't agree, who cares? It's my life.

Roberta thinks my intention to woo Claire back with friendship and service is romantic, while Jeff keeps screwing up his face like someone shit in his turkey club.

Roberta becomes frustrated with her husband's attitude, and gets back on the boat for a little nap, after touching my arm and giving me another flash of her assets, presumably to make me feel better.

Jeff is too busy formulating his rebuttal to my intentions. I know how he operates, and I can't wait to hear the expert advice he's going to impart. I may go over my one or two beer limit today.

Jeff puts up his hands in defense before he even opens his mouth. "I know you think I'm gonna try to convince you to give up on her, but that's not what I'm gonna do."

I raise an eyebrow and roll my eyes. This should be good.

"I think what you need is a distraction. Now wait, hear me out."

I close my mouth again and float on my back. "Go ahead."

"Now I know you've had some women lately, but

they become a nuisance, right? They're in your space. But you need a little harmless fun while you're trying to get Claire back...to keep your ego and other parts satisfied."

I bolt upright and say, "You are *not* suggesting hookers, are you?"

"Of course not. What kind of a guy do you think I am? Jeez, no." He looks up towards the boat to see if Roberta is still ignoring us and continues. "No, I am suggesting Russian Internet women."

"*What?*" I narrow my eyes as if squinting might help me find Jeff's brain. "So, you mean cyber-sex? Internet porn?" I guess I'll have to cross boating off my list of activities because both Jeff and his wife are crazier than loons.

"No, that's not what I mean. They have sites for Russian women who want to meet men from the US—"

"Like mail order brides?"

"No. Well, sort of. But no. You just talk to them online, and if you like them you can chat with them in the private...you know, like that Skype thing they have now."

So, he *is* talking about cyber-sex with desperate foreign women who want to come to America, and be saved from bad living conditions. That's a *great* diversion. I wish I had come to Jeff sooner. So much better than hookers.

"I don't even know what to say to this...idea."

"It's just a little diversion until Claire comes around. She'll never know, and you can still have a little fun with other women while you're waiting. You don't have to worry about them showing up on your doorstep or interfering in your plans. Think about it."

"But isn't that using these women? They're real people."

"No, they like it. They're putting themselves out there. I'm not saying all of them are going to go to the private…you know…but even talking to them and exchanging pictures, could be a meaningless, but fun escape. Like a little harmless flirting. And if one of them turns out to be great, then you can arrange to meet her. Crazier things have happened. People meet in strange ways these days, and nobody needs to be the wiser."

I swallow the remains of my now warm beer, and lean back against the anchored boat. "So it's just like meeting someone online on one of the dating sites, except in order to see them in person, it's a long plane ride."

"Exactly, so you would never do that for casual encounters. Now, it's not the same as a real live woman here with you, but you need to stop that if you want to pursue Claire. It's just a little harmless fun. Think about it."

He wades over to the ladder and starts climbing. "Another beer?"

I agree to more alcohol as I ponder my well-meaning buddy's words. It's not anything I would have thought of, but as long as I don't make any promises it could be interesting. Plus, it wouldn't hurt for me to work on my communication skills with women. I would never admit it to my wife, but she's right. I suck at communicating. I don't know what the hell to say to women, and that's why I can't find a good one.

And why I let the best one get away.

I don't think I'd take this too far because it feels like moving into deviant territory, but what do I know? I was sixteen the last time I was truly single. Maybe what used to sound creepy when the Internet first started up is the norm now.

I accept my second cold one, and relax for the first time today. This little method of satisfying my 'needs' actually could help me in my quest to convince my wife that she 'needs' me.

After all, she's the one who dumped me, and she wouldn't want to start over with a man with a bruised ego.

And I know Claire has no desire to visit Russia.

Yep, that's right. You really can rationalize anything if you try hard enough.

CHAPTER THIRTEEN

Claire

"Who names their children after Bible characters?"

Rachel spits her drink, and my eyes almost pop out at our friend Audra's unknowingly sacrilegious statement. Bible *characters*? My mother would die, but that's hilarious.

"Shit, now I have sangria on my best partying shirt! It's bad enough my boobs have leaked milk on the rest of my wardrobe." Rachel grabs a bunch of napkins off the bar and starts dabbing at the reddish purple stain on the left boob of her glittery pink tank top.

She huffs at the futility of her efforts and storms off to the ladies' room.

I glance at Audra, still waiting to see if she gets it.

"What did I say?" She grips her wine glass and smirks. "Okay, so I guess they're not *characters* because a lot of people think it's *real*, so they are what? Historical figures?"

I shake my head and survey the room. "It really doesn't matter what you call them, but the guys in question were definitely not from this time period."

The Tobacco Warehouse is hopping tonight, and the bar is crowded with people of various ages, but the under-thirty crowd is mostly downstairs at Metromix, the dance club counterpart of this establishment. Justin gave me the full low-down, enough to keep me firmly planted up here.

Rachel returns in time to join the conversation. Unfortunately, she hasn't made much headway with her stained shirt. But at the rate she's going with the sangria, soon she won't care.

"So, what were you guys saying before I soiled myself? Oh yeah. Our friend the heathen here was saying something about Bible characters." Rachel gives Audra a playful grin and they share a laugh.

"Claire went to a speed dating event at a church. You know, one of those ones where they do faith healing with snakes." Audra is doing this on purpose now.

"Audra, all churches are not like that. Claire, how did you end up…?" Rachel turns to me and gasps. "Oh, it was your nutty church lady neighbor who roped you into that?"

"Yeah, and I figured why not? Now I have a bunch of answers to that question."

I go on to crack them up with the stories from the event—from the guy who was confused about the female reproductive system to the disappointed buffet eater to the favorite Bible verse missionary.

And of course, I end with the suspected spanking man-whore.

They are both wiping their eyes, and now Rachel has smeared purple eyeliner on her other boob. Now they almost match, as if she was trying to draw nipples on her shirt.

My sloppy friend grabs my arm, probably more to steady herself than emphasize her point, and says, "Why would you go to something like that? You should come to our church—everyone is so nice and I think we have a singles' group." She hiccups and looks behind her as if the sound came from someone else.

"No, no, she doesn't need any church singles anything. She needs a proper date with a normal man. I'm going to think very hard on it and come up with a good prospect." Audra nods towards the bar and says, "In the meantime, there are plenty of men here. We should be in the thick of it. Rachel can reel them in with her purple spotted titties, and you can have the lot of them."

Audra isn't a lesbian, as far as I know, but she never dates. I think she has just soured on the whole thing. Maybe by the time I'm in my forties I'll be ready to give up, too.

We amble up to the bar, keeping a watchful eye on Rachel. She doesn't get out much, and it's no wonder with a pre-schooler and a six-month-old baby. Who I have yet to see. I am hoping Rachel doesn't remember that.

We locate a couple of stools and Audra and Rachel sit. I'm too wired, so I decide to stand, rocking back and forth on my new leopard print stilettos. Oops, maybe I better stop doing that—it really throws off the balance.

Audra signals the bartender for another glass of wine and says, "The cheek of that one guy, though. Thinking you were going home with him. In my day, a man would at least ask for the shag outright." She accepts her wine and turns back around. "But you could have gone along with it. What's the harm, really?"

"No, I want a relationship. And I don't care how good looking he was—he made me mad and I am not one of those women whose passion is fueled by anger. Ron and I never had makeup sex when we fought."

Now Rachel is teary-eyed.

"What's wrong, love?" Audra turns maternal for a brief flash.

"Stop talking about men and sex!"

I say, "But you have a husband, Rachel. Remember George?" He's nothing special to *me*, but I wouldn't think she's had enough sangria to erase the memory of her marriage.

She stomps her foot and now she has a new splash of sangria on her top. Hmm...that almost looks like a third boob.

"Of course I remember him. I remember how dull and stupid he is!"

Oh my God. Here we go.

We spend the next thirty odd minutes comforting Rachel, telling her that it's normal for new parents not to have sex a lot, and of course he still loves her, and we would be happy to babysit so they can go out on date nights...wait a minute...*we would*?

I don't think Audra has ever held a baby, and I am avoiding them for my own selfish reasons. Now I can't even remember which one of us offered that catastrophic suggestion. And who are we to give advice to a married mother about anything?

The guy next to us pays his tab and slinks off, probably sick of listening to crying women. I don't blame him. Something has to salvage this night, and bring our mood back up to a decent 'girls' night out' level of festivity. I know...

"Hey, let's check out downstairs."

Audra abruptly looks up from patting Rachel's shoulder and says, "I thought you said we were too old—"

I shake my head vigorously and lead Rachel off the

barstool. "No, I said this bar up here can get *old* quick. And it has. The men are starting to look more like my father, and the music is a snooze fest. Pretty soon the jazz quartet will be coming out, and we'll have to resort to slicing our wrists with the butter knives."

Rachel is eyeing the cutlery on the bar and I realize that any suggestion of self-harm probably isn't a good idea in her fragile state. Damn these men! I hope both of the kids are pooping and throwing up on George right now!

We pay our tabs and make our way through the crowd out to the sidewalk. The entrance to the basement club is actually around the corner, and it is manned by a huge, imposing muscle-bound bouncer.

Luckily Richmond isn't one of those cities where the clubs are so exclusive that they won't let you in if you don't look a certain way. Basically here if you are human, have US currency, and most of your essential body parts are covered—you're in. Oh, and proper ID of course.

However, muscle guy takes one look at Audra's grey hair, my middle thirties 'trying to be hip' attire, and Rachel's 'mom meltdown,' and waves us on down.

I can already feel the music in my chest and the heat from the crowd on my face as we descend the narrow steps. I actually prefer rock music, but there are no clubs catering to people my age who want to bang their heads.

Audra is already starting to bop her head like it's London in the eighties. She really has no concern whatsoever that she could easily be the mother of everyone in this place.

A girl bops up to us and says to Audra, "Hey, I love your hair! My friend just dyed her hair grey, too. It's such a cool look."

Audra smiles and doesn't tell the girl the truth, as she runs off. Audra yells to us over the music. "See, if you just do nothing, eventually you're in style."

I look around the room and spot several girls with very unnatural hair colors, and a few of them do look grey, not blond. Who knew?

I touch my long, blond hair, which is highlighted, low lighted, side lighted, light bulbed...

"Hey, gorgeous. Wanna dance?"

I stare at the young man, who is wearing a skin tight blue shirt and the skinniest jeans I have ever seen. They look like denim leggings.

My first inclination is to point him in the direction of a more suitably-aged partner, but then I decide—fuck it. I'm stuck here now, and it's still more fun down here than it was upstairs with the grandpas. Tonight does not appear to be the night I solve the mystery of the missing thirty-something men.

'Skinny jeans' grabs my hand and drags me out to the dance floor, where there are so many bodies flailing around, I needn't worry if I look stupid. The strobe lights make it impossible to see, and the music makes it impossible to hear, so I do the 'dance like no one's watching' thing that embroidered pillows in craft shops encourage.

For a few seconds I actually feel unburdened as my new young friend and I gyrate, and I attempt to keep my heart from blowing up from the thumping bass. For some reason rock seems more balanced than this repetitive dance music. I think it's because they use actual instruments.

Oh, shit. So much for dancing like no one's

watching.

I could avoid him but his eyes lead me off the dance floor. 'Skinny jeans' doesn't even seem to notice, and he's quickly sandwiched in between a girl with pink hair and someone whose gender I can't easily identify.

"Hi, Justin."

He offers me a seat at his tiny high-top table, and I wonder who he's here with. I guess a guy like Justin can go out alone and not have to worry about being lonely. He's only a couple of years older than my dance partner, but his education and corporate position have matured his appearance a little bit. He's wearing normal looking black jeans, and a regular fitting grey knit t-shirt. Casual, but put together.

"Claire, I can't believe you're here. I thought I scared…I mean put you off this place for sure the other day. What are you drinking?"

I tell him I was having wine upstairs and he is off to the bar. I notice that he chats it up with a couple of the people at the bar, and they appear to be *his* people. Similar age, upscale trendy types. I don't know why he feels the need to talk to me. It must be fun for him to watch me squirm in this environment.

As if he needs more teasing material.

"So, I saw you out there dancing and I had to look twice. Who are you here with? Oh, you're not on a date, are you?"

We both glance back at my dancing partner and his cohorts, who are now doing some kind of synchronized hand motions, and we both laugh.

"I guess he's a little young for you, huh?"

My mood darkens, even though he's right. "Yeah, everyone here is too young, but my friend was upset, so my other friend and I brought her down here as a diversion."

I point out Audra and Rachel, who are talking to a couple of girls who are probably telling them that they wish they had such cool moms.

"Oh, did she break up with her boyfriend?"

I roll my eyes and say, "No, her problem is a bit more grown-up, but...never mind, I'm going to join them. Thanks for the wine."

I hop off the barstool and Justin is right behind me.

I turn back and say a little sharply, "Where are you going?"

He looks sheepish and says, "Oh, I thought you wanted to introduce me to your friends. I'm not that embarrassing, am I?"

I take in his blond hair, emerald eyes, and tall, strong form and sigh. Yeah, he's embarrassing.

I don't even answer as we reach my tired looking pals. The girls they were talking to have just walked away, but they almost fall over their own feet ogling Justin.

I ignore the retreating admirers and say, "Hey, this is Justin. My co-worker. Justin, this is Audra and Rachel."

He shakes their hands and Audra begins to say, "Oh, he's the one who—"

"What? It's so loud in here. I can't hear you." I take advantage of the crowded bar area, and give her a slight elbow in the side to shut her up.

"Rachel, I understand you're having a rough night." Justin moves closer to her, and droops his mouth in sympathy.

Oh my God, is he really going to try to offer advice

here? He really has some nerve—I know he's enjoying this way too much, and Rachel has serious problems.

I stare into his mocking, gorgeous eyeballs and say, "Justin, Rachel doesn't need your help. She's married and she has little children."

"Oh, how old?"

Rachel proceeds to show him pictures of her kids on her phone while Audra smiles like she's been hypnotized and I stand there stewing. Even Audra is charmed by this?

"Beautiful family you have there. So I don't understand. Your husband seems like an okay guy. He's not mad that you're out with your friends, right? And he's home alone with the kids taking care of things?"

"This is true, but he's *so* boring." Rachel is whining now and we really need to get her home.

It is hard to believe that George approved of this night out. Things must be very tense between them.

I bite my lip and say, "Rachel, where did you tell George we were going tonight?"

She looks confused, as if she has once again forgotten he exists, and then smiles. "Oh, I told him we were going to one of those 'wine and paint' nights at the place in the mall."

Audra and I look at each other in mutual horror, and Justin appears perplexed. He likely has no idea what she's talking about.

Audra says, "Rachel, love, the mall is closed since half nine, and it's after midnight. Hasn't he been calling? He must be worried sick."

I grab Rachel's phone and see that he hasn't called. Hmm…maybe the babies have worn him out so much that he doesn't notice she's still out. That could be good, except…

"I'm not sure how to say this without freaking you out, but those places give you your painting to take home. So you need to bring home a painting if you want George to believe your story." I cringe and brace myself for the…here it comes…

Rachel starts bawling and Audra takes the mostly empty glass of sangria out of her hands.

Justin backs away slightly and yells into my ear, "What is she going to do?"

"I don't know. She surely has the wine part down. He'll believe that. Maybe we can tell him she drank so much wine she couldn't finish her painting?"

"Rachel, what are you doing?" Audra's shouts interrupt our conversation and we both follow her pointed finger.

Rachel has stepped over the posh crowd Justin was chatting with earlier, and she's on top of the bar, attempting to pry a picture of the Richmond skyline off the wall. As if that isn't enough, her skirt is hiked up around her waist, her underwear is showing, and if she leans too much farther she is going to knock herself, and about fifty bottles of booze, to the ground.

We all rush the bar screaming her name, just as one of the bartenders finally spots her and puts up his hand to brace her. Unluckily, his hand is on her stomach, right between the band of her white 'just married' cheeky bikini and her C-section scar.

One of the female bartenders yanks Rachel's skirt into place, and they awkwardly pull her down to the ground.

"Who belongs to this one?" The older woman is clearly used to drunken shenanigans, but I doubt this one is a common occurrence at Metromix.

Justin bravely steps forward and lifts Rachel up over the bar, careful not to knock anyone out or expose any more of my friend's honeymoon undergarments.

I don't know what's sadder—going home to your husband without proper proof of your lies, or going to a hip bar wearing the only non-granny panty underwear you've owned in five years.

I quickly settle all of our tabs, and we haul Rachel to the street level. Justin follows us and asks if he can be of any further help.

"No, we're okay. Go back to your friends and have fun. And thanks for helping out."

He frowns but says, "Okay, if you're sure. And it was no problem. I hope everything turns out okay."

"I'll fill you in at the office on Monday."

He leans forward to give me an awkward hug, but stops short and just squeezes my arm.

Now Audra is trying to talk some sense into Rachel. "Do you honestly think that a *photograph* of the Richmond skyline was going to pass off as a *painting* you did at a 'wine and paint' class?"

"No, I *wasn't* thinking. Help me to think!"

Now Rachel is sitting on the curb with her head between her legs.

"I know what to do." Audra suddenly springs into action, and pleads with me with her eyes to follow along. "Let's get some food in you, and we'll call George and tell him we're at the diner and lost track of the time. Then we'll take you to Walmart—that blasted American rat trap is open all night—and we'll buy you a painting. And a shirt, too. We can't let you go home in that mess."

I wrinkle my forehead and say, "Seriously? You

think that will work?"

We get Rachel up off the curb, and each hold up a side of her limp body. She's starting to resemble a rag doll, and I do agree she needs to eat and sober up.

"Yes, of course it will. George probably has no idea what she was wearing when she left, and they probably have a shirt just like this one anyway, or at least a plain tank top. And their art work probably comes from the 'wine and paint' shop anyway."

We laugh and hobble down the street, a pathetic threesome. So much for a fun night on the town and drumming up any decent men prospects.

As we round the corner to the parking deck, a young girl shrieks and points at my feet. 'Oh, I love your shoes, my mom has a pair just like them."

I smile and grit my teeth. Not so much at the girl, but at a theory of Ron's. He was always telling me that animal print clothing and shoes were for middle-aged women trying to look hot.

Again, I hate it when Ron's right.

Ron. I get to see him tomorrow. He better not give me any attitude. Too bad I can't meet a nice guy like Justin, only older. Although, scratch that. He's not that nice. He's probably hysterically laughing at the bar right now, making fun of us and imitating Rachel hanging off the bar with her ass hanging out. All he ever does is make fun of me. Jerk. I'm so sick of men.

Audra startles me by breaking our silent, twisted walk of shame and blurts out, "I know the perfect guy to set you up with!"

She looks so damn excited about it; I hate to tell her I just swore off men ten seconds ago. "Okay, who is it?"

"My neighbor. Finn. I think he writes about cars for

some magazine. He's very cute, actually looks a bit like that Justin hunk, but older. Probably just your age. Never married, no kids."

I look for excuses to say no, and the one that always comes to mind is that guys my age who are childless still want kids some day, and I can't deliver. But everyone keeps telling me that's not necessarily true, so I shouldn't pre-judge.

I'm tired and this night has beaten me down, but who am I kidding? I'm not swearing off men.

"Is he one of those guys with the perfect sports car you can't drop a crumb in?" I think of Justin getting out of his fancy convertible every morning.

Yes, I know I'm really reaching now for reasons to reject this guy before I even meet him.

"Oh no, he's not the posh type at all. Very down to earth. He drives an old clunker. Very practical kind of guy. I don't think he's one of those guys who writes about the latest hot sports cars. Now that I think of it, it's probably like one of those mechanic's magazines you'd see in the toilets at your old uncle's flat."

We finally reach Rachel's car and turn our attention back to the logistics of two people driving three cars. We decide that we will have to leave her car. Hopefully it won't get towed, but if it does at least George will know that we kept her from driving drunk, and he probably has no idea where the 'wine and paint' place is located.

And if he does figure it all out, it's not the end of the world. Or her marriage. She needs to learn *some* lesson from this night. Nothing will get better between them if she hides everything from him.

However, I do agree that he doesn't need to know about her bar climbing stunt.

Audra has Rachel buckled into the passenger seat of her car, and I lean in and say, "Okay, fine, I'll meet him. Give him my number, but I'm busy this weekend."

She nods and waits for me to get to my car to follow her on this ridiculous trek.

There is no way I want this guy to think I'm free at such short notice. And I also don't want him anywhere near Ron. If he happens to be decent, he doesn't need to meet my soon-to-be ex-husband and general contractor.

On second thought, I am not allowing Finn to pick me up at my house. That eliminates any thoughts of him getting lucky, and it provides some distance and an easy escape, should the date turn out to be a disaster.

I may not have met anyone online yet, but I'm learning how to be a savvy, modern dater. Just because Audra knows him, it doesn't mean she *knows* him.

CHAPTER FOURTEEN

Ron

I'm up too early on Saturday morning, but I'm actually excited.

Things did get a little weird on the boat last night, but once the conversation moved away from me, things settled down and we had a nice evening on the water.

For the record, I did not exceed my three beer max. I am not going to become one of those guys who hits middle-age with a gut.

I should hit the workout room in my apartment complex before I go over to Claire's, I mean *our* house, but I don't want to run into Stacy. I still haven't addressed that problem, but I don't feel like fighting her off today, or explaining where I'm off to. I should just buy a treadmill and get my free weights out of storage.

My wife is not an early riser, so she asked me to come over around noon. She said she was going out with her girlfriends last night, and she'd probably get in late.

Not wanting to piss her off, I didn't question her further, and sure enough she volunteered that she was going out with Audra and Rachel. This 'being friendly' thing really does the trick. Without me putting any pressure on her, Claire can relax and let her guard down.

But I wasn't worried because Audra is like an old spinster, and Rachel is married and has little kids. I'm sure it was a tame outing.

However, I will address this whole 'girls' night out' thing when we get back together. I don't mind once in a while, but after she was sure she'd never be a mother, I felt like Claire was going out too much, drinking, and just generally behaving recklessly, especially for a married woman.

I can't believe George let Rachel go—I think she just had a baby a few months ago. I've only met the guy a couple of times, but he seems like a bit of a wuss. Plus, Rachel could be hormonally off the ledge and he doesn't want to rock the boat. I know what that's like. He could be hanging onto his own sanity by a thread.

Sometimes when I see people in these situations, I am grateful we couldn't have any kids. Of course I would NEVER tell Claire I feel that way, but with her aversion to adoption and the puppy mother thing underway, I think I'm safe now. Don't get me wrong, I would have been glad to be a father, but I am just able to see the bright side of both options.

Now Claire and I can do things together as a couple. Hobbies…like…okay, I can't think of anything.

I'm not going to buy a boat because she's afraid of the water. Our musical tastes aren't the same, but we can agree on a few bands from our high school days in the nineties. Maybe we could see a few shows—Richmond has a couple of decent concert venues.

And travel…we've been nowhere because all of our time and energy was spent trying to get pregnant, recovering from miscarriages, and fighting about all of the above.

Maybe we could start small with a beach trip—like Nags Head. Claire does like the beach, even though she won't go in the water. She likes mini-golf, and they have tons of that shit down there. Hmm...there are a lot of kids there, though. Maybe a more adult beach destination would be better...we've never been to any of the islands.

We'll figure it out. The important thing is that we'll be together, and stronger than ever.

It's not even ten. She'll have a fit if I show up this early, and if I call she won't answer if she's not up and ready for the day. I don't want to start things off on a bad note, but I'm so antsy.

I eye my computer, and I feel like it's taunting me. Jeff said he was going to e-mail me the links to the sites he was talking about. We never did discuss how he has such a vast awareness of this fishy foreign Internet dating world, but I didn't want to ask in front of Roberta.

However, her exhibitionist behavior screams 'attention starved,' so maybe he does have an Internet sex fetish thing going on. If he's fooling around on these sites it's totally wrong, but I am not going to be the one to fuck up my friend's long term marriage over something that is essentially harmless.

At least that's what I'm telling myself.

I reach for my laptop and realize that I am about to find out how harmless it actually is. After thinking about it last night, I came to the conclusion that my initial reaction is probably correct. This whole thing is insane, but my curiosity is killing me now.

Sure enough—Jeff has sent the links. I open up the first one and it essentially looks like an American online dating site. I haven't signed up for any of those, but I took a look. I'm not paying to belong to a site to help me meet the same women I can meet by walking out my front door.

Stacy has profiles everywhere.

I scroll through the Russian women and see that I do have to sign up and create a free account, if I want to be able to talk to any of them.

Do I want to do that? I think I do. I can't resist seeing more. Some of these women look pretty attractive, but I'm not an asshole and I realize that this could all be fake, and all of these women really have mustaches, double chins and pointy toenails.

However, in the video chat I don't see how they can trick anyone, unless there is some wizard type technology that changes appearances on Skype. I know the Cold War is long over, but can we really trust the Russians?

I should have gotten more sleep last night because now I'm making up movie plots about magical spies and covert dating conspiracies. *That's* where they're getting to us now.

This is what happens to me when I listen to Jeff.

I fill out the basic free profile so I can get into the site and look around for real. I can always go back and fill in more details once I decide if I am serious about this or not.

Probably not.

I scroll through the women in my age range, and see a lot of common Russian names. At least common enough that I've heard of them.

Lyudmila, Svetlana, Tatiana, Alexandra, Natasha…

What am I doing? I just wasted an hour looking at these far away, most likely fake, women, when a real woman—my wife, who I love, is five minutes away and just waking up.

I close the computer and text my little sleepy head.

Claire

I told Ron to come at noon, and now he's texting me at ten-thirty. I'm not surprised. He's never been too concerned with my boundaries, so why start now?

Maybe this was a bad idea.

Speaking of bad ideas, Rachel purchased a painting at Walmart and brought it home, pretending she created it at her perfectly tame 'wine and paint girls' night out' event.

Luckily Audra drove her home, since they live closer to each other. I would never have been able to keep a straight face when George inevitably asked to see her creation, like he would his son's pre-school finger paintings.

I wonder if he asked to see Audra's version, since all of the participants paint from the same still life at these events. This issue did actually come up in Walmart, but then we realized if we bought three of the same painting they would be *identical*, which is not the case when three people of varying skill levels paint the same thing.

But the most ridiculous part of all of this is so obvious, and it didn't hit me until I got home. Walmart does not sell *paintings*. They sell prints. There is quite a big difference. I wouldn't mind being a fly on the wall this morning when George tries to figure out how the instructor turned all of the paintings into 'ready to hang' prints at the end of the night.

Plus, Rachel was a mess — does he really think 'wine and paint' night gets that wild?

Needless to say I was up pretty late, and I don't need Ron pressuring me to get over here, and start what may prove to be a stressful day.

Dixie was fine in her crate when I got home, so I was

able to relax. I decided to read a book to unwind from the craziness of the night, but I picked a slightly creepy one, and then I had bad dreams.

That was one thing Ron was good for. He was always there if I had a bad dream, and he didn't get mad if I woke him up to tell him about it — except when they started to center around the pregnancy losses. But that's also when Ron started *causing* the sleepless nights with his insensitivity and…

Yes, this is undoubtedly a bad idea. However, he is only coming to paint. I don't need to look perfect, and do full makeup and hair. I responded, and told him I was going to jump in the shower, and he can use his key to get in and start taping — the color is going to be gorgeous!

I know what you're thinking — why do I need to take a shower first if it doesn't matter how I look? And why does Ron still have a key to the house?

Well, I don't need to be *stunning*, but I *did* spend the night in a bar, and who wouldn't want to shower? Maybe put on a little lip gloss? Some eyeliner? I don't even like the mailman to see me without some eye definition.

And as for the key, it's still his house and he's never abused the privilege. For now, it's just easier to let him keep it.

Dixie follows me into the bathroom, and watches me turn on the water in the shower. That's her cue to run since the water monster might get her. I have learned that she's one of those wiener dogs who is super afraid of any wetness touching her body.

I, on the other hand, love bathing and showering. I could stay in here for hours. Okay, maybe not *hours*, but a long time. It drove my father insane when I was growing up. He used to bang on the door and yell at my mother for allowing me to shower for more than five minutes. Come to think of it, Ron also berated me for enjoying a lengthy, therapeutic cleansing. These men just don't understand the at-home spa experience.

And they are also cheap bastards. Apparently water is the same price as gold.

As the hot water soaks my hairspray-matted hair, I grab the coconut milk shampoo and think of dancing with 'Skinny Jeans' last night. That was so much fun, even though I felt ridiculous and Justin caught me flailing around like a wet noodle. If only I could find an age-appropriate man who likes to do things like that. I am sure they're out there, and I just haven't been looking in the right places.

I sniff my rose petal body wash and begin lathering. At thirty dollars a bottle, this stuff is intoxicating. If Ron knew I was buying something better than Suave shampoo and Ivory soap, his head would blow up.

I laugh to myself and replay Audra's words regarding this blind date she's foisted upon me. I am very hesitant to try this tactic again, but Audra is a level headed woman. She's been single a long time, and she knows what it's like out there. Like Rebecca. However, Audra doesn't bother to date any more. That part worries me—like she's a Mormon making wine recommendations.

I'm just being overly paranoid. Audra has a PhD in Genetics—not that the subject has anything to do with human behavior (or maybe it does—I know nothing about science), but she's smart. Hmm…but she did think of the Walmart painting idea.

I rinse my hair and sigh. I also wonder why she's not interested in this guy, but then again she is quite a bit older than him. Perhaps she feels the same way about Finn as I do about Justin. If I knew a fantastic, single young woman I would set her up with my gorgeous, but exasperating co-worker.

I finish shaving my legs—no, not for Ron! It's summer time and I do it every day. Plus, I don't want him to think I've let myself go like some reclusive, depressed divorced woman on the brink of a…

"Claire!"

I hear my name, and it sounds like it's coming from the bottom of the stairs. I know that summons all too well. Even when he was welcome to climb the stairs to find me, he always chose the yelling, as if it was irritating that I wasn't perpetually sitting on the couch, in case he needed me for something.

I chastise myself for getting pulled into past bitterness. He's here to help me and I invited him, so it's not reasonable to be mad at him already.

I scoop my hair up in a towel and hastily shrug on my soft, blue bathrobe.

Standing at the top of the stairs, I yell down, "I'm right here! Oh, there you are."

Ron is at the bottom of the stairs, with Dixie jumping on his legs. I seem to have forgotten that we have a normal suburban home staircase, not the one from Tara in *Gone with the Wind*. There is no need to shout.

"Hey, do you want me to get started in the dining room?" He bends down to pet the jumping wiener bean, but it's not calming her down a whole lot.

"Yes, you can start taping. The paint is in the garage, along with all of the other supplies."

I hope I bought the right things. I insisted on taking care of all of it. The guy at Home Depot helped me, so I'm sure it's all right. If not, I can always run back out. I can't let Ron do everything.

"Okay, well come on down and show me."

Ron's neck is craned as he stares up at me. He is smirking, so I know he's playing with me. He knows damn well I don't want to come down there like this.

"I'll be down in a few minutes. I just have to get dressed and…anyway, go look in the garage."

I turn around and exit gracefully, quietly closing and locking my bedroom door.

No, I don't think he's going to follow me up here. It's just a thing I do. I come from a family that locks doors.

I quickly pull on a pair of knit gym shorts and a purple tank top, swiping my lips with the frosty purple gloss I wore last night (it was right on my dresser!) and while I'm at it, I put on some eyeliner and mascara. That makes my cheeks look pale, so I sweep on a little blush.

Okay, yes I just did my whole face. I peer intently into my magnifying makeup mirror and wipe off some of the eyeliner. I can have a heavy hand with it—it's so hard to get the sides to match in thickness, and by the time I achieve parity, half my eyelid is black.

Satisfied that I look decent (who cares anyway?), I head downstairs to get Ron started. I don't plan on sticking around watching him all day, and I promised Dixie a walk.

Ron is in the dining room, wearing cargo shorts and a UPS t-shirt. I used to tease him all the time for wearing those shorts—why does he need all those extra pockets? I used to carry his wallet, keys, sunglasses, etc.

everywhere we went together. I guess they help for solo outings so that men don't have to resort to purses or 'man bags.'

I am just about to ask Ron if he's checked in the garage yet, when he turns around and points to my office and says, "Your little bundle of joy peed on the carpet in there."

"Oh, she gets excited, and when you let yourself in she probably got nervous and peed."

I brush past Ron and his stupid judgment of my dog mothering, and pick up the furry offender. I kiss her little head and say, "Did you pee-pee on the carpet? Do you have to go outside?"

Ron winces and says, "She's never going to learn if you baby her that much. My dad used to swat our dogs whenever they had an accident in the house or misbehaved. Just a little smack to show them who's boss."

I glare at Ron and take deep breaths to avoid telling him what I think about his father.

"Well, that's not something I am going to do. It's none of your concern. Let's go out to the garage and get—"

"Sure, I know you're too soft for that, but you know they have puppy classes at the pet stores. You know, like obedience training?"

He smiles as if his suggestion of training will make me forget his earlier recommendation of smacking my three-pound baby. He probably wishes he could have sent me to wife obedience classes.

And obviously I know they have fucking puppy classes. I'm not a moron.

I sigh and put Dixie back on her bed by the window

in my office. The pet stain remover spray is in the kitchen, but I'd rather get Ron set up first before I work on the carpet.

He shrugs his shoulders and gestures with his hands palms up, to indicate his innocent confusion over my dirty looks. "What did I say? You don't want her peeing…okay, fine, let's get the paint."

As he follows me to the garage my phone beeps. I popped it into my shorts pocket before leaving my bedroom in case I got a call from Finn. I know I shouldn't be so anxious, but it's a habit from my childhood conditioning.

My mother taught my sister and me not to keep a man waiting. Also, don't bother them when they're working or watching football. Thanks, Mom—this has all helped so much! Meanwhile, she tells my father he's an idiot, refers to his favorite sport as 'the goddamn football,' and basically does whatever she wants. Maybe she figured we'd do better if we didn't act like her.

My first inclination is to ignore Finn's call with Ron breathing down my neck, but fuck it—it's none of his business. I answer the phone, hoping now that the unknown number is actually Finn's. I hold my breath for a split second, realizing it could be any number of weirdos my number has been distributed to in the past year. I never add anyone as a contact if I don't plan on ever talking to them again.

It's Finn! He sounds very normal and we make plans to meet while I point out the paint, tape, rags, and brushes to a slightly red-faced Ron.

What's that all about?

CHAPTER FIFTEEN

Ron

Sunday rolls around and I'm in the apartment workout room. I was hoping if I got here early enough I could avoid Stacy lurking in the hallway. Like my wife, she's not up and at 'em at seven in the morning.

Speaking of my *wife*, she had *nerve* making that date right in front of my face yesterday. I mean, I know we're separated, and she thinks we're getting divorced, but that took balls. I don't remember Claire even having marbles.

I tried to ask her a few casual questions to scope out the competition. She was already annoyed with me for mentioning some dog training ideas, and I didn't want to alienate her any more. I was able to switch back to 'mildly detached' *friend* behavior, and show polite interest in her date while masking my jealousy.

Not that I'm actually *jealous*. This is just another fix-up one of her friends dredged up. I can only imagine this guy's story. I'm sure after the date she'll be telling me about how ridiculous it was over a glass of wine in the bathtub.

Okay, maybe just over a Coke in the kitchen, and take-out Chinese while I finish painting the dining room. Baby steps.

I just thought of the bathtub since it's one of the things that Claire loves that drove me crazy, and I couldn't comprehend. I've actually made a list of those things to remind myself to integrate them into our conversations so she can see I've changed.

Things Claire loves:

1. Long, hot baths (preferably alone and with a book)
2. Small, yappy dogs (I added the yappy part)
3. Donuts (she doesn't care that the fat circles will kill her)
4. Shoes (practical for work, and slutty for going out, which I prefer for home use)
5. Mini-golf (silly activity, but it's the one 'sport' she's good at)
6. Ridiculously loud rock music (I think she's going deaf)
7. My chest (this could come in handy in a pinch)

I know that sounds manipulative, but I sincerely want to get her back, and I know she craves a guy who *gets* her. I'm stopping to *get* some donuts on the way there today.

I did *get* her when we were younger, but somewhere along the line, we got *way* off track. I could relate to the 'pre-pregnancy crisis Claire,' but all of these experiences changed her. She used to be more fun, more outgoing. But then of course she also drank too much and made a spectacle of herself. I see a little of that behavior resurfacing now, but it's no longer fun.

Come to think of it, she's never been all that stable, but my influence was calming. I need to move back into our house before she reverts back completely to her younger self. If I time it right, I'll get a fair and balanced Claire, just like that Fox News her mother watches all day. My father may have lightly tapped a misbehaving dog, but he's a liberal, tolerant kind of guy. Not like *her* parents.

Things went okay with Claire yesterday—overall. She didn't seem to want to discuss her latest blind date, and I got that, so I dropped it.

I didn't make any comments about the paint color she chose for the dining room. I used to tell her that these crazy, loud colors she always picks are terrible for resale value. The average person does not want a Berry Cobbler dining room. She makes things way too complicated.

But I held back, even though I know I'm going to have to repaint before we sell the house. I don't know when that will be, but I would actually like to get out of that neighborhood and have a fresh start somewhere. Maybe even out of state.

I know I'm getting ahead of myself again.

I quit bench pressing because I'm just not in the mood. I should probably just join a gym where there are other guys around to spot me, and some positive energy pumping through the place. And Claire won't mind me going out—I don't want to make the mistake of smothering her.

I was trying to save money by using this shitty apartment gym, but once I move back into our house, I'll have more disposable income again. I'm not a cheap guy, just practical. For instance, last night I insisted upon buying dinner, even though Claire wanted to do it to thank me for my work. She gave in when I reminded her that the deal was that I am going to get more money when she buys me out, so she *is* paying me.

It's hard to say that with a straight face.

So I cleaned up a little, and said I was going to grab Chinese from a place we love. She was in a much better mood by then—probably because her dog peed outside and her walls were red—and she suggested that we order from a new place that delivers, *and* she offered me her shower to clean up.

This was a *big* score in my book. A woman doesn't let a guy back into the private parts of her home, or herself, unless she's softening towards him. I was careful to show my gratitude by being the perfect dinner companion, and not pushing for the second, more desirable private access. We laughed and reminisced about the old days, and I was cautious about steering clear of any topics that upset her.

I could have used the shower to push for something, but I acted appropriately distant and casual, as if Jeff asked me if I wanted to shower at their house after boating all day.

On second thought, that's a bad example. It's more likely that even Roberta would follow me up the stairs far more easily than Claire would.

I still have a lot of work to do.

I also spent a lot of time playing with Dixie. She's a cute little thing, but Claire is way too permissive with her. She's an animal and she needs to know that Claire is the pack leader. Hopefully she doesn't do too much irreversible damage and I can turn it around after I move back in.

I may even add another dog to the mix once I get a handle on things again. I was thinking a nice chocolate lab. A real dog. And Labs are nice dogs, and would be unlikely to mistake Dixie for a hotdog and gobble her up.

This is another thing I would NEVER say to Claire, but watching her with the dog makes me wonder how permissive she would have been with a child. It makes me even more sure that everything happens for a reason.

I wanted to stay later, and tried to delay my departure, but Claire said she was tired from being out late the night before, and maybe she should get to bed so we could get an earlier start on the painting today. I didn't argue and I left to the sounds of her praise for my good work and selfless assistance.

Okay, she just thanked me for coming over, but I know she was very grateful by the big smile on her pretty face. She wore a lot of makeup for me. Claire used to let her guard down with all of that primping when we were married. She may not be willing to admit it, but she wanted to look good for me.

And even though I have backed off my declarations of love, I still said it. It has to be on her mind every second—wondering if I still feel that way, if I meant it, and if I've changed my mind.

That kind of tension is very sexy.

Despite overall positive progress, I still left feeling restless and unsatisfied. It's those moments when I would previously visit Stacy, or go to a bar and pretend to be interested in drinking to see if I could find a short-term solution to my problem.

But now that I'm committed to 'Operation Reconciliation,' I am not going to behave that way. As I was congratulating myself for my restraint and good judgment last night, I walked into my apartment and turned on my computer. I am not one of those guys who checks messages and e-mail on his phone all day, especially if I'm already with the one person I have any interest in hearing from.

So I was surprised to see that I had about twenty messages from Russian women who wanted to get to know me better. All of them were written in broken English, the way you would expect Russians to be imitated in a bad comedy movie starring someone from the cast of Saturday Night Live.

Jeff was right. There is no shortage of available women out there. I smiled and reminded myself that this could all be fake, and that all of these smiling photos could be a cover up for…what? Desperate, unattractive women in the US pretending to be Russian beauties? Desperate, attractive Russian women hoping to snare sad, lonely American men into green card marriages?

Apparently there really was once such a thing as mail order brides. Does that still exist?

I decided that these answers are unimportant because I am just doing this as a joke, a distraction, a game. So who cares if these women are serious?

Except as I start to read their messages, it seems like they *are* serious. Some of them are pretty, and some of them not so much. They look like real photos of real women, not glossy magazine shoots of fake women designed to trick pathetic American men.

So I changed out of my paint clothes into some sweats, and spent the rest of the evening reading all about the chicks that want me.

I'm not really this full of myself—I find it all funny,

and the humor is one of the main reasons I signed up.

That, and extreme curiosity and boredom.

I scrolled through all of the messages telling me about their lives, their hopes and their dreams of coming to America. A couple told me about how great it is in Russia in the hopes that I will want to visit. That actually seems like the better option if a guy was serious about this. You could meet a whole bunch on one trip, and then get the hell out.

If one of them comes here, how do you escape them?

I was just about to close my computer and call it a night, when I spied a message from Natasha. Her English was better than most, and her soft brown eyes, high cheekbones and long, shiny brown hair framed a face that was warm, beautiful and…

Oh my God, what the fuck am I doing?

Claire

Ron was helpful, but as I expected he got a little full of himself and started giving me puppy rearing advice— as if he's the damn dog whisperer.

And I *know* he was biting his tongue when he saw the paint color on the walls. He was probably counting to ten to keep from berating me about it, but all he said was, "A color this dark is going to take several coats for full coverage."

Really? Like I don't know that?

So I did something very out of character this morning. I got up *early* with the intention of *painting*.

Okay, *two* things.

Ron already did all of the taping and the first coat, so I figured how hard can it be to apply a second coat? This way it cuts down on the time he has to be here, and the amount of comments I have to endure.

I pour the paint in the tray thingie after a difficult time prying open the can. I swear, why is everything so hard? I'm not *that* weak, but maybe I should join a gym. I think part of my aversion to that activity is Ron's obsession with it.

I'm finally all set up, and I even have the foresight to put Dixie in my office, behind the gate. I had to buy special, expensive gates because baby gates don't fit properly in these doorway openings. But that's fine since these are more secure—they can hold back a much bigger dog. There's a picture of a German Shepherd on the box, just sitting there like a doof behind the barrier.

Speaking of doofs, I am not doing that great with the painting. It looks *way* easier when Ron does it. But I plug along, listening to my favorite head banging music while Dixie lays down and pouts in her prison.

I know when Ron gets here he can just let himself in, so it doesn't matter if I can't hear the door over the music, *which has just been turned down at my favorite part of a semi-favorite Breaking Benjamin song!*

I slam the paint brush down on the tray and stomp off into the family room.

Ron bursts into a fit of laughter as soon as he sees me, but I am not going to be dissuaded from yelling at him for touching my music. He always did that shit when we were married, and how much paint could I possibly have on...

I glance at my reflection in the microwave door and join him in hysterical laughter.

"Oh my God, how did I get paint on my...is there paint in my hair, too?"

"It's on your nose and your chin, and your...elbows! How did you manage that?"

He is doubled over and coming back into the kitchen with his 'asking for forgiveness for teasing me' face, which no longer works.

I walk out into the entryway to look at myself in a real mirror, and it is quite a sight.

He is right behind me and I quickly turn and say, "I'm trying to be more independent, and don't think you can divert my attention from the fact that you switched my music to that stupid *grunge* station."

Getting XM Radio was not helpful for our marriage.

"Claire, Nirvana is *classic*. This newer shit you listen to is for idio…I mean, kids."

Now I am really stewing, but I want this job done as soon as possible so I can salvage some part of my Sunday for…I don't know what, but maybe some peace and quiet. Or very loud music of MY choice!

I find it preposterous that he was professing his love last week, and now he is back to his usual jerky self. Of course, I did reject him but that's because he doesn't get it. I left him for a *reason*…many of them…and I don't see any of those things changing. He says he's just helping me out as a friend, but this is a hard 'friendship.' It's more like a 'rubbing my nerves with a cheese grater' ship.

"Okay, you aren't here to debate music. You agreed to come over and do this job, and you're right, I should just let you do it. I don't even have to be here. I am going to get cleaned up and take Dixie for a walk."

I stomp back into the dining room while Ron is backpedaling like a clown on a unicycle in the circus.

"I'm sorry. It was just cute that you tried to paint and got it all over you. It's good for you to try to do things. And here, I'll put your music back on. This one isn't that bad…Shinedown…this guy is a good singer…Claire?"

He joins me in the dining room and focuses on my face, which is turning purple as I cover an audible gasp, blinking my eyes furiously at the scene before me.

"Dixie, what have you done?"

While Ron and I were arguing in the other room, Dixie managed to get past the 'heavy, metal gate' (ironic that she did that while heavy metal was playing — maybe it inspired her), and apparently she proceeded to jump in the paint tray — yes, I left it on the floor!

If that's not bad enough, she came running to greet me and now there are Berry Cobbler paw prints all over the wood floors. I lean down to deal with the damage and she jumps on me, applying paint to the rest of my body and clothing.

"I'll get some rags. Just hold onto her." Ron rushes out of the room and I hear him under the kitchen sink, searching for the stash of old towels we have always kept in there for emergency cleanups.

I don't know what's worse — the mess itself or the fact that Ron is here to witness my screw-up.

Definitely the latter. How did he not notice the hole in the island? That's right, it's on the other side. Whew…

We get Dixie cleaned up as best we can, and I pick her up for a trip to the dreaded bathtub.

Ron goes to work on the floor and says, "I've got this. Just take care of the little furry menace. It's really both of our faults for arguing and ignoring her. This is how little kids get hurt when their parents are fighting and not watching them."

I choke back both a scream and a fresh batch of tears, as I grip Dixie tightly and turn towards the staircase. "Well then I guess it's a good thing we didn't have any kids, since we are so irresponsible."

He throws down the rag and yells after me, "Claire, I'm sorry. I didn't mean it like that."

Ron

A few hours later I am finishing up the painting and I hear Claire coming in with Dixie. After our argument, she and the dog got cleaned up, and she took her to the park. Obviously she took her a few other places because she's been gone a long time.

I really fucked up. Old habits are hard to break. I always changed the music when I came home. How the hell can I have a conversation with my wife listening to that crap? I could have turned it down to a normal volume instead of changing it, but I guess I keep thinking Claire will realize she's wrong if I do things subtly.

I should have learned my lesson by now.

But the dog—that's a handful right there. She's cute, but she's not dumb. She's stubborn and laughing at Claire, who needs to take control.

I call out to Claire in greeting. "Hey, look I'm all done. It looks great, doesn't it?"

My paint job looks perfect, but I still think the color is headache producing. But I am keeping my mouth shut.

She slowly saunters into the kitchen. I hear her put Dixie down and throw her keys and purse on the island. She pauses a moment, and I know she's probably rehearsing a speech, or she's trying to put on a happy face like nothing is wrong at all.

She stands in the doorway with her arms folded and says, "Yeah, I love it. Thanks." A small grin escapes her lips, but I know it's for the color, and not for me.

I lift my hand up with the intention of running my fingers through my hair, but stop midway because of the amount of paint on it, and the memory of Claire's earlier paint smeared appearance.

We share a laugh at this realization when I widen my eyeballs at my dirty hand. That's how I know we still have a connection — no words were needed.

"You're welcome. Hey, I was thinking — "

Her phone starts beeping and she puts up a finger. "I'm sorry, I have to get this."

She walks back into the kitchen and Dixie comes running in to greet me. I quietly pet the little monster while straining to hear her mommy. It sounds like she's making plans. Probably with the blind date jerk.

She laughs and comes back, clutching her phone. "Sorry, that was Audra's friend calling to set up our date."

"Oh, yeah. When's that?" I keep petting Dixie so I don't have to meet Claire's eyes. The poor dog must think I'm going to wear a hole in her with all of this exaggerated attention.

"Tomorrow night." She smiles wistfully and then continues. "So, are you all done with this room?"

I stand up and stretch. I wouldn't mind a nice soak in the big bathtub upstairs. I have paint on me, just like Dixie did, and she got a bath. I consider making that flirtatious remark, but decide not to press my luck. A couple of hours ago I made her cry, so I'm lucky she's talking to me. Even the donuts I brought didn't help. It's nice to see her smile, even if it's only because she has a date with another guy.

"I just need to finish up the trim. Hey, I know. I could come over tomorrow night and do it while you're out. I could watch Dixie and keep her out of mischief, and be out of your hair before you even get home from your date."

I am not leaving his house until she comes home, but she doesn't know that. I'm really not *worried* about this guy. All of these dates turn out to be losers—I just wish I could put an end to her need to look for another man. I keep thinking she will eventually get sick of it and give up, but I guess it hasn't gotten bad enough yet.

Just in case this one goes okay, if I'm here she can't bring him home, and it might dissuade her from going to his place, knowing that I might know how long she's been out.

"Okay, that sounds like a good idea. As much as I hate to admit it, I can't possibly do the trim myself. I would destroy all of your work. Just let yourself in. I'm meeting Finn after work on the other side of town, so I'm not coming home first."

She proceeds to rattle off a list of puppy-minding directions, and I zone out. I can handle dog sitting, but I'm not sure I can handle Claire out with another man.

No matter how long the trim really takes me, it is going to take me exactly as long as it takes Claire to pull into the driveway after this date.

CHAPTER SIXTEEN

Claire

Monday morning is dragging as I fixate on the nonsense of this past weekend, my date tonight and my screwed up life in general.

I am trying to review resumes for this executive administrative assistant position, and my eyes are blurring. If our CEO, Tim, could keep an admin for more than a few months I wouldn't have this problem. But then of course I may not have a job because our relatively high turnover keeps me in business.

I don't understand what he could possibly be doing to scare away all of these assistants, though. He's a nice guy, or at least it seems like it. I've never had any issues with him. He chews gum a lot, which seems to be a nervous dieting habit. He explained to me one day that he doesn't eat if he's chewing gum. When I look at his ever expanding waistline, all I can think of to say is—I didn't know gum was so high in calories. But since I need to keep my mind numbing job, I zip my mouth shut.

Hmm…here's a recent college grad. Maybe that's the problem. I normally place much more experienced admins with Tim, and they probably get bored. There isn't enough going on around here to stimulate a seasoned professional. Plus, if the rumors are true I think Tim may have a roving eye that Mrs. Tim doesn't know about.

But that's none of my concern. And even if it becomes a problem, Rebecca will have to deal with it. I'm almost certain that employee sex scandals fall under employee *relations*.

I glance down at my outfit and hope it's okay for my date. Dating really is a nightmare. When I was married to Ron, and even long before, dating was about sitting on the couch watching a movie with a big bowl of popcorn, or going to visit family, or if I begged — a weekend at the beach.

God, we were boring. But at least I didn't have to worry about my wardrobe so much.

Today, I chose a sleeveless black shell that flares a little at the waist and a dark violet cardigan. The skirt has a floral pattern that pulls the purple and black together with a few more subtle hues. I can just take the sweater off when I leave, and switch to the higher strappy sandals, ditching the frumpier work pumps.

I am trying to be a little more daring in my work wardrobe, but I still try to avoid low cut tops or toe-baring shoes. Of course I don't have all that much on top, and I could get away with the shoes, too. I don't think anyone at Bella Donna has a foot fetish. Unless Tim...no, that's ridiculous.

Just to be on the safe side, I might start screening applicants for toe coverage, as well as MS Office experience and good organizational skills. I make a note to add Cecilia Griffin to the pile — recent local college graduate with a major in communications.

A knock at my door breaks my train of thought, and I look up to see Rebecca in *her* office uniform of a black pencil skirt, sensible black pumps, and a light blue button down shirt.

"Hey, how was your weekend? I meant to stop by first thing in the morning, but I had to meet with the accounting department."

"The whole department? What happened?"

"Apparently Debbie brought in cookies her daughter was selling for school, and someone ate all of them and didn't pay. So I was asked to solve the problem."

I was about to ask why their manager didn't handle it, but I decide to let it go. At Bella Donna, anything that management wants to avoid conveniently falls under human resources.

I smirk and say, "Come in and close the door. I have a few minutes for gossip before I have to get these resumes to Tim."

She scurries in and discreetly closes the door. We just pretend we're discussing 'sensitive HR matters' if anyone complains about the closed door. Given enough time sequestered in here we could solve all the world's problems. Or at least maybe a few of our own.

I proceed to catch Rebecca up on my weekend with Ron in the house, and tell her about my date tonight.

Rebecca crosses her legs and says, "He sounds promising. Your friend Audra is a pretty stable chick, right? She's a scientist, so she probably did some experiments or calculations to prove your compatibility."

I ignore her feeble attempt at humor and say, "I hope so, because nothing I've been doing seems to work. At least Ron will be done with the painting tonight."

Rebecca checks the time on my computer and says, "Shit, I'm going to be late for lunch with Tim. He has some new ideas for employee morale boosting." She stands up and as she opens the door she adds, "Monday is a weird day for a date, don't you think?"

"I thought that, too. He said 'Monday's suck anyway, so let's have our blind date then.' I thought that was kind of a jerky thing to say. I think he laughed, though."

I wrinkle my nose and purse my lips. I didn't analyze my conversation with Finn enough because Ron was breathing down my neck and...

Justin picks this moment to waltz on by and offer, "I would never say such a thing to a beautiful prospect such as you, Claire."

Rebecca shakes her head as she watches him disappear down the hall. "He's unreal. How does he always manage to catch us talking about something—?"

She jumps as he reappears in the doorway. Squeezing Rebecca's shoulder and smiling at me, he says, "You two are the only people in this building who ever talk about anything juicy. It's dry as a bone on the second floor, ladies. Dry as a bone."

He emphasizes the last word as if we should feel sorry for his lack of moisture. Does he want us to spray him with a hose? I smirk to myself, but if I say anything like that I will just add fuel to his fire, as my mother would say. I don't want to encourage his flirting, and besides—I find it somewhat insulting. He's just a kid and he thinks it's great fun to tease the old single women.

Rebecca obviously doesn't care about appropriate office conversation as she replies, "Don't look at us—we haven't hit menopause yet. Maybe you should get your office moved down here."

Justin's smile has magnified, and now there's a twinkle in his green eyes. "I would love to, but unfortunately those nerdy IT guys are like robot monkeys, and can't be left alone."

He turns to leave, and grabs the doorway one last time and says, "Claire, have fun tonight. Oh, and I would change into something with a little less...neck coverage." He fingers his own neck to indicate where I went wrong with my wardrobe choice.

Rebecca and I are quiet for a moment as we recover from Justin's audacity. She finally breaks the silence and says, "Listen, text me if you need an 'out' tonight. You're meeting him right in my area and I'll be home."

"Okay, I will. Hey, do you think it's odd he wants to meet in the Dairy Queen parking lot? There are a couple of restaurants over in that shopping center, but wouldn't it make sense to just meet at one of *them*?"

"Maybe he wants to give you a choice. Ooh, Chez Francois is over there. I bet he wants to treat you to a gourmet meal." She raises her eyebrows and widens her eyes in exaggeration of her excitement. "Lighten up, I'm sure he will be very nice and normal. Even if you end up at Franco's, the pizza is great."

I smile and thank her again as she dashes off to her meeting. After Tim is done with her, he'll want to see some resumes. I am dialing Cecilia's number right now. Hopefully, both she and my date will be normal and fill a need.

Just very different ones.

Fortunately, Cecilia sounds great on the phone and she's interested in the job. I send her resume, along with a few others, over to Tim for review. For the rest of the day, I work on a Power Point presentation on company policies and procedures. I can't believe we have travel or relocation policies. No one ever travels on business, and no one is ever hired from outside Richmond.

The boredom drones on until five o'clock mercifully arrives, and I leap out of my seat to get this date started. I hit the ladies' room first to change my shoes, freshen up and apply an evening layer of makeup.

I laugh to myself as I think of my father giving me grief about my makeup in high school. 'Claire Marie, why don't you just use the paint roller to put it on? I have one in the garage.' Then he would mime the paint roller makeup application for me, just in case I didn't get it.

Speaking of rollers, I should text Ron to confirm he's still going to my house to paint the trim tonight. And take care of Dixie.

Hmm…on second thought, I really don't want to get involved in a dialogue with Ron as I'm off to meet my date. Instead I type out a quick text to Jane, asking if she can let me know when she sees Ron pull up at the house. If he doesn't show up, she can go over and let Dixie out.

I pop my phone back in my purse, blot my lips of the extra drippy gloss I've applied, and close the ladies' room door behind me.

I survey my appearance and wonder if Justin would approve. I could walk past his office and ask, but I am not the type to indulge in flirting with insanely hot, younger men.

Instead, I do the sensible thing and hightail it to the parking lot and my date with an age-appropriate, adult man, who has been fully vetted by a veteran, single woman with an advanced degree for my dating enjoyment.

I put some music on to quiet my crazy thoughts, and

drive out of the office complex while checking my teeth for errant lip gloss in the rear view mirror.

I still don't understand this Dairy Queen parking lot thing. I hope he's not one of those guys who wants to leave one car somewhere, and drive together to another location. I'm sure he's not an axe murderer, but I prefer to drive myself when meeting strangers.

The other weird thing is his car. Audra told me he's not the least bit pretentious about cars, and he drives a beat up, old jalopy. Yet when he texted me this afternoon to confirm our meeting time and place, he said to look for a frost blue Jaguar convertible.

I am guessing 'frost blue' is the actual name the car manufacturer assigned to the color. Any man who is that descriptive with color on his own is an odd bird.

Audra could be confused. Maybe someone else on the street owns the crappy car and she thinks it's his. If he has a Jaguar he probably doesn't park it on the street in the city, and Audra is not at all concerned with material things. Until not too long ago, her own rear car doors were tied together across the back seat with strings, so they didn't pop open while driving. Even *I* think that kind of problem warrants a trade-in.

I didn't want to see a picture of Finn because I didn't want any pre-conceived notions, and people often don't look like their pictures. Finn did say that Audra showed him pictures of me and he couldn't wait to see me in person.

I hope I don't disappoint, although I think I look better in person. When someone points a camera at me, I get all squeamish like my mother. Every time she sees a camera, she screams, 'Are you taking my picture?'

I want to tell her that we need to have photos of her

for her grandchildren, but the chances of her having any are bleak with one infertile daughter and one blissfully single one.

I have no problem spotting Finn and his frosty mobile. Wait, don't you get Frosties at Dairy Queen? No, never mind…I think that's Wendy's.

It's easy to spot such a high end car at six o'clock in the Dairy Queen parking lot. This is a weird shopping center. It's kind of sandwiched between the upscale side of town and a neighborhood of more modest, older homes and apartments. So there's a high-end wine shop next to a laundromat, and then fine dining at the other end of the complex.

Finn is leaning on the car as if he's not at all concerned about smudging or scratching the paint job. What if there are buttons on his back pockets?

I park my car and take a good look at him, before he looks up and spots me. He's texting vigorously on his phone—hopefully he's not setting up *his* escape phone call if we don't hit it off. I know I just did the same thing with Rebecca earlier, but in my defense it was her idea. I was planning on bravely soldiering on through any dating adversity.

I sigh and check my teeth for lip gloss again.

Finn is tall-ish. Maybe not as big as Ron, and he's definitely not as beefy and muscular. But he looks like a good-looking, fit sort of guy. He's wearing a nice striped button down shirt and the usual business casual pants. They're black, not khaki. I hate the color khaki. It's an ugly word and it reminds me of baby vomit.

I feel a momentary pang at the thought of baby vomit. You know you are suffering from maternal longing if you think wistfully about the bodily functions of the child you'll never have.

I take a deep breath and decide to push aside the dark, senseless thoughts and focus on my date. He has goldish brown hair, cut in a short neat style, and a strong jawline. No facial hair, but that can always change. I forgot to ask about his eye color, but I am soon to find out because he's heading over to my car. I leap out to meet him halfway, hoping the big minivan next to me will block his view of my old, crappy Honda Civic.

"Hey, you must be Claire? I hope you don't think I'm too forward, but I was worried you were too afraid to get out of the car and having second thoughts about meeting me."

He smiles and I can feel my face redden. I had no idea he saw me. Maybe the phone was just a ruse and he was checking me out in a sneaky way, too.

"Hi. No, I was just finishing up a conference call. It's nice to meet you."

I extend my hand and Finn lightly touches my shoulder to move me out of the way of the minivan that now wants to exit the DQ parking lot. Since it looks like the driver is a distracted mom yelling at her kids, he probably wants to make sure our date doesn't begin with me getting run over. Even for me, that would be my worst blind date yet.

And why the hell did I blurt out the stupid conference call excuse? It's six o'clock and I'm sitting in my car waiting for a date. What kind of job would I have that would require that level of dedication? Now I feel like my standard 'work is boring' speech isn't going to fly when he asks my favorite question, 'Claire, what do you do?' That one is truly pins in my eyes.

I break the awkward silence and say, "Wow, that's a

nice car. And I'm not even a car person."

He can obviously figure that out by the old trash can on wheels I'm tooling around in. Me and my 'high profile, after-hours conference call job' could use a fancier ride.

He laughs a bit too much, but I cut him some slack for blind date stress. "That's not mine. I get to borrow some pretty nice vehicles as part of my job. Everyone wants a great review in the magazine. I would never waste money on such a lavish car. Your Honda is practical—I bet you'll get way over 200k miles on it."

"Yeah, my ex-husband always wanted me to have a new car every few years, and I thought it was wasteful since I don't really care. So I'll be keeping this awhile."

He glances over at my vehicle and says, "Actually that's looking pretty new. You could even get away with trading down to an older model and pocket the difference."

I start to open my mouth to respond to that, but I can't quite get my head around someone thinking I should get an *even older* used car. Maybe he was the one who helped Audra tie her back doors together.

When I just smile and wipe a bead of sweat from my forehead he says, "Oh, I'm so sorry. I don't know why we're standing out here in this heat. Do you like Dairy Queen?"

"Um, yes for ice cream. Did you want to get some after dinner?"

Now I realize we didn't specify that we were having dinner. Did he think meeting at six gave me enough time to eat first? People with high level positions like mine don't have time for that.

"Oh, I thought we'd get it all here. That's why I

suggested meeting tonight. Monday is 'buy one get one free' hotdog night at DQ, and you can't beat that."

I squint at Finn, partly because the sun is in my eyes, and partially because I don't know if he's serious. This is already getting weird, and that's too bad because I have now noticed how his eyes are a very pale blue and match his car. I don't normally like blue eyes, but his are soft and dreamy...

If he turns out to be a total whack-job, at least he's a good looking one.

He is smiling so I now assume he's teasing me again. I find a lot of men think they need to make a woman laugh. Apparently there was a survey a few years back that stated 'makes me laugh' as the top criteria for women in picking a mate. I would say 'has normal brain' would be tops, but maybe I'm being too picky.

I return his grin and say, "That's funny. So where did you want to eat, really?"

Now he's slapping his leg so I know he was kidding. Whew, I was worried. Now that I look at the building, there is a banner sign for the BOGO on the hotdogs. He just read that while standing here, probably trying to find a good ice breaker.

"I really had you going, didn't I?"

His smile fades slightly as he turns his head to survey the shopping center for possible choices. My guess is that he hasn't picked a place and now he realizes he should have been more focused on a plan, rather than joking around.

I am totally flexible, but he doesn't know that so he may be needlessly stressing.

I smile wider and say, "I'm totally flexible."

I was just about to suggest getting pizza at Franco's

when he blurts out, "Let's go to Chez Francois. One of the guys at the Jaguar dealership was telling me all about it. Apparently the chef is really from Paris."

I am taken aback by this complete switch from a meal that costs five dollars to one that might cost a couple of hundred, and I'm not sure if he's kidding again.

I was about to say it's a bit much when I remembered that this is a blind date, and my policy is to pay for myself anyway. I don't want him to think I'm cheap or poor, especially since my job is supposedly *so* important, so I do a quick mental calculation on my checking account to decide if I can afford this meal. Oh hell, if the prices are outrageous I'll just get a salad. I never eat much on dates anyway, and I could use a little luxury.

"Wow, that's quite an upgrade, but please know that I will be paying for myself tonight."

He smiles and agrees. "If you insist."

CHAPTER SEVENTEEN

Claire

This place is gorgeous. I'm so busy staring at the art work on the walls, and the chandelier in the center of the room, that I just nod numbly when Finn asks me if I approve of his wine selection.

A little wave of panic goes off in my head as he gives the water the order. Bottles of wine in restaurants like this can cost more than whole meals in a regular eatery. This may be so pricey that I'll have to eat macaroni for the rest of the month, like I did in college. My parents gave me plenty of food money, but I saved it for shoes.

Now I have to waste money on dumb things, like my mortgage. Perhaps I should talk to Ron about selling the house. I should downsize — not my *car* — but I don't need a four-bedroom family house. I think I'll bring it up tonight if he's still there when I get home.

The waiter hands us our menus, me first of course. I'm relieved to see the prices are on the menu, but then I'm not relieved because there isn't an entrée under thirty dollars. Crap. It's hot out, but it's cool in here. Maybe I wouldn't look too obvious if I ordered the fifteen-dollar soup? I could always grab a couple of hotdogs at Dairy Queen after Finn drives off.

I smile and Finn must think that means that he has pleased me, and that someone of my stature must be hard to impress. Seriously, what did Audra tell him? I don't even think she understands what I do for a living. She probably just said I work in publishing.

"So what looks good? I think I'm going to have the lobster in cognac and tomato sauce."

I read the description and note the price. Now I really feel like a loser if I order soup.

Oh, fuck it. Since when do I care about money?

"I think I'll have the filet mignon."

The waiter suddenly appears, "That's an excellent choice, mademoiselle."

He gets extra points for not calling me madam, and now I remember that I also have to factor this guy's tip into the equation.

He presents the wine to Finn, who looks a little out of his element with the tasting, sniffing and swooshing circus that everyone does when they order wine in a fancy restaurant. I've watched my father do it many times, which makes it very unsexy to me. I'm actually glad to see Finn struggling. Maybe there is hope for this date.

The waiter fills both of our glasses and scurries away, leaving us to finally start a real conversation. Once we do, things are flowing pleasantly. We're covering the usual topics—place of birth, family background, career, hobbies.

Finn refills my wine and although my stomach is grumbling, I sip it. I guess the food takes a while to prepare in a place like this.

"So, yes my job is fun. I wouldn't call it glamorous, but I get to travel a lot and play with cars. I meet a lot of people on the road. And the per diem is amazing. You wouldn't believe how much money I've saved by pocketing the cash and staying at dive motels, and eating microwaved meals in the lobby."

I grin and take a gulp of wine. It *is* delicious, even though I know it costs more than my whole outfit.

Hmm...I'm not sure if he's joking again. In my agency recruiting days, I do remember contractors traveling on a lower budget to benefit from per diem rates, but Finn's case sounds pretty extreme. Maybe that's how he affords to eat out this extravagantly when he's home.

I finally reply, "Wow, you've got it all figured out, haven't you?"

I try to focus on his soft blue eyes and not worry so much about everything that comes out of his mouth. Relationships need time to develop. You can't make snap judgments. After all, I first met Ron when he was copying off my paper in English class. And he turned out fine, well...never mind, that's a bad example.

Once again he just laughs and I don't know if he's messing with me. I need to ask Audra if she gets his sense of humor. I'm guessing she doesn't. American humor flies right over her scientific genius brain.

"So tell me about your job, Claire."

I struggle to hold back a grimace and give him the basics. English major in college. Publishing company. Human Resources. Recruiting. Training. Blah, blah, blah.

"Oh, you're a recruiter? Audra just told me you worked in publishing. I have a friend who's looking for work. I'll send you his resume."

I blink hard and say, "What does he do?"

Finn waves his hand as if my question is a fly he's swatting away and says, "Oh, I think he's a *chemist* or something. But he can do anything. He's smart guy."

I lean back in my chair and summon a fake smile. Why does everyone think a recruiter is a job genie? And no, he can't do *anything*. We don't do any experiments on the molecules and atoms in the fucking manuscripts.

And there are people who have experience doing the *actual job* we're hiring for. I want to ask if his friend would like to be our CEO's admin, and be in charge of party planning and ordering bushels of chewing gum.

Instead I say, "Sure, send it over."

Where the hell is our food? I should've had a later lunch knowing that dinner would be a non-event on a date.

Unfortunately, Finn has now moved on to the topic of relationship history. I was hoping not to tackle this one on an empty stomach.

He shares, "It was a short marriage. We were much too young. You said you and your husband were high school sweethearts?"

"Yes, we were also too young, but together a long time." This conversation is heading into a depressing zone and I need to brighten it up. I smile and continue, "But, he's painting my dining room right now, so the 'friends' thing is working out okay for us."

In his enthusiasm for responding, he almost spits his wine. "Yes! It's so beneficial to be friends with an ex. If you can get something done for free—"

"Well, it's actually not for—"

"I have many exes who help me out on a regular basis with all sorts of things. One picks up my dry cleaning because it's on her way home. Another one sews for me, if I lose a button or break a zipper. My ex-wife still brings me dinner on Thursdays. That's why I didn't pick that day for our date. Someday I'll probably have enough exes to feed me at least most of the weekdays."

This is getting to be too much. Is he fucking serious? He has enslaved his exes, and they go for it? I can't resist saying, "Wow, you must be continuing to give them something they want."

I don't normally make overt sexual references when on dates with strangers, but I can't help but call this guy out on his obvious 'friends with benefits' relationships.

He visibly bristles and says, "No way. That's the worst thing to do. Then you get locked into all the emotional stuff and the friendship can't flourish."

He studies my reaction for a moment and adds, "So you're not...you know...with your ex, are you? Painting is a big job to do for free."

So is weekly dinner for the past ten years, but I bite my tongue and say, "No, he's actually not doing it for free. We are adding it to the price when I buy him out of the house."

"Oh, I wouldn't do that, but I guess it's none of my business."

He's right, and I don't know why I'm telling him all of these private things. What happened to talking about music and hobbies on dates? I could tell him more about my mini-golf obsession, and he could tell me about how he likes to bury his cash in the ground like a squirrel.

I am feeling very queasy — don't they have a piece of damn bread in this place?

He rubs the stem of his wine glass and says, "You know, I am glad for the way things turned out with Holly, and I'm so grateful that we didn't have any children."

"Did you not want any?" I eye the empty bottle of

wine, but since my electric bill is due tomorrow, I lick my lips and suck up my thirst.

His eyes widen and he says, "Oh, I definitely do. Just not with the wrong woman. I wasn't ready, you know? I'm sure you felt the same way with your marriage. High school sweethearts and all."

This is the point where I can continue to smile and change the subject, or be myself. I need to get used to being truthful about my situation. Even if I get a little teary-eyed, so what? This is who I am and what I have to offer. Or don't. And I don't think Finn and I have much of a future anyway.

"Actually, I can't have children."

I go on to explain the abbreviated version of my pregnancy losses and subsequent hysterectomy last year.

His face shows concern and he replies, "Oh, Claire, how awful for you. So your husband left you because of it? I can see how that would happen, but how terrible."

He reaches across the table for my hand and I pull it back.

I steady myself and say, "No, I left him because of his insensitivity over our situation."

I can't believe Audra didn't tell him this important fact about me. I get that she was protecting my privacy, but maybe I should encourage people to share my story for pre-screening purposes. Knowing Audra, she didn't even think about it. To her a hysterectomy is the same as having your gall bladder out. She always acts like the desire to reproduce is a bit unusual, like eating pickles for breakfast or collecting toe lint as a hobby.

So here I am explaining myself and trying not to become emotional in front of a guy who is obviously a cheap, manipulative…hey…I *don't* have to talk about this anymore!

Just as I am about to stand up for myself and regain my dignity, he says, "Oh Claire, there are so many other options. If I were you, I would explore all of them."

I let him pat my hand this time, and the human contact feels nice, even though it's coming from a guy I'll never see again.

I feel my eyes tearing up now, because of this minor act of kindness, and I'm not sure if I'm crying for my loss, or because I'm so mad at myself for putting myself in these situations.

I stand up, accidentally rattling my silverware, and excuse myself to the ladies' room. "I'm sorry, I'll be right back."

I swipe under my eyes instinctively, to catch the smearing mascara, and Finn says, "Don't worry. Take your time. I'll see where our food is — I think we're both just famished."

He smiles and I make a beeline for the room marked 'Femmes.'

I pull out my phone and get ready to text Rebecca. I'm not sure how that will help, but it may calm my nerves. I really do want to eat this meal, and maybe Finn isn't a prospect for a boyfriend, but we could be friends. Never mind — I could be penciled in for cat litter changing or dinner delivery on Tuesdays.

I know that sounds preposterous — a selfish bastard like Finn would never own a cat.

I should just call Rebecca, but I don't want anyone to hear me, and there is always some slowpoke in the stall taking ten minutes to pee. What do women *do* in the bathroom? And they're not playing games on their phones, because I've been waiting with my legs crossed in ladies' rooms since I've been out of diapers—back when 'playing games' meant Monopoly in your living room.

I send Rebecca a string of texts that have enough misspellings for her to assume I'm drunk, or I've been kidnapped by someone who failed English.

She writes back a series of sad-faced emojis, followed by the red angry ones and then the one for poop. I am assuming that means she thinks Finn is full of shit, which I wholeheartedly agree with.

'Sorry he's a jerk. Just eat and get the hell out of there. I'm home and right around the corner. Stop by after if you want to vent more.'

I thank her but I probably won't do that. I just want to get home, but now I remember that Ron is there. What a mess of a night. Mondays do suck.

Maybe I should just go home and have sex with Ron. He's available, willing, familiar. Yes, he's a jerk too, but he doesn't have any brainwashed slave girls, and he doesn't wash and save paper plates.

I don't know if Finn does that, but doesn't it seem like he would?

I blow my nose and the lady who was sleeping on the toilet comes out and gives me a sad smile. "Are you okay, honey?"

Even though Finn isn't my ideal guy, I don't want him to be accused of abusing a blind date in a five-star French restaurant, and this lady may decide he's done something terrible. I assure her that I'm fine, and she's so nice that I now feel bad for wondering if she fell in the toilet.

I dry my eyes and repair my makeup. I wasn't full-out bawling, so it's not a complete train wreck. I toss the paper towel in the trash, grab my purse and calmly walk back to the table.

I can see already that Finn is no longer sitting there. I'm sure he used my absence as an opportunity to use the men's room, and who wants to be gawked at after your visibly crying date left you sitting alone?

I approach the table and see a wonderful delight — our food is here and it smells amazing! I know it would be rude to dig in before Finn, so I sit down and…wait, what's this?

There is a folded piece of paper on my chair. This can't be the check — or is the bill so high in this place that they put it in a more discreet place?

My eyes bulge, and my hand shakes with rage as I read the following:

Claire,

Sorry, but this isn't going to work.

FU

OMG!! Not only has he left me here to eat *alone*, but this expensive restaurant was *his* idea, and I *strongly* doubt he paid the bill before he ditched me.

And FU? Seriously, was that necessary? What the hell did I do to him? What an asshole.

I look up to catch the waiter's attention and I can see Finn in his car, fixing his hair in the mirror. I really want to run out there and jump on the car and cut off the convertible top with my butter knife — wait, I ordered steak. Even better!

The waiter breaks into my demented plotting with an offer to bring the check. He doesn't even ask any questions. I guess if he's been in the waiter business for a while, he's seen it all. He's probably hoping I have enough money to pay the bill.

I rummage through my purse for a pen and paper to jot down this asshole's license plate number when I see him pull out of the parking lot, but I miss it. Shit, now I'll have to get Audra involved, although it serves her right. How could she be this clueless when it comes to judging character?

I continue to watch, just to see which way he turns, not that it will help me. I'm not much of a detective. Oh, he pulled into the gas station and convenience store across the street.

How convenient.

I toss the waiter my credit card and tell him I will be right back, instructing him to leave the food.

Just as I get my car door opened, Rebecca calls. I pick it up and blab a blue streak, giving her the basic rundown of the story in under ten seconds.

"Whoa, slow down. So he ditched you at the restaurant and he's at the gas station? Are you talking about the Wawa across the street? I just got here, too. I needed to pick up a—"

"Perfect. Keep an eye out for a jackass with beautiful eyes and a car to match."

As I gun the gas out of the parking lot, I think about how I'd like to make both his car and his eyes less pretty—where are these aggressive thoughts coming from?

Obviously I am not going to cause him bodily harm, but I am going to confront him. This is unacceptable. However, I *am* eating that dinner. Rebecca doesn't know it yet, but she's having Finn the fucker's lobster.

I pull into the Wawa lot and park on the side, right next to Finn. I guess he needed to pick up some dinner since he didn't get to eat and it's not 'free meal Thursday.' I'm surprised he didn't hit the DQ for the hotdogs. If he does, I hope he gets an extra explosive bout of diarrhea.

He's not in his car, so I lean up against the side of the building and shimmy to the entrance. Rebecca is standing in front of the building. I'm glad to see she's wearing decent clothes. She often comes to stores like this in pajama pants, and I really don't want to eat alone.

She stops me and says, "He's inside. What are doing? You look like someone who can't ice skate holding on to the wall. You realize the flatter body doesn't make you invisible, right?"

"Oh shut up, this isn't funny. Are you sure it's him?" I attempt to wipe the brick wall residue off the back of my clothes, and hope that no one spit on it, or left their chewed gum as a souvenir.

She says, "Yes, the pretty boy got out of the pretty car. It is a shame he's such a jerk — he's cute. So he left a note? Give it to me, but before — "

"Wait, listen." I point to the store and draw Rebecca's attention to the music playing on the outdoor speakers designed to entertain the gas pumpers.

"Oh, come on. Stop it. You hate country music. And I was just going to say you better not do anything stupid like — "

"What? Carve my name? Bash the headlights with a bat? Slash all four tires? Or any of the other lovely ideas Miss Underwood suggests in her hit song?"

"The gleam in your eye is scaring me. And this guy didn't cheat. You barely know him. So what if he — "

I hand her the note, she takes the two second pause necessary to read it and says, "Oh, hell yeah, he's goin' down."

"I knew the FU would make you see it my way."

Before we get a chance to plot what we are going to do to Finn's pretty car, which isn't even his, I see him approach the counter to pay for his merchandise. Shit, it's too late.

I take a deep breath and say, "There he is. I'm just going to go in and have a chat with him. If he apologizes, I promise I won't do a thing. If not, then...I'm not sure yet. I think Finn's fate is in his own hands. You stay here. I don't want him to see you."

"Why not?"

"I may need you."

Hopefully I won't need her to bail me out of jail because seeing that smug dick chatting up the clerk makes me furious all over again. If that young girl knew what he did she would smack his head on the counter (there's that pesky violence again). I bet she's seen her share of trouble in here, especially late at night. These convenience store chicks are tough.

But since I am not anywhere near as tough, I am just going to talk really loudly.

"Hey, Finn. What's up? Did you come over here to pick me up a little treat? Maybe a bouquet of these pretty flowers? Oh, cigarettes. How nice. You smoke in addition to being a royal jackass. FU, too!"

I hold my note up triumphantly and then realize that no one in the store has any idea what I'm talking about, and I sound like a whack-job.

He nervously grabs his discount brand cigarettes from...Sharla...and says, "Claire, really? We're in public. I left the note to *avoid* a scene. And you really didn't understand the note, but since you've chosen to freak out and humiliate both of us, I am not going to explain any further."

Sharla rolls her eyes, and we move over so she can take her next customer. She says, "Hey, don't go too far, I wanna hear how this drama turns out. It's been a boring day and I so enjoy a lover's quarrel."

"We are not lovers!"

We yell this almost in perfect unison.

I fold my arms and continue to spew my anger. "How could you leave me there to pay that bill alone? That's a sick thing to do."

"Well, you didn't want to eat at Dairy Queen—"

"You were *serious* about that?"

Sharla chimes in with, "Wow, that's low. You don't take a fine woman like this to Dairy Queen. What are you, in sixth grade?" She shakes her head and wrinkles her face in disgust.

He ignores Sharla and says to me, "There is nothing wrong with DQ. Obviously you're a snob with your fancy job. *'I was on a conference call.'* Really? I'm not impressed. I thought when I saw your car that we were of the same mind. I was even planning on buying *two hotdogs* so we would each get an extra one. But no, you had to ruin it."

Sharla laughs and elbows the guy paying for his beer. "Ooh, big spender. I'm getting excited just thinking about all those hotdogs. Johnny, can you take me to DQ after my shift ends?" She bats her eyes and Finn's face turns even redder.

He lowers his voice and says, "I could see you had a snobby attitude about the hotdogs so I suggested the most expensive place. I figured if the date went well I would pay and expense it—pretend I took the Jaguar guy out. And if you blew it, then you could pick up the whole tab. I will not be used for a meal, Claire."

I ball my fists and scream, "What are you talking about? I was always going to pay for myself. You are the cheapest, rudest, most delusional—"

Sharla cheers me on, and says, "There you go, baby girl—give it to him good. I've got a bat behind the counter if you need it."

Johnny grabs her hand and she laughs. "I'm not going to do it—it's just funny because that car bashing song by that skinny, little bitch was just on. I love that song!"

Johnny and Finn both roll their eyes as if to agree that all women love that song, and we're a bunch of man haters, and isn't life so hard for them.

Assholes.

"Look, Claire. We are not compatible, and I am sick of getting stuck spending money to find a woman. You can't have children and I'm sorry you can't, but—"

"You said you'd do *anything* if you were me?"

"Yes, *you* should. I am getting someone pregnant the old-fashioned way."

Sharla shakes her finger and Johnny laughs as she says, "Hmm…no sir, I don't think there's much chance of that with your attitude. You know they have battery operated boyfriends that replace dicks like you—"

Johnny stops her as an elderly lady comes to the counter. It's nice to see he has manners. If Johnny stopped wearing the hat that says, 'who farted?' he might be cute. Definitely a better catch than this…GRRR…

I am speechless at this point and my food is getting cold across the street. I see Rebecca's face pressed in the window. "Fine, I give up. You're a terrible person. Goodbye."

"Hey, I have to go to the men's room. Sharla, Johnny…please make sure she doesn't leave until after I do. That car out there is not mine, and I don't want the Carrie Underwood wannabe getting any ideas. It's for her own good."

Sharla smiles and tells him not to worry, and he skulks off.

Then she whispers to me, "I really have that bat if you want it. You do whatever you want and I'll tell him I saw you get in your car and drive away. What a jackass."

Rebecca runs back into the store and grabs my hand.

"What are you doing in here? You need to leave. Obviously you made your point, and there's no reason to stick around."

"Relax. I am not going to do anything too crazy, but he needs to be taught a lesson. Don't you think, Sharla?"

Rebecca looks at the clerk as if she's wondering how she's already gotten involved on a first name basis.

My new ally Sharla says, "Miss Claire, I think your pretty friend here with the big boobies needs to stay inside and distract our man long enough for you to leave him the appropriate message."

She winks, and Rebecca sighs and says, "Incredible…okay, fine. But you better not do anything to get yourself in trouble. He's not worth it."

I thank my new and old friends, and rush out to the side of the building. Luckily, Finn was so worried about his precious borrowed ride that he parked it as close to the back of the building as possible, which backs up to the woods. There is no one around at all, and all the other customers are getting gas out front.

I bend down and peer under the car, beneath the back bumper. The color is so pretty — I think I may try to find a similar one for the kitchen. Why not keep Ron around for more painting? It's not like I'm finding any other men to help me out, and he *wants* to do it. And I'm compensating him.

I discreetly pull my keys out of my purse and drop them, and bend over to pick them up.

Before I stand up I quickly carve a little something for Finn to remember me by — *way* under the bumper.

Realistically, no one will ever see it, and I know that. It's a pathetic attempt at vandalism, but it makes me feel better. He's just lucky he didn't abandon and insult a tougher woman. Rebecca likes to pretend to be all calm and in control, but Sharla isn't the only one who'd be looking for her Louisville Slugger if this happened to her.

I stand up, but then decide to crouch back down again to quickly take a picture with my phone. No one will believe I did this unless I have proof, and the girls deserve to see it.

I jump in my car and drive over to the farthest gas pump. I might as well fill up while I'm here. I have another credit card, and with all the driving I do with my long commute I always need gas.

Finn exits the store, walks all around his car and peers inside. He hesitates for a moment, probably trying to decide if the lack of visual damage is enough to ensure his safety, or if I had time to plant a bomb I just happen to carry in my purse for blind dates that go wrong.

I replace my gas cap as Rebecca appears beside me.

"What did you do?" She's looking partly accusatory

and partly excited. I'm guessing her few moments with Finn didn't help to improve her opinion of him.

"Did you talk to him?"

"Yes, he stared at my chest the whole time, and Sharla screamed at him that women have eyes." She bursts into a fit of giggles. "That guy is going to need a new convenience store. That was quite a show in there." She stops laughing when I don't join her. "I'm sorry. Seriously, what did you do?"

I show her the picture on my phone. Carved in very sloppy 'keymanship' it says what simply sums up our meeting.

FU.

She smiles and rolls her eyes. "You know he'll never see that, but I get that it made you feel better. You know what's even funnier, though? He introduced himself to me when I told him I couldn't help but see that beautiful car outside that matches his eyes."

"You're good." I smile at my loyal friend and add, "Why is introducing himself funny?"

"He said the crazy lady yelling at him about the stupid man-hating Carrie Underwood song was out of her mind, but it's only because she didn't understand his message. Guess what his name is?"

I am losing my patience. "I know his name. It's Finn!"

"Yes, it's Finn. Finn...*Underwood*."

FU.

CHAPTER EIGHTEEN

Claire

I'm so grateful that Rebecca chipped in for that outrageously expensive, but delicious dinner. It ended up costing me a little less than a mortgage payment, and that reminds me of how that expense will be going up soon, putting fancy meals and other luxuries even further out of my reach.

And I am clearly not going to be seeing any more money from Bella Donna Press any time soon, and finding a man to ease my burdens is also proving to be a fruitless effort. Yes, I think tonight would be a good time to approach Ron about selling the house and splitting the profits.

On second thought, I am in a weakened state after my spectacularly disastrous date, and I know Ron is just going to say that he could move back in, and that would solve all of my problems. In his mind that solution works, but it's not what I want, and I need to be at full mental capacity to counter his arguments.

My defenses may be low, but if I just review some of the jerky things he's done in the past, I can stay strong enough to get him out of the house tonight without incident. I have plenty of unsavory memories to choose from, but going down that road is depressing. Hopefully he'll be gone, and I can just cuddle up with little Dixie for a positive end to this shitty day.

My eyelids feel heavy as I get off at my exit. This drive is also getting old. I'm tired of living on this side of town, with work and everything else so far away. I could hang out on my side of the river more often, but it just never seems to work out that way. My area is oversaturated with families, older people, fanatical churches and all-you-can-eat buffets.

I could have done without meeting Mr. FU, however, on any side of town. I probably would be treated much better by one of the truckers who hang out at the rest stop at my exit off 95. I'm not finding that the men with the good jobs and better clothes have any more substance, but Finn was truly one of a kind. I can't believe I never asked his name.

However, if I had I don't know that I would have even put two and two together. 'FU' was a clear summary of his actions, so it was the appropriate message to convey how he felt about me and our meeting. He thinks his name somehow explains his note, as if it's fine to ditch a woman during dinner on a date, as long as you leave an honest note while she's in the bathroom.

I pull into the driveway and glance at my phone out of habit. Audra has already sent a text asking how it went. I'm going to wait to respond. Or just never talk to her again.

I sigh and plop my phone in my purse. I am dying to know what Finn had to say for himself. I wonder if he received the same text from Audra, but I bet he's been busy shoving cheap hotdogs in his jerky face, and smoking his nasty cigarettes.

Ron's truck is still here, and no matter how long I sit in my driveway, it isn't going to magically disappear.

On the bright side, he probably finished the trim and Dixie isn't alone, so it's unlikely I have any doggy gifts to clean up.

I open the front door and it's eerily quiet. The lights are on in the dining room, but nowhere else. I instinctively tiptoe, as if we were still married and Ron was upstairs asleep.

He better not be upstairs asleep! Or awake.

I put my purse down in the kitchen, and Dixie's little head pops up on the family room couch. The rooms are open to each other, so I can immediately see that Ron is sleeping with Dixie on top of him. For some reason, that makes my chest tighten and a lump in my throat form.

I stifle the tears that threaten to spill out of my exhausted eyes and greet the little nut, who has come running to me. I whisper to her quietly, but I don't know why. Ron needs to wake up and go home now.

He stirs on the couch, which is much too small for his body, and sits up, rubbing his face. "What time is it?"

"A little after eleven. The dining room looks good." I didn't actually see it but I can't think of anything else to say. I fill Dixie's water bowl and give her a treat to settle her down.

Ron stretches his big arms and widens his eyes. "I guess you had a good time." He nods his head in the direction of the front door. "So is he outside waiting for me to leave? Or parked around the corner to be sneakier about it?"

Dixie picks this moment to run back to Ron, jump on his lap and lick his face. She's really not helping.

They both stare at me and I could either laugh or cry from the absurdity of his question. Unfortunately, when I'm tired things don't seem as funny, so I opt for letting the floodgates open.

Ron picks Dixie up and places her on the seat next to him, and then stands up and walks across the room to take me in his arms.

And I let him.

I shouldn't. I've had a bad day. Night. Week. Month. But I'm sad and lonely and Dixie just isn't able to offer the comfort level of a human. This feels very familiar, despite all of the very good reasons it's a bad idea.

But it's just a hug.

Ron wordlessly leads me to the couch, which quickens my heartbeat, but also sends off more warning bells in my head.

But instead of trying to kiss me or make any move to take advantage of this situation, he gently guides me onto the couch, fluffs the pillows behind my head, places Dixie on my lap and takes off my shoes.

I stretch my toes and he sits next to me with my legs in his lap. He begins slow circles and kneading motions on my weary feet. It feels like heaven. Ron has very large, strong hands.

I mumble, "I don't know if this is a good idea", but it comes out as more of a moan, which only makes it worse.

"Shh, it's fine. Feet are very non-sexual, unless you're one of those weirdos who steals women's shoes and licks them."

I laugh, even though he may have made that up. I've never heard of such a thing. I was only joking about the shoe fetish thing. I lean back and give in to his expert touch.

"There you go—just imagine I'm one of those dudes at the nail salon giving you a pre-pedicure foot massage.

Do you want me to talk to Dixie about you in a foreign language to make it a more authentic experience?"

He proceeds to bark and Dixie looks up and tilts her head. I laugh again and close my eyes. I guess he listens to me more than I thought because I know he's never been in a nail salon, but he's nailed the description of the experience.

As he rubs away my tension, I am falling asleep but also feeling aroused. Maybe I'll just have some nice dreams for once.

That's if I can get him to leave.

Hmm, I wonder if Ron *has* been in the nail salon. I remind myself that I don't know what Ron has been up to this past year, and I can't assume I know him anymore.

"So, what happened tonight, Claire? You can tell me."

Ron

I want to kill this fucking guy. I mean, he *is* making this intimate moment with my wife possible, but he still deserves punishment for what he did.

But what Claire did is hilarious! I had no idea she had it in her. Not that she actually *did* anything — the guy is never going to look under his car before he gives it back. I'm just proud of her for standing up for herself.

I know — I could set up the FU guy with Stacy. That would be a match made in heaven. She would flip him over her shoulder and step on his head if…

Yeah, Stacy is a little nuts and unfortunately she's been calling me all night. I'm still avoiding her, and the larger problem of ending things with her. That's why these casual things don't work out. Someone always wants more and there's no good way to get out of it. I could just be very direct with her, but I know she will be super pissed off and tell Claire.

It's not like I'm doing anything wrong. Claire was the one who wanted a divorce, and she can't expect that I've joined a monastery. But I know Claire, and she hasn't been sleeping around so it's just another way that I'm the bad guy when we get back together. It's something else she could hold over my head.

The dog loves me, but I don't know if that's enough to make up for her womanly jealousy. And then I have to be careful with the dog because if I act like the dog is a baby replacement, she'll eventually lash out over that, too.

I know it seems like I can't win, but I plan to be victorious in a short while. I just need to figure out how to get Stacy off my back without getting *on* my back. She likes to be on...never mind, I'm listening to Claire's story. She's wrapping it up, and I can see that telling me has made her feel better.

"I'm sorry to lay all of that on you. It's not right for you to have to listen to my troubles. So how was Dixie tonight? I don't see any paint paw prints anywhere."

"She's been good, but she needs a lot of attention. And you're out a lot."

She's looking annoyed and I backtrack. "I mean; you're just having fun. Well, not fun exactly, but maybe this single girl lifestyle isn't making the puppy training easy."

Now she's stiffening and moving away from me on the couch as I dig a deeper hole. But seriously, I can't just blindly go along with everything she does just because I want her back. The dog does need more supervision and she...

"You're right." She looks me in the eye and continues, "I have been distracted and I know just what I need to do."

She pats my hand now, but I resist the urge to pull her to me. I must move very slowly because she's very vulnerable right now, and I could fuck up all of my progress if I'm not patient.

I'm waiting for her to say that she wants me to come over more often to help her with Dixie, because her puppy likes me so much. Or something even more...forward moving.

But instead she jumps up and blurts out, "Jane gave me the number of her pet sitter. Now where did I put that? I'm going to call her first thing tomorrow and get her over here for a consultation."

She roots around in her purse for the scrap of paper she undoubtedly scribbled on. Claire is not very organized. Another thing that drives me crazy about her.

A pet sitter? So much for being her knight in shining armor.

She pulls out what looks like a receipt and says, "Here it is. Melody. She sounds very sweet. Jane's been using her for years and you know they have a whole zoo."

She looks at the time on the microwave clock and says, "It's getting really late. I should go to bed."

"You sure you don't want a little more foot rubbing? It was definitely relaxing you." I move my hands in the kneading motion and she comes back to the couch.

"Okay, maybe just a little more. But hands don't go above the ankle." She wags her finger at me and smiles.

"Jeez, even the pedicure guy gets to rub above the

ankle."

We're back to joking and Dixie is back to laying down on her mommy. Claire is getting sleepy, and I probably should encourage her to go up to her bed, but I don't want to break the closeness.

When I hear her breathing change to the slow, steady rhythm of slumber I've listened to since I was a teenager, I cover her with one of the many blankets in the room. Dixie stays burrowed underneath, and I plant a feather light kiss on Claire's forehead.

Just when I move to pull away she reaches up and touches my face. With her eyes closed she runs her fingers along my chin, and I take this as a sign to lower my head and kiss her lips.

It's a fleeting moment, and I'm not sure if she was already dreaming of someone else, but I'll take it.

I whisper into her ear, "I don't suppose you want help getting into your pajamas?"

She rolls over and says, "Shh, you're very bad. Very sleepy now." I take that as my cue to leave and slowly back away when she stirs again.

In a low, slurry voice she says, "Hey, I'm sorry, I shouldn't have done that. It was a bad day…but thanks."

Her eyes are still closed and I'm glad she can't see the disappointment on my face.

When Claire is very tired she can act like she's drugged. That's why I have always dissuaded her from using sleeping pills or drinking too much. I've always been able to relax her, except of course near the end of our marriage, when all we did was fight.

At least I made her feel comfortable enough to kiss me, even if she regrets it, or thinks she should. At least I think she kissed me, and I hope I didn't misread the signals.

But knowing my sentimental wife, she'll remember that it felt good.

I make it to the front door and she mumbles a little louder. "Hey, I have an idea for a color for the kitchen."

I laugh to myself and call out, "Okay, tell me tomorrow. Good night!"

I close the door before I am tempted to go back in and continue where we left off. That was enough progress for one night, and I don't want to risk back sliding.

I have to get up for work in about six hours and I don't know how I'm going to wind down enough to sleep. This is another one of those times when I would have stopped by to see Stacy. Even though I've ignored all of her calls tonight, she'd let me in without any hesitation. I'd get a little beat up for going missing, but she'd just wrap her legs around me and…

Nope, I can't do that so I should stop thinking about it.

I get in my truck and delete all of Stacy's messages without listening to them. I glance at the texts, which are colorful to say the least.

I also have a bunch of new e-mails. I open up my account and see that my newfound popularity is coming from the Russian dating site. I must have twenty-five new messages from women who think I am 'strong American man.'

Hmm…I do have one from Natasha. The first line is— 'you are so much kinder than other men on computer.'

I bet I am. I don't care what Jeff says, this sort of thing is a magnet for degenerates and weirdos. On both ends. But I like Natasha.

I feel bad communicating with her because nothing will ever come of it, but I remind myself that she could easily be an old lady with a mustache and support hose playing on the stupidity of lonely men. But I'm not sending any money, so why would she bother being deceptive?

I'll read the rest of her e-mail when I get back to my apartment. I don't feel like I'm leading her on. It's like having a pen pal in school. We did that when I was in third grade. My teacher matched us up with kids at a school in Canada somewhere. My friend was Jacques. It wasn't much fun writing to a little French dude, and our friendship fizzled pretty quickly. He didn't know anything about baseball, and I was discouraged that his English writing skills were better than mine.

No, I haven't said a word to Natasha to make her think I am serious about anything. I told her I am just interested in making new friends and I'm not over my divorce. Women like that sensitive crap, but it also puts up a barrier.

As Claire would say, I'm going to hell, but we made progress tonight. I am not going to fuck that up for anyone, especially not a woman on the other side of the world. Or the one in the apartment above me.

Luckily, Claire has a lot of white walls for me to paint, and if I play my cards right I'll be back home in no time. She'll give up on these pathetic dates, and I'll be rubbing her feet and tucking her in for good.

And repainting all of the damn walls so I don't get a headache from the rainbow, and *then* someone will buy the fucking house.

But first thing first. I can't wait to hear what color

she wants to paint the kitchen.

Claire

I could use a vacation. It's another beautiful morning and I am stuck in the horrendous 95 traffic on the way to my boring, dead end job. I really do need to put some effort into something other than finding a man, but the thought of updating my resume is almost as bad as going on another blind date.

Okay, not quite *that* bad.

Ron was so sweet last night, and for a second I almost considered giving up on dating and giving him another chance. But then I came to my senses. The only reason he's being so nice is because we're not together. If we reconcile, then all of the problems that drove us apart will just bubble right back to the forefront. Nothing is solved — we are just dancing around each other in the 'friend' space.

Yep, the marital discord is hiding under the surface, like Finn's initials under the Jaguar bumper.

I laugh to myself as I take a moment to call Melody while sitting in the pile up at my exit. She answers on the first ring and I tell her that Jane referred me and I'd like her to come over as soon as she can to meet me and Dixie.

By the time she's done gushing about Jane's animals, I am off my exit and pulling into my parking lot. We agree to meet tonight after work. She has some forms for me to fill out, and I need to give her a key to my house.

This will be so much better than dealing with Ron. For a small fee I can come home to a dog who has been taken out, played with and watered. There won't be anyone there to rub my feet when I get back, but there also won't be any chance of sleeping with Melody after a disappointing date. So clearly the better choice.

Except...I don't know...it felt so good being with Ron last night, and he's so good with Dixie. Yes, he's shown a *little* of his controlling side, but all men are a little bit like that. After all, he is entitled to opinions. I'm sure we're not the first couple to argue about paint colors.

But of course I'm forgetting the larger issue, sweeping it under the rug and focusing on our more mundane conflicts. When I lost my fertility he just wasn't there for me. Sure, he made meals and brought me to doctor's appointments. But he wasn't upset about it. Not really. Not like I was.

I felt like he was relieved in a way. Like he thought sex would now just be about...well, sex, and not about getting pregnant. I was crying every day and he was showing me websites of vacation destinations. He said he was trying to cheer me up, but what he didn't understand is—I wasn't ready to cheer up.

My phone rings and I assume it's Melody again. She must have forgotten to tell me something. She did seem a little scattered.

I get out of the car and start walking to the building because it's getting very hot without the air conditioning on.

"Hello."

I don't hear anyone right away and then a low volume voice says, "Is Ron there?"

I frown at the phone and reply, "Ron? No, this is Claire. His wi...ex-wife. You're calling my cell phone. Who is this?"

My first thought is there's a family emergency and someone still has my number? But Ron doesn't have a sister and this is definitely not his mother.

The caller laughs and says, "Oh, I'm sorry. This is Stacy."

Who the hell is Stacy? She's acting like I should know, and I usually have a pretty good memory.

"I'm sorry, Stacy. I'm drawing a blank. How do you know Ron?"

"Wow, he's never even *mentioned* me. Men, I tell ya, right? I thought you might know where he was since he wasn't answering his cell last night. Sorry to bother you."

I still don't know who Stacy is, other than that she's miffed at Ron for not...duh Claire, obviously it's a new girlfriend. Well, that puts everything in a different context. I guess he's keeping all of his options open.

"It's no bother. If I see him, I'll tell him you called."

"Thanks, but I'll see him at home later. Oh, and Claire?"

"Yes?"

"He *will* be signing those divorce papers very soon so don't worry your blond head about it."

And the line goes dead.

I fling my phone into my purse, almost missing and smashing it on the pavement. I would actually love to smash something, but Ron's head isn't available (I may need anger management soon).

I pull open the heavy doors to Bella Donna's lobby and try to smile at Amanda, the perky and sweet receptionist who has not yet ruined her life.

I could call Ron and confront him, but what would I say? I'd just look stupid. I kissed *him* after coming home from a *date* (well, sort of) — so how can I complain that he seems to have a woman in his life? And who knows if there's anything really going on. She could be someone who just has a crush on him, or maybe he has his own blind dates gone bad.

Maybe we could set her up with Finn.

One thing is for sure—I know very little about what's been going on in Ron's life in the past year, and *I* share *way* too much with him.

I make it to my office, and see that Rebecca sent me an e-mail asking if I'm okay. I tell her I'm fine and don't mention Stacy. Or Ron. Or kissing. Or any other dumb shit going on in my life. If I tell her anything, she'll be here in a heartbeat and I don't feel like reliving it all over again.

I scroll through a few actual business e-mails and then I see one from another person I don't need to deal with today. Justin.

He wants to know how my date went.

Can't everyone mind their own business? I know Rebecca means well, but Justin is just bored. It's not my fault he's some kind of child prodigy genius. He should be working at NASA or in some lab where they turn sheep into fruit.

I know I should exercise more self-control, but Ron, Stacy and let's not forget FU, are all competing for space in my angry brain, so I quickly type and send:

'It was just fucking great!'

Hopefully I don't get fired for using profanity in a company e-mail, but I don't think Justin will rat me out.

I expect an immediate response—something obnoxious and snarky and highly inappropriate. But instead he picks today to be serious.

'Sorry to hear that. Really, I am. Lunch on the patio at noon? I'll bring the food and we can plot the poor guy's

doom?'

I'm well beyond plotting Finn's doom, but the e-mail makes me smile. And I don't have to give him any details. Right?

I agree to meet Justin and that was the biggest mistake of…okay, only of the *day*. So far. I make so many lately that they are piling up on top of each other, like dirty laundry in a whorehouse.

It's a few minutes into lunch and already Justin is wide-eyed and in hysterics over my story. It *is* funny and I can't blame him for laughing. If it happened to someone else I would fall off my chair.

But I am tired and edgy and I have this thing with Justin where I always feel like he's mocking me and…

"So why did he ditch you? Wait, you were wearing your work clothes? I've told you how you need to spice it up a little on dates. Come to think of it even for the office. I think Gladys in payroll is wearing that same skirt today."

Normally that would be a silly, harmless comment but two things are happening in my brain.

Thing 1 – I feel old and unwanted and unattractive…you get the picture.

Thing 2 – I didn't tell Justin about my infertility because it's none of his business.

This combination is not good for my mental health, and now I see that there's mayonnaise on my fucking sandwich!

I jump up and throw my nasty food onto the table, just missing Justin's tuna wrap, and scream. A wordless scream like a total whack-job. Justin stares at me because who wouldn't? I'm completely insane. And now a couple of smokers get scared and start choking on their cancer…ahhh…that just reminds me of that cheap asshole Finn…

I turn away from the table and run back into the building, screeching to a halt in the lobby, right before I get to the main reception area. There are people quietly sitting on the uncomfortable sectionals, and Amanda is pleasantly answering the phones.

Maybe that's because Stacy isn't calling *her*!!

Before I can catch my breath, Justin is right behind me.

"Claire, I'm assuming you didn't like your lunch, but it must be more than that. Are you really that upset about that guy? He's just one man. You have to keep tryi—"

"Shut up!"

Now I see a couple of heads craning to peer into the back hallway and I curse myself for choosing this spot to have my emotional collapse.

Justin grabs me by the shoulders—he's very brave, and says, "Claire, get a grip. Jesus. I know…punch me."

"I am not punching you. What good will that do?"

"It will get out your anger. I can take it for all the men—"

I wiggle free from his grasp and smash my pathetic, bony little fist into his abs.

"Ow, that hurt!"

Unfortunately, it was me who said that. His stomach is like a slab of cement. I thought Ron was in shape. Damn young people!

As I'm massaging my hand and checking for broken fingers, Amanda peeks her head around the corner.

"Um, hey Claire. Your one o'clock is here."

I sigh and look out into the lobby to catch the eye of

a very thin young girl with spiky black hair.

Cecilia. She looks interesting—maybe Justin will latch onto her and leave me alone.

"Okay, sorry Amanda. I'll be right there."

She darts away and doesn't even acknowledge Justin.

He frowns and says, "I told you my stomach could take it, but seriously are you okay? Hey, I just had a great idea. Why don't you come out on the boat with me and my friends this weekend? It is a young crowd but so what? You're trying too hard with all of these old guys. I know you're serious about your future, but is your biological clock ticking that loudly?"

Now the remaining blood drains from my face and my hands get clammy. After this interview, I am going home sick.

"I have to go. Thanks for..." I can't finish my thought because even though I think he meant well, I am not any more grateful for the past hour than I have been for the past twenty-four.

Something major has to change, but right now I need to talk this porcupine girl into working at this dynamic company. Hopefully she saw Justin before he wisely slithered away—we should put his picture on our recruitment brochures.

If we had any.

CHAPTER NINETEEN

Claire

"**O**h, I love all of Jane's little furry guys and gals. And the feathery and scaly ones, too!"

Melody gushes over my friend's menagerie while giving Dixie an all-over body massage. That's what I need—a massage. Maybe regular therapeutic touching might make me less inclined to let Ron…

Thank God no one can hear these twisted thoughts.

I finished my interviews at work for Tim's admin, and now I'm interviewing Melody to be Dixie's personal assistant. Melody is definitely getting the job, and I recommended that Tim hire Cecilia. She has good credentials, makes good eye contact and has a firm handshake. The rest she can be taught.

"Oh, I just love these little weenie doggies. And they live forever. I used to sit for a pair—Bert and Ernie—they both lived to be twenty-one. Isn't that amazing?"

As amazing as that is, I still don't like to think that Dixie is going to die before me. I mean I do hope I outlive her, but I feel like she's a ticking time bomb of impending grief. Dogs should live much longer.

I think I'm just being overly morose because I've not been sleeping well, or eating well, and…oh shit… the doorbell rings and I peek out the front window. Why is he here again?

As Melody continues to rattle on about the joys of

wiener dog longevity, Ron is standing on the porch. He did ring the bell, as opposed to using his key, but it does perturb me a bit that he's here unannounced. What if I had a man…never mind, he knows that's not happening.

"Oh my, who is that, Dixie?" Melody jumps as Dixie flies off her lap to the front door, sliding on the entryway wood floor and smacking into the powder room door.

I wince for her, but she shakes it off and hops all over Ron as soon as I open the door.

Melody says we're just about wrapped up since I have signed the paperwork and given her a key, so she'll be leaving.

She bends down to say goodbye to her new furry client. "Bye, bye sweet Dixie. I'll see you soon. Mommy probably has lots of dates."

She blushes when she realizes this man could be one of my dates. Melody has been married a long time, so juggling men isn't something she knows how to do.

Nor do I.

Melody smiles at Ron and I say, "I'm sorry, this is Melody—Jane's pet sitter. Remember I told you about her last night?"

Ron shakes her hand and says, "Yes, of course. Seems like the little one likes you. I'm Ron, Claire's husband."

Melody's eyes freeze and mine narrow.

"Oh, I'm sorry." She raises her hand to her mouth and says, "I must have misunderstood. I thought you were divorced, Claire. I guess I'm getting senile. Better go."

She smiles like I do if someone asks me if I like jazz, and runs down the porch steps.

I drag Ron all the way into the house and take a very

deep, loud and exaggerated breath before saying, "My *husband*? Really?"

His laughter only makes me madder, but then I soften. "You are such an asshole." Said with a smile I can't suppress; it doesn't have much of a serious effect.

"You have to admit that was funny. Her face when I said I was your husband—after she said Mommy has lots of dates."

I fold my arms and try again to scold him with my pursed lips and heavy sighs, but it's still not working. "You're impossible. That was mean, she's a nice lady. Now is there a reason for this visit?"

I'm really hoping he's not here to talk about last night.

He runs his fingers through his hair and says, "Yeah, I came to talk about last night."

Shit.

I back up into the kitchen, and he follows me, smiling just enough to make me sweat a little. He's going to force me to talk and it's my own fault, so I decide to start.

I mean I back against the counter with Ron just inches away from my personal space bubble and say, "I'm sorry about what happened. It was wrong of me to let you kiss me, or even to let you rub my feet. We need to keep our distance if we're going to be friends, and I didn't mean to lead you on. I was just tired and I had such a bad night…are you going to say anything?"

He crosses his arms across his big chest and leans back against the counter opposite me. "Thanks for all of that information, but I really just came to say I can paint the kitchen if you tell me what color to get. You said you had an idea last night before you drifted off into la-la land."

He's smiling and I know he's playing with me again. I am so sick of being teased by stupid men. My father used to do it. My uncles. I am an intelligent woman and I don't like being treated like a little...

"Claire, are you mad? Your face is getting red."

"Stop smirking at me like a big, dumb jerky fucker!"

This only makes him laugh more. I walk over to the kitchen table and sit down, burying my face in my hands.

He follows me, keeping a safe distance on the other side of the table, and says, "I really am sorry. Listen, I do want to paint the kitchen, so just let me know when you decide on a color."

I lift my head and say, "Frost blue."

We both start laughing again since I told him all about Finn's car.

"Hey, I've been thinking." This seems like as good of a time as any to pitch my idea. "Maybe we should sell the house and split the proceeds. It really is too much for either one of us alone, and this way we can both move on and get smaller places that suit us better."

He sits back and looks around the room, into the family room where we used to snuggle on the couch and watch TV. We're sitting at a table where we ate dinner together every night for years. I know he's thinking these things, too, but we have to be strong and fight the urge to go down memory lane.

"Yeah, okay. That makes sense. You were the one who was adamant about keeping the house and buying me out, so it's a good plan."

His smile has weakened and he stands up. "I better go. Let me know when you're ready for more home improvements."

I follow him to the door, with Dixie at our heels. He bends down to pet her belly before saying, "I'm sorry, too. About the kiss. I was wide awake and I knew you were in a vulnerable place. But it's okay. We're okay now, right?"

He opens up his arms for a hug, which seems platonic and harmless, and how do I snub a hug at this point?

As I let him embrace me and get lost in his huge upper body, I try to push thoughts of his bare chest out of my head. Thank God he hasn't been working on the deck or doing landscaping. If he takes his shirt off, I won't be able to control myself.

For some reason all this sexual thinking reminds me of the phone call I received this morning. I was going to let it go, and I should...what's he going to say? And what does it matter?

As I settle into the hug, I say into his chest, "So who's Stacy?"

Ron

On the drive back to my apartment, I assess my response to the inevitable question that was just dropped on me.

I weaseled my way out of it as best I could. I don't know what kind of a moron I am to think that I could keep Claire and Stacy apart forever, but I wasn't expecting Stacy to reach out to Claire directly.

What I really want to know is how she got Claire's cell phone number, but I suppose it's a no-brainer if you're a conniving bitch. All you do is wait until the guy you're banging has to take a leak, and then search through his phone for numbers of his exes. Easy enough.

I'm one of those people who doesn't have a passcode on my phone. I know I should, but I absolutely hate passwords. There are websites I don't use anymore because I refuse to make up another code with a capital letter, a number, a Chinese character and a picture of a farm animal.

So because of my resistance to secured technology, I had to quickly explain Stacy to Claire. Unfortunately, 'who's Stacy?' didn't give me much to go on. It would have been much easier if Claire had immediately told me the story of the phone call right after the dog lady left. I can't believe she didn't start yelling and poking me with her fingernail, and accusing me of being a sneaky, selfish bastard.

But no, she was sly about it, and since I *am* a sneaky, selfish bastard I told a 'sort of' truth. I started to say she lives in my building, which is true, and then Claire stared at me a good while until I said, "She's a friend who—"

I didn't have to finish the lie because Claire finally lost it and blurted out, "Well, your *friend* called me this morning and I didn't appreciate it."

I think Claire needs to go back to the doctor. I still say her hormones are all over the place. One day she's mad at me, the next day we're laughing together. Then she's kissing me, and then turns around and demands I sign the divorce papers. She's telling me about her dates and then she tells me everything is none of my business. She's seriously out of whack.

I thought the hug would settle her down after she got annoyed with me for teasing her, but it seemed to push her in the opposite direction. Or maybe she was just trying to keep from mentioning the Stacy incident and then she snapped.

Either way, I was able to convince her that Stacy is a bit of a loose cannon, and that I've helped her out with a few home repairs (I'm starting to look like a boy scout with all this helping out women I'm supposedly not sleeping with) and she must have gotten a hold of my phone.

Claire seemed to believe that Stacy is nuts and that she's a lonely chick looking for a man, and she has set her sights on me.

Before I left I said, "Let's just get this house sold so I can get out of that apartment. And you can be closer to the action. And the better dating opportunities."

My smile always leaves Claire charmed, and she shook her head at me as I waltzed down the driveway, waving behind me.

She's so confused by my mixed messages, but here's why I know Claire is not over me. If she was, it wouldn't be so easy to pacify her when she's mad. I also know that she wouldn't even *get* mad if she didn't care. Claire is an emotional girl, and when she has no emotion over something, she ignores it completely. Even when we were married she would not kiss me or laugh with me when she was really angry and hurt.

And she's doing those things now.

My first instinct when I left the house was to drive straight to Stacy's apartment and confront her, but that's exactly what she wants, and I am not playing into her shit. I am renting this apartment on a month-to-month basis, and I don't think I will be renewing any more than one more month.

I pull into my apartment complex parking lot, and get inside as quick as I can, locking the door and the deadbolt behind me. Stacy can throw her Amazon body against the door if she wants, but I am not dealing with her. If she makes enough of a scene, one of my neighbors will call the police.

I kick off my shoes and grab a cold bottle of water out of the fridge, thinking about calling Jeff to get myself invited on the boat this weekend. I would also like to tell him about my e-mails with Natasha. There isn't anyone I can talk to about this and I am starting to feel like a dick.

Of course Jeff is going to applaud my efforts with no concern for the feelings of any of the women involved. He's one of those guys who sees the Internet as an anonymous playground. I can't help but wonder if he's going down the slide or riding the teeter-totter himself, but I don't want to know. If they split up, then I'll have Roberta at my door, too.

I scroll through my messages again. Natasha is a nice woman. Or at least the 'character' of Natasha, if this is all a fantasy. She has now sent me a lot of pictures, though, so it seems real.

She said I am one of the few men she has met online who hasn't asked her for nude photos or cyber-sex. While that does sound fun, I can't go there. I feel like enough of a shit for lying to Claire about Stacy, and I don't want to add 'taking advantage of desperate foreign girls' to my resume.

Shit, I'm about one step away from being as bad as the FU guy.

The funny thing is that Natasha doesn't seem desperate. She seems normal. Accessible, even though she's far away. Simple, but not stupid.

I told Claire once the house thing is settled that I will

sign the papers. And I guess if we get that far and my plan to get her back still isn't working, I'll have to give up. And I will—I have *some* pride.

There is nothing wrong with having a back-up plan. Claire could be making a date with another guy right now.

She's not over me, but…I can tell she *wants* to be and I don't know if I can change that. So in the meantime, I am going to live my life. I'm really not such a bad guy.

'Dear Natasha, it's another beautiful day here in Virginia. I loved the pictures of you and your sister at the fair. We have one like that…'

Claire

I lay in bed tossing and turning. That damn Ron!

I know he wasn't telling me the whole truth about Stacy, but why should he? I *apologized* for kissing him—what's more of a rejection than that? He doesn't owe me any explanations. Although it would be nice if he asked his 'friend' to stop harassing me. Hopefully that was an isolated incident.

No, I have no claim on Ron and I don't want one. I just wish I could stop imagining his arms around me.

I decide to get up and get a glass of water when my heart almost stops. The old security alarm in the hallway starts beeping, and I mean 'wake the dead' beeping.

The shrill noise is hurting my ears and I need to make it stop. I run for the stepladder and climb it unsteadily, reaching for the…

Oww, I grabbed it and fell off the ladder. Luckily the hallway is carpeted but…oww…

The fucking thing is still beeping and now I remember that the battery needs to be removed. It's probably ancient. This happened once with the smoke detectors a long time ago, and Ron had to replace all of the batteries. I should have just gotten rid of this stupid thing—I don't pay for the service anymore, and its archaic technology. Just one of the many things I have ignored while licking my wounds and looking for a stupid man who can change batteries and deal with beepy things.

I can't get the batteries out and it won't stop screeching! I could smash it with a hammer, but I don't even know if I have one. I could put it in the trunk of my car or the mailbox. It would probably be loud enough to bother the neighbors but maybe not. It could be muffled enough so no one will notice and tomorrow I can borrow a hammer or...I don't know, I'm really tired. It's like three in the morning and can't...I wrap it up in a towel and put it by the front door while I search for shoes.

Oh my God, who is that out in front of the house? At first I think of Ron, but that's not his truck. It looks more like a van.

I could just go back to bed, but I have my beepy thing and I also can't rest if there's a rapist van in the cul-de-sac. But if I call the police what would I say? Anyone on the street could have a visitor. I'm just being paranoid because it's the middle of the night. I am a wimp and everything always seems scary at this time.

But you do hear stories about maniacs in vans who prey on unsuspecting women. Maybe whoever is out there tried to get in the house and the alarm went off. Maybe I didn't cancel the service. Or I did, but they never turned it off. Wait, they would call me if I still had the service.

I grab my phone and think of who to call. Ron. No. Bad idea. But he could talk me down. No, I need to leave him alone.

I press send on his number by accident. Goddammit! Why did I do that? I promptly hang up. I'm sure he has his ringer off anyway. He won't even see the call until morning, and I'll just say I dialed him by accident...or maybe he won't even ask.

The sound is still so loud, and I can't believe Dixie hasn't woken up. What the hell kind of guard dog is she? Once she gets in the crate for the night, it's like she's off duty and Mommy is on her own.

Not that a three-pound dog is any protection.

I can't think of any way to smash this thing and I don't want to make a big mess, so I creep out the front door with the intention of putting it in my mailbox. While I know that sounds preposterous, it's all I can think of. I could throw it into the woods behind my neighbor's house but my throwing arm isn't much better than Dixie's.

I realize that doing this slowly is a bad idea because now I am going to wake the entire neighborhood, so I sprint to the mailbox and slam the offending noise maker inside, which does the trick of muffling the sound. I stand for a moment and catch my breath, only to have it taken away almost immediately with, "Hello, Claire."

If my name was Clarice it would have sounded exactly like that horrible psycho in that movie Ron made me watch years ago. I had nightmares for months!

But now my nightmares are right in front of me and I'm all alone with Joe the creepy, drunk lovesick painter!

Fortunately, my lungs work better than my legs, which are frozen to the driveway. My screams draw Mike out of his house in a few seconds. He's got a baseball bat and Jane is right behind him.

Jeez, they react quickly.

"What the hell is going on out here? First there's an alarm and I see nothing out here—now screams! Claire, is that you? Who is that?"

Mike rushes over, bat drawn and Joe covers his head and falls over onto the lawn.

Jane crinkles her forehead and says, "Is he playing dead or did he pass out?"

"Joe, what are you doing here?" Mike bends over and yells at him while Jane says, "He's supposed to paint at our house in the morning."

"I'm just here early...so I don't forget..."

And he's out again.

Mike tosses his bat on my front lawn and says, "Okay, it looks like he was sleeping here so he'd be on time for his painting job. Makes perfect sense if you're a drunk. Janie, we need to find better help. Poor Claire almost crapped her pants and I'm out here wielding a weapon in my underwear."

Jane sighs and pulls her bathrobe closed, looking around to see if any other neighbors have bought tickets to this show. "I'm sorry, he paints a very straight line. Hey, isn't that Ron's truck?"

CHAPTER TWENTY

Claire

No amount of under eye concealer is going to help me today. I should have called in sick, but then Ron never would have left.

Yes, Ron, my knight in shining gym shorts, slept over.

On the couch!

But still. Every time we say goodbye and wrap up some dramatic exchange with what feels like closure, one of us (me) does something stupid to start it all up again.

Only this time, I didn't even make it twenty-four hours. The only positive outcome was that Ron had a hammer in his truck and let me beat the shit out of that fucking beepy thing! I would rather be robbed than have a thing in my house that makes that noise. I can't believe I was ever tricked into buying the stupid service in the first place, but when we moved in we were the only house on this street and the salesman spooked me.

As you can see, I spook easily.

Mike and Jane dealt with Joe, and I apologized to Ron for calling him. I was very surprised that he came over just from a few short rings with no message, but he said that when he tried to call back and I didn't answer, he got worried. I had left the phone in the house so that explains that.

I felt so guilty for bothering him at that hour so I invited him in—of course, what else would I do?

By this time Dixie was rattling her cage, so I let her out, took her out to pee, and we started her bedtime ritual all over again.

And even though the Joe thing ended up being ridiculous and no threat whatsoever, I was still a little distressed. I could see Ron was beat so I didn't want to make him drive home, and I did feel safer with him in the house.

He told me that he always keeps his phone on at night now, since he worries about me being alone and he knows I get nightmares.

This melted me and when he kissed me good night, I kissed him back—again. Like an idiot.

It was a sweet kiss, and while I was expecting him to try to take it further, he promptly laid on the couch and was out cold.

I am beginning to think he is doing this on purpose to toy with me. Why not try for more if he could get *that* far? But maybe he did the same thing I did the other night—a habitual kiss initiated while half asleep.

Needless to say I was up all night, until ten minutes before my alarm went off.

Ron was already downstairs ready to leave, but he said he would stay with me if I needed him. I assured him that I was fine and had lots of work to do.

Now I'm sitting in my office wondering if the cafeteria has any toothpicks to keep my eyes open, and if Justin would come by so I could have something to punch.

I may take up drinking. Joe may not have his shit together, but at least he's oblivious to all of it. When I left for work this morning, he was outside getting his ladders out of his van and whistling.

I don't feel like talking to Rebecca, even though she'd definitely listen. This level of stupid behavior is only for family.

No, I'm not going to call my mother—I'm just exhausted, not masochistic.

My sister answers on the first ring. "Cole & Barnaby Real Estate, Jackie McDonald speaking."

"What do single people do?"

"Excuse me? Who is this?"

Poor Jackie. I shouldn't mess with her in the office—she is super serious about selling real estate. She's quickly rising to be one of the top producers in the DC metro area. Since we live two hours apart, I don't see her that often and sometimes a girl needs her sister.

"It's your sister. I'm looking for your expert opinion."

I'm also ducking out of my office because I can hear voices that could be coming my way, and I don't want to be interrupted or overheard.

I head outside to the patio area with the smokers and Jackie says, "What are you talking about? We do whatever we want."

The smokers are eyeing me warily after the sandwich outburst earlier in the week, so I walk around the corner to the more private side of the building.

I was really hoping Jackie would give me some literal advice. She's four years younger than me, but she's single. *Happily*, single. She dates occasionally, but rarely talks about it, and when she does it's in a pleasant, conversational way. With me it's an angst ridden 'death of the soul' sort of theme.

"Claire, are you there?"

"Yes, I'm here. Sorry, I had to find a private spot. So obviously I know we can do whatever we want, but what if you don't *know* what that is? Exactly?"

"Are you okay? Mom said she hasn't seen you in weeks, and you still haven't brought Dixie over."

"I know she wants to meet her grand dog."

"It's not like that. I know it's hard for your mind to avoid that comparison, but it's a puppy. Some people just really like to see freaking puppies. Mom is bored and—"

"Okay, I'll bring her the damn puppy!"

Now I am lightly tapping my head against the brick building. I want to point out that it speaks volumes for my overall mental health that I am not actually banging it. If that starts up, I would hope one of my co-workers would stop puffing long enough to intervene.

Can you imagine if I went back to my desk with brick indentations on my forehead? Tim would refer me to one of those doctors who prescribe the protective head gear. On the bright side, I could join a woman's hockey league.

Jackie isn't letting me off the hook, and on some level I knew that calling her would result in an emotional vomit session. I tell her all about the Ron situation, and a little about the bad dates. They don't really matter so much, at least not the details. 'I am a douchebag magnet' sums it up for the purposes of this conversation.

Plus, Jackie would not approve of vandalizing private property or punching co-workers.

I also leave out the Stacy part. It's really not relevant to my problem. Whether or not Stacy is anyone in Ron's life almost doesn't matter. He clearly isn't with her, and doesn't want to be. If I wanted him back, whatever that is would stop. Wouldn't it?

Jackie takes it all in with very little interruption (she's so good at that—if someone were telling me all of this it would take an hour because of all my yelling and theatrics), and says, "What I don't understand is why you are so adamant about needing a man. I mean, we all need one for *some* things at times. And being in a good, healthy relationship is one of life's greatest blessings, but why chase it so hard? It hasn't even been a year since your split from Ron. Don't you want to focus on yourself? Develop your hobbies?"

Now I remember why asking single women for advice is fruitless. I love my little sister, but we have lived vastly different lives.

She knows I don't have any 'hobbies.' My main hobby since I was sixteen was being Ron's girlfriend, then wife. I know it's pathetic and I'm embarrassed to say it, but I never had a chance to grow up in that way. I grew up *with* someone else, and no one seems to get that it makes me different. It makes Ron different. It's something we share.

I do like mini-golf, but that's hardly a league sport. I can't really say shoes are a hobby, or eyeshadow. Even Dixie isn't a hobby. I guess if I did something dog-related with her that could be a hobby, but I don't know what that would be.

"I see what you're saying," I finally reply. "But you don't understand where I'm coming from. I am used to being in a relationship, continuously for many years. It's a normal state of being for me, and it's a normal instinct to seek to replace what I lost, or gave away. Pushed away. Whatever. Ron is the same way. He's doing it too, and it's like we're both starting to realize that it's not easy out there, and maybe all marriages have rough spots and you just—"

"Claire, stop. I do know all of that. And you're right, it's hard for me to relate. And you know I don't have anything against Ron, but don't you feel like you're beating a dead horse going back down the same path? There are so *many* paths, and you've barely tried any of them. You haven't even tried online dating."

"Yeah, I'm sure that will be the big solution." I lean against the building and shoot daggers at the nosy women from accounting staring at me. What, they can smoke but I can't talk on the phone?

I lower my voice and turn my head again, saying, "It's not just because I want a man, and he happens to be there. I think I still have feelings for him."

"Sorry, hold on. My boss is at the door."

I hear a muffled mutual exchange in the background and she returns. "I'm sorry, but we have a hot prospect in the lobby who wants to see one of the insanely expensive condos in the heart of Georgetown, and it's my listing. Cha-ching! So I have to run. But I'll leave you with this food for thought—if a gorgeous guy who loves wiener dogs, mini golf, *and* shoes moved in across the street, would you forget all about Ron?"

I can't help but laugh at that visual. "Ha, ha…too bad I can't place *that* order and get it filled. Although, I'm not sure that guy would be straight. But yes, I guess I would drop Ron like a hot potato. However, my neighbors are all boring married couples with little kids. No hot guys are moving to Locust Lane."

I need to let Jackie go, and I should get back to my desk, but what I really wanted to work up the nerve to ask her is what she thinks about sex with an ex. Just to clear the cobwebs in my head and other places!

But I already know what she'd say — get a vibrator. I am thinking that is the key to her uncomplicated life. Her boyfriend lives in a drawer and only comes alive when she flips a switch.

"I think you should do some things you enjoy and get out of the house. Take Dixie to a dog park. There's lots of men at those places, so I hear. I wouldn't be caught dead any place where random dogs could jump on me."

My sister has a childhood fear of dogs she hasn't gotten over. I swear, she even gets nervous if a Yorkie passes her on the street.

And she acts like *I'm* the nut for wanting a man.

We say our goodbyes with promises to get together soon, and I promise to call Mom so she stops bitching at Jackie over my absence.

I lean over the patio railing and close my eyes. The sun feels good.

I scan the deck for anyone who might grab me for a quick 'walk and talk,' and when I don't see anyone I march back to my office with a purposeful stride, like someone who has an important meeting to get to.

I used to be a human resources professional who liked humans. But lately I've been a little preoccupied and I have an important task to attend to this afternoon — researching dog parks.

Ron

Every day this week I have eaten my lunch in my truck, alone, talking to Natasha.

Well, obviously not actually *talking*. Just e-mailing on this 'highly addictive, not good for me at all' dating site.

Now things have escalated to her asking if I want to Skype. That feels way too personal...and real. And of course my asshole meter is about to blow — I keep telling myself I'm not leading her on, but I kind of am. And never mind that I'm doing this behind Claire's back.

However, Claire is openly dating *and* trying to divorce me, so I'm not doing anything wrong as far as she's concerned.

The rationalizing part of my stupid brain is working over time, but I do need to look at this logically. Does Natasha really expect that I'm going to come to Russia to see her? Or send her money to come here? Why would I do that, even if I had the money?

I mean, even a guy who is a complete troll can find a woman in this country if he has that kind of dough. I don't really get how this works, and I'm not clear on the audience for this site. I know it's not 'mid-thirties UPS drivers who are still in love with their exes, but have too much time on their hands and dickhead friends who lead them down the wrong paths.'

That would sound really bad in their advertising campaign.

To my credit, I've been ducking Stacy like she's a swarm of killer bees. I'm sure women would say that's also an asshole thing to do and I led her on, too.

What I want to know is — how in the fuck do you have anything to do with a woman without being accused of leading her on? Are we only supposed to talk to women we're sure we want to marry? And how do we decide that if we can't talk to them, get to know them, or God forbid *touch them*?

Being shackled to one woman since high school has

not done me any favors, and I don't know any single guys to talk to about this stuff. And if I did, they probably wouldn't be helpful.

I envy women. If Claire has a problem she can call her sister, her mom or any number of women friends and they come running to her side. Nobody really takes into account that I don't have that. When things went bad for us and she lost all those babies, no one was running to comfort me. I was expected to either *do* the comforting, or get the fuck out of the way to let the pity party through to the *real* victim. Even my own parents behaved this way!

Feeling sorry for myself isn't going to help, and I am rapidly painting myself into a corner, and the only way I see to go forward with what I really want is to spend more time with Claire. So I need to literally paint myself *out* of the corner by painting our house.

I can see Claire wants to be with me. If she didn't, she would go out when I'm there. I don't need her there to paint.

Last night, or should I say, early this morning, was bizarre to say the least, but I have to thank the drunk painter and the battery manufacturer for that one.

The fact that she called me in her time of need was *huge*. That's a big shift—earlier in our separation she would do *anything* to avoid asking for my help. She smashed her finger once trying to hang a picture, she hired an exterminator to spray for bugs when all she needed to do was get something at Home Depot. The back door was sticking and she could barely open or close it.

I know all of this stuff because I keep in touch with Mike, and he is almost as useless as Claire with home repairs. I think he enjoyed telling me how badly she was coping without me—kind of like some stupid male bonding thing. He meant well, but it frustrated me more, and I wasn't about to come to her rescue if she didn't want me around. I was angry then, but I've softened considerably.

I slept under the same roof as my wife last night for a total of three hours, and I want more of that.

Stacy is still a wildcard and a loose end. I can't believe she called Claire—what a bitch! Since I've been avoiding her, she went around me to try to fish me out of my hole. She's more like a tactical warfare expert than a research librarian. But I'm not that dumb, and she can't prove anything to Claire. I will come clean eventually, once Claire and I are back together and everything is great.

So why am I talking to Natasha? It's *easy* and she's the one bright spot in my day that is free of complication. Once I move back into my house, and I tell her I got back together with my ex, I'll just close my account. It will be the truth, and she will just move on to the next guy in her queue.

Who knows, maybe she's talking to a dozen guys like me, telling them all the same crap. Or she has a boyfriend or even a husband she hates, and she's doing this to get back at him.

And if she's looking for a free ticket to the US, she's got the wrong guy for multiple reasons.

Nope, I am going to keep painting myself out of the corner by coloring Claire's world. She thinks I'm not romantic, but see what I did there with that analogy? Or is that a metaphor? I don't know—it's something poetic. I'm not the English major.

I'm going to pick up some paint that matches a frost blue Jaguar. I looked it up online and I found a perfect match. I know exactly what Claire wants, and little by little she's going to get all of it.

Claire

"Okay, Dixie, let's meet some doggies!"

She's excited, but that's because she has no idea what's going on. She popped her little head up as soon as we arrived, and I think she's just thrilled to be out of the house. I raced home after work, changed and jumped back in the car to take my baby to the closest dog park, The Bark Yard.

Ron sent me a link to some paint swatches, and I'm shocked that he spent time trying to find a color that matches what I described. I would have expected him to go right home after work and take a nap after last night's debacle.

I'm trying this dog park thing because I need some fresh air and it's good for Dixie. I'm not discounting Jackie's wisdom — there are plenty of romantic comedy movies where couples meet over a love of dogs.

However, Jackie is not seeing how much Ron has changed. The old Ron would never have taken the time to do something just for me. He's normally very self-centered — and I don't even think he's played tennis lately.

I'm still not sure I believe him about this Stacy chick, but I've met my fair share of whack-jobs. What if the 'drunk skunk' or the 'unholy church speed dater' got a hold of Ron's number and fed *him* a bunch of crap about me? There are a lot of crazy, desperate people out there. And even if he did sleep with her, so what? We're not together and I can't expect faithfulness to a bond *I* severed. Right?

It makes perfect sense, but it still makes my stomach hurt. She's also probably not playing with a full deck if she's stalking him. I'm hoping she doesn't know where I live, but luckily I don't leave Dixie outside for any length of time. You never know when you're dealing with a potential bunny boiler, so it's best to stay clear of her.

I wrangle Dixie into her harness, which isn't easy as she jumps at the window, trying to get out into the world. Her little sniffer is going crazy. Even through the closed up car she can smell the fresh, new scents of the park.

I turn her around to see if the harness is on properly and she sneaks in a lick. Yuck! One thing I hate is dog kisses!

Speaking of kisses, I need to stop kissing Ron. And letting Ron kiss me. I'm blurring the lines and making it harder to be objective, but he *has* been there for me lately, and that feels good.

I have a loving family, and some loyal girlfriends, but it's not the same thing. They all have their own lives. That's what is so hard about being single—not having that *one person* who is always there for you. I know lots of long term singles would say you have to be that person for yourself, and that sounds good on paper, but it's not realistic. Sometimes you want big, strong arms around you and a…

I finally open the car door and place Dixie on the ground, and begin running to keep up with her tiny legs. She's kicking it to the dog park—I don't know how she knows that's where we're going. We could be going to the basketball court or for a walk on the trail, but she's leading me to her people. I wish I had that instinct.

There are only a few people on the little dog side, which is much smaller than the expansive fenced-in area for bigger dogs. The small dog area is also fenced, and it's big enough to provide ample running room for tiny dogs. Dixie *thinks* she's a marathon runner, but she's only a short-distance sprinter.

There's a young couple with a little, fluffy white dog, and an older lady sitting down with a shaking Yorkie in her arms. I can't imagine the dog is cold, but I don't know why she would bring it here if it's that terrified.

Maybe she's like me, and she just wants to get out of the house because she let her 'not so great but only human' husband go, due to possible stubborn short-sightedness.

Or her old man is home watching TV and he thinks little dogs are annoying.

I unclip Dixie's leash and let her roam around. Her nose is on the ground and she's frantically taking it all in. She'll sniff every square inch of this place before she even thinks about greeting other dogs.

She runs over to me and smacks me with her paw, as if to say, 'thanks for bringing me to this cool place.'

I pet her little head as we are startled by a very deep, gruff bark from the other side of the fence.

I feel something warm and wet, and...oh great, Dixie has peed on my foot.

I immediately hear laughter from the other side of the fence. A young guy in a backwards baseball cap says, "Hey, I'm sorry Buster scared the piss out of your little wiener."

Buster is a Rottweiler and his owner isn't as young

as I first thought, but too young for me. And he thinks he's so funny! Little does he know, his dog scared a few droplets of pee out of me, too. That's some terrifying bark!

I smile and tell him it's okay (I don't really want to discuss pee with a smart ass stranger), and he throws a frisbee to Buster, after thoroughly checking me out. I'm sure he thought I was younger from afar as well, but once he got closer and saw the laugh lines and less than perfectly toned legs, he retreated.

I watch Buster jump with his muscular body and retrieve the frisbee in midair. I'm not a fan of big dogs, but they are interesting to observe. So powerful and strong. I now notice that all of their owners seem to be men, and a few couples. Dixie would easily be a snack for any of the dogs on that side, and if I want to meet men, that side is where I would need to hang out.

I look down at my little one, who is still jumping on my leg. I pick her up, and look in my bag for a baby wipe to clean my foot.

Neither Dixie nor I are off to a good start with this activity, but there's hope for her. I decide to join the old lady on the bench and see if her little dog can calm down long enough to make a friend. Who knows, maybe she has a son who's single and doesn't need a dog that doubles as a horse.

I wish I could make up my mind about what I want, and figure out how to get it.

CHAPTER TWENTY-ONE

Ron

"I do like that color!" Claire's eyes shine as she holds the paint swatch up to the kitchen wall in the best light.

I try not to smile too smugly, and can't resist teasing her. "So, it was the same shade as the guy's eyes? I seem to remember you telling me that when you were getting a foot massage the other night. I thought you preferred brown eyes. I'm disappointed that you've crossed over to the other side."

Claire and I both have brown eyes, and it was always our thing.

"I do prefer brown *eyes*, but I hate brown walls. It looks like poop."

I laugh and she looks up, staring into *my* eyes. I am not going anywhere tonight unless I am asked to leave.

"So do you want me to get started tonight? I'm here anyway and I've got the paint and all the supplies."

She hesitates and says, "Are you sure you want to spend all of this time over here? Have you even played tennis lately or hung out with any of your friends?"

"No, but I want to help you. And besides, if we're going to sell the house, we need to work on making it show better. Isn't that what Jackie would say?"

Her smile is back at the mention of her baby sister, and she agrees that I should get started. She also offers to make dinner.

"We could eat in the dining room and close the pocket door to avoid the paint fumes, if you get that far before dinner's ready."

I was thinking of a spot on the second floor for dessert, but the night is young and I need to pace myself.

Claire

This is all feeling very domestic, but not in a bad way. I've spent so long being mad at Ron that I've forgotten how great it can be when we're getting along and everything is clicking. We did spend close to twenty years together.

It's not just my lack of luck with men that's causing me to think this way, although I can see why a casual observer would say that's why I am reconsidering my feelings for Ron. Yes, I suppose if I met someone who was just *perfect* for me it would divert my attention away from Ron. But I haven't, and as far as I know neither has he, and I feel like that means something. All of our time as a couple counts for something.

Dixie is behaving a bit better lately. I have set her up on the floor with some chew toys, but she's curious about Ron's activities. You'd think she would be used to painting by now, but every day is like starting all over for Dixie. She gets a clean slate, except for remembering Mommy and food and where to find her ball.

If only people could have the same ability to forget and start over.

I'm just throwing together some chicken before the paint fumes get to be too much, and my hungry little piglet is now by my side. At least this will keep her out of Ron's way.

I'm breading and frying some chicken cutlets, like my mother taught me long ago, and throwing together a salad and some rice. Ron doesn't really eat carbs, but if I don't have a starch I'll be starving later.

Since Ron is still taping the kitchen while I'm cooking, we can eat in here. I begin setting the table and catch him watching me.

"What?" I glance at the table and my clothes to see if I've splattered grease all over myself.

He goes back to taping and says, "Nothing. I was just thinking this is nice. I mean, it's nice of you to make dinner. I've been pretty much existing on take-out."

I know that's not true. He doesn't like to waste money and he eats healthy. However, even though he's not a big spender, he will never be on line at the 'buy one get one hot dog' night.

He's just trying to show his appreciation, which is also new. Ron is not one to gush his thanks.

"It's no problem. I don't have any reason to cook anymore, and I get sick of eating out, too."

I mostly eat microwaved meals and donuts. Shh…

Ron

I'm back to painting and Claire's in the kitchen, cleaning up. Dinner was good. She's not the best cook, but my food needs are simple.

We shared some laughs—she likes when I tell her stories about my work day and all the nutty customers I meet on my route.

"She asked you to look at the mole on her back? Eww, I can't even finish my dinner now."

It was so awesome to see her shake with laughter.

Dixie was indulged with people food, but I didn't say anything. When I move back in there will be plenty of time to reverse the dog's bad habits. I have more important goals right now—like making Claire shudder for other reasons.

Claire started cleaning up the dinner dishes and I got back to work. I offered to help, but I knew she would say no. She never let me help when we were together, and she said she wants me to be able to finish up early and get home, since I must be so tired from last night.

I'm *not* going home early — I'll sleep when I'm dead. It's time to ratchet things up a notch.

"Oh, shit, look what I did now? I love this shirt."

Claire turns around from the sink and shuts off the water. "Oh, what happened? Oh, you didn't know you were going to paint tonight and you didn't wear your work clothes."

She narrows her eyes and dries her hands as she walks over to survey the damage. Frost blue paint on a black shirt is pretty glaring. I did a good job.

"Do you mind rinsing it, and putting some stuff on it to soak the stain?"

I am already pulling the t-shirt over my head before she answers, being careful not to get paint in my hair.

On second thought, that could lead me up to the shower again, but I need to be a little subtler than that.

Claire

I take the shirt out of his hands and almost drop it. He *has* been keeping up with his workouts. Shit.

This is *not* fair. There should be a 'shirts on' rule for people who are no longer in a relationship. No matter what. Okay, if the paramedics had to come and zap him with those heart starter things, then *maybe*. I would never take my shirt off for *any reason* unless I was dying, so it's wrong that men can do it so casually and torment women…

Now he's watching me stare and I feel my cheeks

burning. I'm not much of a blusher and it's preposterous to allow a man I've been seeing naked since I was sixteen to fluster me now.

Did he do this on purpose?

No, that's silly. I'm just being paranoid now. He's just trying to paint and he made a mistake. He's not so perfect, even though he thinks he is. I'm actually glad he did something stupid.

"Claire, are you going to spray the stuff?"

Shit, I'm still in the same spot.

I flinch and say, "Oh yeah, sure I'll do it right now. I was just noticing you have a mole that looks a little different. Speaking of moles, as we were earlier, you know? You might...want to get that checked out...or something..."

Now he's smirking and I decide to stop my super idiotic speech. I don't have to worry about anything happening between us now with all this sexy mole conversation.

My washer and dryer are upstairs, in the hall across from my bedroom. I find it to be convenient, since that's where I take off my dirty clothes. I've never been more grateful for its location now as it buys me some time to collect my thoughts and get myself in check.

Last week, Ron said he still loved me. He did take it back, sort of. But that was only after I refused to go down that road with him. He's been here a lot and he's being very patient, but for the first time since I met him I can't accurately read him. The mixed signals are maddening. Does he love me? Just want sex? Is he bored? Is he trying to torment me for leaving him? Genuinely being friendly and helpful?

I have to figure out what's really going on before I

let things get out of hand.

I soak his shirt with Shout and lay it on top of the washer. I peer into my bedroom and see the book I had been reading a few weeks ago (not the scary one—I put that on the bottom of the to-read pile).

Reading is one of my passions. It may be a boring hobby to a lot of people, especially Ron ('why do you always have your nose in a book?'), but I enjoy being swept away to other worlds and losing myself in the ups and downs of fictional people.

I need a good escape, both from my thoughts and from interacting with Ron. I descend the steps holding my copy of a popular chick lit novel like armor.

"Your shirt is soaking—I think the stain should come out since we caught it right away."

"Great, thanks." He barely looks up and concentrates on his task, which gives me an extra few seconds to marvel at the way his muscles flex when he reaches up…

AAHHH!!!! Stop it!

I start to sit down on the couch, then decide to plant myself on the lesser used loveseat, which will position me with my back to the bare-chested temptation.

I fidget to get comfortable and soon I am joined by my little snuggle buddy. Any time I am sitting or lying down, Dixie takes advantage of the chance to lay on me.

So now, where was I? Oh yes, the heroine was about to quit her job and move across the country to be with her long lost…

"Hey, Claire. Could you help me for a second?"

My heartbeat quickens and I drop my paperback, almost hitting Dixie. Good thing I'm too cheap and poor to buy hardcovers.

"Sure, what do you need?" My voice sounds a bit shaky and I'm hoping he doesn't notice.

"Come over here and take this curtain—I need to get the rod down."

I lay my book down on the couch, but then move it to the coffee table as I see Dixie eyeing a new, tasty treat. She will put anything in her mouth.

I take a short breath and calmly walk over to take the curtain.

He won't just hand it to me like a normal person, and he starts teasing me with it like it's a cape and I'm a bull, and *why* I don't just walk away or not engage in this nonsense, I'll never know. But in a matter of moments I'm wrapped up in the fucking rooster printed fabric and guess what I'm doing?

Yes, kissing Ron. And this time I am not resisting, it's not a good night peck, and before long my legs are wrapped around his waist, and the kitchen table I inherited from my parents' house is seeing action like it never has before.

Ron

I love watching Claire sleep. Everything was perfect. *Is* perfect.

I figured if I could get her in close proximity I could at least get another kiss in, but she caved faster than I thought. And the beauty is that it was really all her doing. *She* reached for me, *she* escalated things, and *she* even pushed the painting supplies aside on the table.

But not too roughly—Claire doesn't really do reckless, wild abandon sort of things.

That's why I know she's serious about me. Us. I think she was trying to resist because she's stubborn, and she doesn't want to explain to her friends and family that she forgives me and she was wrong.

Or that there wasn't ever anything to forgive— which is really more the point.

But I'm not dumb enough to say that. I've learned some lessons. In the past when one of us had an argument with our wives, Mike used to say, "Do we want to be right, or do we want to be happy?"

I used to scoff at his philosophy as being wimpy. I didn't want my balls dragged around on a chain just because I was married, but then all of a sudden I wasn't married anymore. And Mike was. So I think he's on to something.

Claire also had a chance to come to her senses and tell me to leave after our tabletop activities were concluded, and the passion subsided. But she didn't. *She* was the one who moved the proceedings upstairs, so who was I to argue? I find it's best to keep my mouth shut and let Claire lead when I want something to go a certain way. It may sound manipulative, but I'm just helping her get out of her own way, and she gets what she wants in the end. And I don't get nagged or accused of controlling her.

She jumps up when her alarm goes off. I've already called in sick for both of us. Two sleepless nights in a row, and an extra workout have really worn me out. Plus, if we both stay home we can solidify our new bond and iron some things out. If we separate, there's always a chance she could change her mind.

She silences her blaring phone and puts her head under the pillow. "I'm calling in sick."

Well, that was easy.

I pull her close to me again and get under the pillow with her. "I already did that."

"You did? Yeah, you must be tired, too." She rubs her face and gropes her nightstand for her phone again.

I stop her and say, "I called in sick for both of us."

I start kissing her neck and she stiffens. "You did what?"

"You're not mad, are you? I knew you'd be in no shape for work. I should have turned off your phone alarm, but I don't know your passcode. Anyway, I called your main office number and the receptionist said your boss was busy, so I just told her I was your husband and you were too sick to come in."

She sighs and punches my arm, but playfully. I think.

"How did you know I didn't have an important meeting or something? And I'm not sure I want everyone knowing my business. Amanda isn't going to say anything, but still—you should have let me do that myself."

"I thought we could spend the day together, and I am predicting we will need a nap later."

She rolls over and sighs at me the way she always does when I'm being exasperating, but she thinks it's funny. "I'm exhausted. I may need to sleep all day."

"Well, we *were* up late, but Dixie didn't help much. I know she was upset when we locked her out when we first came up here, but she wouldn't stop whining and you agreed that was a mood killer. If I remember correctly, you were the one who closed the door in your baby's face."

"Well, she was screwing with my…you know!"

She's smiling so I know she gets me.

"But once you took her out to pee and put her in the crate, the crying was ridiculous. At one point she was rattling the cage like an inmate trying to get the guard's attention before a stabbing goes down. Doesn't she sleep in there every night?"

"Yes, but it hasn't even been two weeks that she's been here, and she's just a baby."

She backs up and pulls the covers tighter to her body. "Besides, she's not used to anyone sleeping up here but me. You being here is different, and therefore scary. She likes you but dogs are very territorial and they have to get accustomed to new things."

"I'm sorry, you're right." I rub her arm and she relaxes a little. "I'm going to go back to the apartment later and get some of my things, and we'll do this gradually. By the time I'm officially moved back in, she'll be used to it and I'll be her daddy."

She still doesn't look happy. What's wrong now? Was the 'Daddy' reference bad? She refers to herself as 'Mommy' to the dog. I'm missing something here.

"Yes, *she* can get used to it, but we haven't actually talked about you moving back in. Last night was great, but..."

I sit up now and realize it's time for a talk *now*, whether or not I want one.

"I only assumed that's what you wanted. That's what this *is*. You're not one to sleep around so I just figured this was your way of...you know?"

Now her arms are folded across her chest and the blanket is almost up to her neck. It's like she's forming a force field between me and her nakedness.

"No, I'm not one to sleep around, but I don't know if you are, and I might like to get a little more information before I put my wedding rings back on and tear up the divorce papers. For instance, does Stacy have any diseases?"

"Oh come on, Claire. I told you she's a kooky chick who lives in my building. She's got a thing for me—I'll get a restraining order against her if she bothers you again. But once I move back in—"

"I know—*everything* will be great."

She's angry but I also see a tear forming, so I know she's more afraid than anything.

I reach out for her and she lets her guard down, letting the blanket fall to a normal breast covering position. I'll take that as progress.

She lays back down and says, "I'm not saying no, okay? But we do have some things to hash out about the past year, and I'm not ready to do all of that this second."

Claire

Ron went downstairs to make breakfast. I really don't eat in the morning and he knows that. I think he was just looking for something to do to break the tension, and clearly sex and sleep were now both off the table for the immediate future.

We are still technically married, so this shouldn't feel that weird, but it does. A lot has changed. I was the instigator last night, but he set the bait. I can't blame him, though. I wanted it as much as he did, but he's right about me. I am not a casual sex kind of girl—that's why it's been a year and I haven't had sex with anyone else. Some of my friends find that mind-boggling.

And I know lots of people have sex with exes, but Ron is going home to get his underwear and toothbrush, so that's not what this is, either.

He can't expect that I am going to go for a reconciliation without talking more about what happened to the marriage, what we've both been doing the past year, and what we've learned. We should probably go for counseling. This isn't just a matter of sleeping together and moving his stuff back.

Or maybe it is, and I am making too much out of it. I do that sometimes.

I wish I could get more sleep, but I'm in the shower letting the hot water caress my overburdened brain. Thank God Dixie decided to sleep in. I guess her shenanigans wore her out.

My fingers are starting to shrivel and the water is getting cold, so I have to get out and face this day.

I can't believe he called in sick for me. When we were married we used to do it for each other all the time, especially in the early days when we had part-time jobs as kids. But I have a real, professional position, and that was quite presumptuous of him.

I turn off the water, dry off and pull on some lounge pants and a tank top, toweling most of the water out of my hair.

I leave Dixie where she is since she's not made a peep, and she's still under her blanket. When I get downstairs I find Ron putting the blue paint cans by the front door.

"What are you doing?" I point to my perfect, frosty blue color.

"Oh, I was thinking of returning these and getting something more neutral. Probably for the dining room, too. Not until we talked about it, of course. I know you love these bold colors, but for resale neutral is best, and now we can move forward with selling and finding another place together. Maybe we could get some other colorful things—hey, you could use a new car—maybe a frost blue Jag?"

"Oh my God, are you *kidding* me? We didn't *decide* to sell, we just talked about it. And what happened to all of that shit about how this color is so great, blah, blah, blah? Did you just do that to lure me into bed?"

"No, I was trying to make you happy, but we have to be practical. Maybe we can save this paint for a new place that we're going to keep long-term. It could go in a bathroom or an office."

"Right, rooms you don't have to see. And did you hear me? I said we *didn't* decide anything."

"It was your idea!"

"No, it was AN idea! You said you wanted to move back in—if that happens, why would we need to sell?"

"You just said upstairs that you're not ready for me to move back in."

"No, I said I wasn't ready for us to *decide*!"

"Claire, you're making no sense. I think you're just tired and emotional."

"I am not tired!" I grab the back of the couch to steady myself. "Okay, I am tired, but I am also *angry*!"

He turns the stove off and rushes to me. "I'm sorry, things are moving fast for you. I guess since this is what I've been hoping for all along, it makes it less of a change for me. I've already thought it all through. I've had more time to adjust while you've been dating."

"Oh right, and you've just been sitting around for a year waiting. Like a *monk*!"

There is no point in bringing Stacy up again, or questioning him about other women in general. I am now questioning my own sanity.

"Claire, please just eat your breakfast—it's getting cold. We'll work all of this out later. You're right—I'm not considering your needs."

He leads me to the table and I glare at the plate he's placed on it.

"You know I don't eat eggs."

"Okay, I'll eat yours. What do you want? I'll make something else for you."

"You also know I really don't eat in the morning." How could he spend almost twenty years with me and not know this? Next he'll be offering me coffee.

"Breakfast is important. You know if your mother was here, she'd agree with me."

He smiles and my stomach churns. This must be how it feels after a one-night stand, except in this case the guy's name is on the mortgage and you can't force him to leave quite as easily.

He sits down at the table pulling the plate of food in front of himself, saying, "Oh, by the way, your mother called while you were in the shower. I heard your phone and wanted to make sure it wasn't your boss calling you back."

I don't have a house phone anymore, so he saw her call coming in on my cell. While I want to muster up some righteous indignation about that, I have to admit that if the situation were reversed, and he had a call coming in, I would glance to see who it was before the name disappeared. Especially now.

But then of course he doesn't have strange men calling asking for me, and promising signed divorce papers. Grr...

"Okay, I'm sure she left a message. I'll check."

I turn to walk back upstairs and he says, "Oh no, you don't need to do that. She told me she'd call you later. I didn't tell her you called in sick, so she thinks you're off to work. I didn't think it was my business to tell her."

"You *talked* to my mother?"

He looks up from salting his eggs and says, "Yes, I just said that. I figured you wouldn't want her to know you were playing hooky from school to play with me all day. Remember when we did that in high school?"

"You *answered* my phone?"

How does he not seem to see that I want to strangle him? He's still smiling like he's performed a great service, like saving my puppy from a bear.

Or painting the kitchen the color I FUCKING picked!

"Claire, why is this a big deal? It was your mother — it's not like some *guy* called."

He laughs and I fume. As if no guys would ever call me. That's what he thinks — that I will settle for him because I can't find anyone else. That makes him far more pathetic than me. And so incredibly manipulative!

He knows the average woman will not put up with his shit, but he thinks his little Claire from high school is still under his spell. Ha! I just haven't seen a chest like that in a long time, but I could go to the beach and look at the lifeguards.

And no, I wouldn't try to have sex with the lifeguards, but I can buy one of those stupid vibrators with the bunny ears like everyone else!

"It doesn't matter *who* was calling. You have no respect for my privacy, and my boundaries. And I *hate* eggs and I *hate* white walls!"

I stop short of adding, 'and I hate you.'

He drops his fork on his plate and I am just waiting for the next stupid comment to come out of his arrogant mouth. How was I kissing that mouth just last night, and now I want to punch it?

"Claire, you're getting hysterical. Remember what the doctor said —"

Until he went there, I had almost lost sight of the thing that pushed me to leave him. My eyes sting with tears as all of his insensitivity flashes through my mind.

"The 'doctor' also privately said that you are a self-centered, immature man who has Mommy issues! As in — you need me to be your Mommy, and that's why you are secretly relieved that we can't have kids!"

I stand a little taller and my eyes challenge him to contradict me now, although his silence just makes me fume even more.

"Here, Ron, eat your eggs — they're so good for you!"

I turn the plate upside down on his head, but I do it gently enough that it stays there, flat to his asshole skull.

I *am* pitiful — I'm not even aggressive enough to break the plate, or cause even a tiny bit of bodily harm. This is why he thinks he can walk all over me.

I choke back sobs while my little wiener baby happily eats the eggs raining down from Daddy Dickhead.

CHAPTER TWENTY-TWO

Claire

I watch the big jerk get in his truck and slam the door. He drives away with no shirt on. He still looks good, but I won't be making the same mistake twice.

Dixie is crying at the door, and I'm not sure if it's because Ron didn't say goodbye to her, or if she saw him as a food fountain.

I pick her up, and head back into the kitchen to clean up the mess. The tears have subsided, but not the anger. It may benefit me to go back to the doctor, but honestly I'm okay when Ron isn't around. Spending all of this time with him lately has kicked up too much buried sadness.

I know—buried sadness sounds bad, but as long as I avoid Ron, babies, pregnant women, my gynecologist's office, the shopping center with Babies R' Us and TV, I'm fine.

Okay, perhaps there's some work to be done, but time heals all wounds. That's what they say—whoever 'they' are. I wish 'they' would tell me where to look for a decent man.

But first things first. I should call my lawyer and find out if there is any way I can force Ron to sign the divorce papers. He's walked all over me and I've had more than enough. We could have been divorced in the state of Virginia six months ago because we don't have any kids.

Hopefully sleeping with him didn't reset the clock, but he has no proof of that.

Another tear squeezes out of my tired eye sockets, and I make a different phone call.

If I had pulled my mother into this from the start, I would have stayed stronger. Of course, that's why I've been avoiding her. Nothing ruins reckless abandon like discussing it with your mother first.

She picks up and I immediately start crying while trying to explain what happened.

"I was wondering what that buffoon was doing at your house so early in the morning, and answering your phone. Well, actually I figured it out—I wasn't born yesterday, and I'm not living under a rock, but I wasn't about to give him the satisfaction of questioning him. He actually told me that you were both coming to see Dad for Father's Day."

"Yeah, he really thought he could take his position back with one…never mind. So now I'm back to where I was before, only I feel stupid and—"

"Claire Marie, that's enough. You are a smart girl, and if you'd listened to your father and me, you would have broken up with Ron after graduation, and had a normal college experience. But you're still young and there's no reason why you can't get out there and find a decent man now."

"I was trying—"

"No you weren't. You were sitting back and letting your friends pawn off all their crazy losers on you."

"But I haven't even told you about half of them."

"A mother knows, Claire. Now why don't you do what all the girls are doing, and get online? I saw a lovely show the other night about couples who got married after meeting on dating sites. It's not creepy anymore, everyone is doing it."

And this from the woman who said if everyone was jumping off the Brooklyn Bridge, would you do it, too?

Ron

There, that's the end of that. I could just mail these back to the lawyer, but I want to see her face. I didn't say anything because I didn't want to continue to argue her ridiculous points. I thought she had changed, but she's still the same whiny, overly emotional girl she was in high school. When is she going to grow up and realize she can't have everything the way she wants it?

I stare at my signature on the divorce papers and it actually feels good. Ronald J. Ratzenberger. I was going to add 'FU' after my name, but after her blind date story, the meaning is diluted. Plus, I think the court may reject that as it's not part of my legal name.

Claire would just say it stands for 'fucked up.' Hey, actually FY is what she meant to carve in that guy's car. Some English major she is.

This is a fresh start for me. I thought I was still in love with Claire, but it was just the lure of the comfort of the familiar, and boy, it *was* familiar. You'd think after a year with no sex she'd be a little more...uninhibited. It started out all wild in the kitchen, but then she was worried about the neighbors seeing in the window and Dixie was crying, and she said the bed will be more comfortable.

Yeah, I've dodged a bullet.

Speaking of bullets, I need to deal with Stacy. I am not moving out of this apartment complex just to escape her, and she's just a woman. A fiery, hot woman, but I think I need someone more balanced.

Stacy would have thrown the plate at my head, but she also would have waved to any neighbors watching us on the kitchen table, and comfort is not in her vocabulary.

Yes, I need *balance*.

The 'doctor' also said that it's very common to initially seek a new partner who is the opposite of your old one. It's called a 'transitional person.' Yes, I went back to see the shrink a few times by myself, but Claire doesn't need to know that.

I'll find someone with Claire's maternal side and Stacy's passion. Too bad Natasha is so far away. I have a feeling she's the kind of girl for me.

I shove the papers in the envelope, and stick them in my back pocket. I grab a clean shirt and head off to the library.

Wait, it's Friday. Stacy doesn't work Friday mornings. Perfect, this way I won't have to keep my voice down when I'm telling her to stay the fuck away from…

I'm barely out my door and the crazy woman is in my face.

"Where were you last night?"

Here we go with the chest poking again.

"It is none of your business where I was, but if you must know, I was with Claire. And you need to leave her alone."

"It's not my fault you're dumb enough to leave your phone lying around without a passcode. I knew you didn't tell her about us!"

"There is no *us*! And there is nothing happening with Claire, either. See these? These are my divorce papers—I am bringing them to her right now, so there is

270

no need…"

I went a little too far there. Now she's smiling and putting her arms around my neck.

"I knew you would sign them. I'm sorry I've been so forceful, but you've been so hard to reach lately. But I see what you were doing—you wanted to end things properly with Claire before starting something serious with me. That's so noble of you. And very sexy…"

I pull her off my earlobe and say, "Stacy, you and I are not going to have something serious. Now stop it."

Her eyes darken and she says, "Then I don't believe you about Claire. You're going back over there to rip up the divorce papers with her—in some kind of symbolic ceremony—like a vow renewal. Do you think you can trick me that easily?"

I hang my head and try the 'counting to ten' thing Claire always used to tell me to do when I got mad. I only make it to three, but I lower my voice this time.

"I am leaving now. This conversation is over and this topic is closed."

If I run I can make it to my truck before she can follow me, unless she has already figured out where Claire lives.

After all, she is a research librarian.

Claire

I finish cleaning up the kitchen and end up opening up a yogurt I don't even want. I take little licks as Dixie continues to lick the floor for traces of Ron's breakfast.

I let my mother do her thing and I thanked her for the advice, but mostly for listening. She's a bit of a whack-job, but she loves me and she's a lot tougher than I am.

I'm going to go upstairs and put on real clothes, do

my makeup and go into the office. Sitting around this house is going to make me stir crazy. I'll just tell Tim I'm feeling better.

And maybe later I'll take a look at one of the online dating sites. It can't hurt. I have peeked at them in the past, but they scare me. However, I need to take some risks if I'm going to get out of this rut.

Speaking of ruts, Justin has a point. My work wardrobe is dull, and even though I'm not interested in any men at work, it's empowering to embrace your sexy, feminine side. I should want to look good for *me*, not just to attract a man.

I have higher heels I could be wearing, tighter sweaters, and push up bras collecting dust in the back of my lingerie drawer.

It's not like I look *frumpy*, but I could 'fix up' a bit more, as my mother would say. And get out more. The night out with Audra and Rachel was a bust, but Rebecca could be fun to hang out with. As a matter of fact, she's an excellent role model. I've been avoiding her for the same reason I haven't visited my mother—I know I've been fucking up and I didn't want the tough love.

I open my closet to survey the contents, and try to pick something a little edgier. I do have this red, lower cut blouse from last New Year's when Jane dragged me out to a boring party with Mike's work friends. It's kind of clingy, but it could work for the office with a tight black skirt. I must have one somewhere—that's a wardrobe basic...what was that noise?

I pull my head out of the closet and follow Dixie's bark, which has moved from 'someone's here' to 'let me at 'em.'

Oh, for the love of…

Ron is running up my front lawn while being chased by an Amazon who I can only assume is…

"Stacy, don't you dare come one step closer!" Ron has used his key to open the door, which I failed to get from him earlier.

Clearly, it was poor judgment when I failed to get it from him a *year* ago.

I could just push him out the door, call the police, and take care of both of the trespassers. However, that's not a permanent solution, and I've avoided confrontation long enough.

"Both of you get in this house right now!"

I'm holding Dixie in one hand and pointing into the entryway with the other. They're both gaping at me and Dixie is trying to wrestle free so she can attack the intruders. Or ask them to pet her belly.

They both comply and I close the front door.

"As much as I hate to do this, I'm not having this conversation in full view of the cul-de-sac. Now Ron, why are you back here? And I presume you're Stacy?"

Stacy is a big girl, with wild hair and big eyes, boobs, everything. I feel like a little dwarf next to her.

"Yes, I am, *Claire*. I'm sorry I had to do this, but I was not about to let Ron trick me into believing he was coming back over here with signed divorced papers. Or trick you into taking him back. When he didn't come home last night—"

Ron's face reddens and he yells, "Stop saying 'home' like we live together when you camp out on my doorstep all night, you crazy—"

I put up my hand and address Ron's stalker. "I don't care where either of you live, now or in the future. Did you just say he was coming over here with signed divorce papers?"

"That's what he said, but I think he's full of shit. He just wants to have me on the side while he cozies back up to you in this fancy house."

I look around and wrinkle my forehead. My house isn't a dump but it's not fancy. How bad is Ron's apartment complex?

Stacy continues without taking a breath. "I've been working at that stupid library for so many years and I will never be able to buy a house like this and—"

"You're a librarian? Did you major in English as an undergrad? I thought about pursuing Library Science but Ron would never have supported me going to graduate—"

"Oh for crissakes! You women are insane. One minute you're at each other's throats and the next you're bonding over career choices. I'm outta here. Here's the papers, Claire. Congratulations, you're divorced!"

He tosses the envelope at my feet and storms out.

Stacy opens the door and says, "Ron, wait...I don't have to be at work until noon!"

I wince at this and can't help but say, "Stacy, why are you chasing him?"

She looks away and now I can see she's falling apart. Why do women get so upset over men? We should pay more attention to our careers. I wouldn't be so bored and Stacy would have a house. Although I suspect she could afford a house and that was just for dramatic effect. Maybe she'd like to buy this one?

"He always comes running to me every time he has a fight with you, and..." She stops herself and leans up against the closed door. "Oh my God, I see what you're saying. All along I've been sloppy seconds! AAHHH!"

Stacy's howling sends Dixie running to hide in my office, and I go look for tissues in the powder room.

I don't think I'm making it into work today, and Stacy needs to look up 'self-respect' in the card catalogue.

CHAPTER TWENTY-THREE

Claire

"Yay, good outside pee-pee, Dixie!"

Jane and I do a little dance in my yard to congratulate the wiener girl on her potty training progress. She actually scratched the door to go outside while I was talking Stacy off the ledge yesterday.

"Let's go sit on my porch with some wine. I just bought some without a cork, but they say that doesn't mean it's cheap anymore." Jane motions to her house and I happily follow along.

Dixie won't stay still on the porch, but I can just click her leash to the railing and she'll settle down eventually. I'm so proud of her. She doesn't need puppy training classes, she just needed a little time and patience.

There's a lesson I need to apply to myself.

Stacy actually isn't *that* bad—she's a little edgy and over the top, but she's had a bad history with men and her self-esteem is in the gutter. I gave her the name of the therapist I used to see. I doubt she'll go, but I think I gave her enough of a lecture to dissuade her from continuing to chase Ron.

I realize that he will benefit as well, but I'm not the vindictive type. He signed the papers. So now that I am about to be truly *divorced*, hopefully the fog will lift, and I'll be less *dazed*.

Sharp, focused, ready to take on the world—or at

least the single men of Richmond.

But that can wait a minute. For now, I am sitting in the sunshine with my best friend, my baby and corkless wine. It doesn't get much better.

"So have you heard from Ron?"

I sip my wine and it's actually not that bad. "He sent me an odd text late last night. Something about getting on a plane, and if the lawyers need to reach him he'll be out of town for a while. Honestly, I think he was drunk."

"He probably just wants to get away and clear his head. *You* should get on a plane, too."

"Yeah, but I have a little one now. I'm content to stay home and enjoy her for the time being. I do need to get a painter…and no, please do not tell me how Joe paints a straight line."

We both laugh and watch Dixie try to break free from her leash. She'll learn to stop fighting and go with the flow.

"So are you going to try online dating?"

"I think so. I went on one of the more popular sites last night and made a profile. It was kind of fun. And there are SO many men out there. I don't know why I was relying on friends to set me up, like it's nineteen-ninety something."

Jane pouts and I add, "No offense, but…your picks weren't exactly…"

Again we explode into a fit of giggles.

"I know for sure I can do better than men who cry over their exes, drunk punk rocker skunks, holy rollers and guys who ditch me with FU notes."

Jane cringes and says, "You *have* had a tough year. No wonder Ron was able to pull you back in."

"He was my whole life for…most of my life. The

Internet is like a well-stocked men store that never runs out of inventory, and I only need one, right? How hard can that be?"

"I wanna see. Let's get my laptop—the Wi-Fi works out here."

Jane rushes inside to get her computer, and I sit back and feel the sun on my face. The porch will be shady later, but the morning sun feels amazing.

Dixie has finally settled down at my feet. I smile at her and she wags her little tail incessantly. I adore her already, and while she isn't a human baby, she's a sweet, lovely little creature. And she needs me.

I'm glad Jane isn't giving me a speech about how I don't need a man. It's probably because *she* has a good one, and she sees the value. I'm not bitter or miserable alone—I'm just a relationship kind of person. I like having a partner. That doesn't mean I can't do better at being on my own, but there's nothing wrong with seeking a companion, either.

Jane comes back and we get the laptop up and running, and I login to the dating site.

Jane loves my profile and is even more excited than me by the possibilities. We've done a search in our area based on my general criteria, and I am encouraged again to see how many single, age appropriate men don't care about having children.

"Oh, this guy is cute." She points to a rather young looking guy with a Rott…

Oh my God, it's the guy from the dog park. I squint to get a closer look and see that he's thirty-five. Wow, I thought he was younger. I guess if you put a ball cap on backwards, you take off the years. I wonder what I could wear backwards for the same effect.

Instead of telling Jane I've already met him, I state the obvious. "I don't think our dogs would be compatible."

Jane glances at the puppy at my feet and smiles. "Yeah, in the interest of Dixie's well-being, we should take him off the list."

We're enjoying the man shopping, and laughing at some of the ridiculous things some people write in their profiles. I knew this wasn't all balloons and unicorns, but hmm…there *are* some whack-jobs out there.

Jane points and laughs so hard, she starts choking on her wine. "Look at this guy—what's with his hair?" She shows me and then we both realize we're looking at Tom.

She frowns and says, "I guess some of the bad blind dates would be on here, too. But we can just ignore those, right?"

We optimistically move on, and I make a mental note to research how to block certain members from contacting me through the site. Although, Tom was so drunk he may not even remember what I look like. And hopefully he'd have some pride.

Jane points to another profile and says, "Oh, this guy is pretty hot. He says he's an auto magazine reviewer…"

Well, if that's not a kick in the ass.

Frugalautolover76.

Jane bites her lip and says, "Okay, let's take a break. You don't have to make your profile live and join right away. Maybe think about it for a few days."

"Nope, I'm doing it. I am not letting a cheap psycho, an asshole ex or anyone else keep me from finding what I want. I know the right guy is out there. Internet dating—here comes Claire!"

Jane does a little 'woo-hoo' dance in her seat and reaches for her wine glass. "We need to toast to your new venture!"

I would raise my glass in a toast if a wiener dog tongue was not currently swishing around in it.

Jane needs higher tables, and now I have to find out how much wine a wiener dog can consume before being over the legal limit. I have a feeling all of Jane's dogs have done this at one time or another, and a few licks won't hurt her.

I remove the mini wino and say, "I guess maybe she does need more training."

I hate it when Ron is right.

THE END

JOIN ME ON THE EDGE

Go here
(http://carolmaloneyscott.com/become-a-fan/)
to become an Edgy Reader, and receive a FREE BOOK
as my thank you for joining!

The fun doesn't stop with the FREE DOWNLOAD!

As a member of my "Edgy Readers Group," you will receive:

- More free books!
- News on upcoming releases!
- Exclusive contests and giveaways!
- Cover reveals!
- Updates on projects and new series in the works!
- Polls asking for your opinion!
- Shenanigans!
- Wiener dog pictures!
- Excerpts!
- Members-only sneak previews and exclusive content!

I can't wait for YOU to join the party!

ROM-COM on the EDGE SERIES

Dazed & Divorced (Book 1)
There Are No Men (Book 2)
Afraid of Her Shadow (Book 3)
The Juggling Act (Book 4)
Accidental Makeovers (Book 5)
Valentine's on the Edge (A Short Story Collection)
Let's Hear it From the Boys (A Short Story Collection)

COMING SOON!

Meet the Neighbors (humorous women's fiction)
Believing in Barbie (paranormal chick lit)
Mismated (Colleen's Story – Rom-Com on the Edge Book 6)

ACKNOWLEDGEMENTS

This is my shortest book to date, so I am going to try to make my acknowledgments short and sweet.

I am loving my mailing list subscribers, who are some very loyal readers. I am very grateful to say they are now too numerous to name individually. I absolutely appreciate the support of my work, but the friendships have enhanced my life as well. I am an extrovert doing an introvert's job when I'm writing, and making new friends on this path is a huge bonus for me!

I still marvel at the support of the writing community, and offer a special thanks to Karan Eleni, Whitney Dineen, Tracie Banister, Rich Amooi, Becky Monson and Geralyn Corcillo for offering ideas, support, and sometimes talking me off the proverbial ledge!

My son, Nick Rissmeyer, is back at art and design school in Chicago, and I miss him terribly. His work on my book covers is a source of great joy and pride for me, and his humor has gotten me through many tough times, in writing and in life. I adore him and can't wait to see all of the amazing things he will accomplish.

My stepdaughter, Jaime, is now a senior in high school, and I have promised that I will write our fairy story before she leaves for college. The fantasy chick lit series we have collaborated on will make its debut in early 2017. Jaime's love of superpowers is evident in the character's strengths. Her superpower is being a wonderful stepdaughter!

My husband, Jim, has signed onto a lifetime of helping me calm my creative, but neurotic brain every night. It's no easy task, and I love him very much for his support and belief in me.

And last but not least, Daisy. My little writing partner is the light of every day!

ABOUT THE AUTHOR

Carol Maloney Scott, author of the Rom-Com on the Edge series, is a frazzled new bride and wiener dog fanatic. She is a lover of donuts, and a hater of mornings. Recently unearthing a childhood passion for writing, she can once again be seen carrying around a notebook and staring into space. Her stories are witty, fresh and real, just like life.

Join her on "The Edge" for giveaways, cover reveals, excerpts, contests and members-only content at
    carolmaloneyscott.com/

WALK THE EDGE
OF
ROM-COM...*ONLINE*

Please check out my social media sites and say hello!

Website
(http://carolmaloneyscott.com/)
Goodreads
(https://www.goodreads.com/user/show/31420814-carol-maloney-scott)
Facebook
(https://www.facebook.com/carolmaloneyscottauthor)
Twitter
(https://twitter.com/CMScottAuthor)
Pinterest
(http://www.pinterest.com/carolmaloneyris/)

Printed in Great Britain
by Amazon

14115473R00169